Richard Davis was born in Surrey. He
attended public school, but left and completed
his education at a crammer. His jobs have
included working in marketing, teaching at a
prep school, and selling insurance. Richard
Davis has been a self-employed financial
advisor since 1980. He is currently at work on
a second novel.

Author photograph by Mark Bayley.

Vermin Blond

Richard Davis

BLACK SWAN

VERMIN BLOND
A BLACK SWAN BOOK   0 552 99484 7

Originally published in Great Britain by
Victor Gollancz Ltd

PRINTING HISTORY
Gollancz edition published 1991
Black Swan edition published 1992

Acknowledgements
'Solitaire' (Sedaka/Cody)
Copyright © Kirshner-Warner Chappell Music
Reproduced by permission of Warner Chappell
Music Ltd
'These Boots Were Made For Walking' (Lee
Hazelwood)
Original Publisher: Criterion Music Corp. and
printed by permission of Lorna Music Co Ltd

This book is set in 11/13pt Melior by
County Typesetters, Margate, Kent

Black Swan Books are published by Transworld
Publishers Ltd, 61–63 Uxbridge Road, Ealing,
London W5 5SA, in Australia by Transworld
Publishers (Australia) Pty Ltd, 15–23 Helles Avenue,
Moorebank, NSW 2170, and in New Zealand by
Transworld Publishers (NZ) Ltd, 3 William
Pickering Drive, Albany, Auckland.

Printed and bound in Great Britain by
Cox & Wyman Ltd, Reading, Berks.

Contents

'It's not necessarily good to go through a stage, you know,' said Gaby – 'it depends which way you're travelling.'

'And which way were you travelling, Gaby?'

'Inwards,' he said softly, and drained his glass.

1

The Undertaker

South Point,
St Osyth,
February 1989.

The builders came today and started work on the roof.
I spotted their truck from the sea wall, approaching
along the causeway, and went down to let them in.
'Bennett & Co.', they have planted a sign. Having spent
the last fortnight tidying the cottage as best I could, I
was disappointed to hear Mr Bennett announce to his
men: 'Mr Palfreyman will be living *on site.*'

It sounded too much like an adventure for me and a
convenience for them, and I shall have to watch out
that I am not exploited. I know that the provisions in
the kitchen were met with dismay – skimmed milk,
decaffeinated coffee, sachets of fruit and herbal teas –
but these are the beverages tolerable to my digestion
and nerves, and if they serve to emphasize to the men
that they are here only as visitors, I am glad. It may
later be necessary to propose house rules, but today
my only plea, again for reasons of health, was that the
use of tobacco be restricted to the loft, where the hole
in the roof provides a natural outlet for the smoke.

From the lane outside, the roof appears merely to be
sagging on account of its age; other roofs in the area
sag equally. In the loft, however, daylight bursts
through where a number of tiles have fallen right
away, and directly beneath this hole is another hole, in
the floor. The likeliest explanation for this second hole

9

is that someone essaying makeshift repairs to the roof has slipped on the wooden rafters underfoot and accidentally pushed a limb through the insubstantial plaster; but it is also possible to surmise, from the correspondence of the two holes, that something long and thin has fallen from the heavens, clean through the loft to the sitting-room below. Although I have explained my position here to Mr Bennett, I caught him looking at me doubtfully on occasion today, and I know he suspects it was I who fell through the roof, for I am long and thin. I did not, of course – that is no way to enter another man's estate – but he is not an unsympathetic fellow, this builder, and if he were to give voice to his suspicion, I dare say that his first words would enquire if I survived the fall without injury. I would have no straightforward answer to that. It happens that I have received injuries from this estate; they are a legacy that passed to me long ago. But though they are not new, neither, it seems, are they mended.

They started playing me up about a month ago, at home, when I took a telephone call.

'Mr Palfreyman?'

'Speaking.'

'Mark Palfreyman?' The voice was slurred.

'Yes?'

A rush of airy laughter, like the fast panting of a dog, swelled in the receiver. Then: 'Hallo, "Undertaker".'

Two weeks later, as a direct result of that call, I woke up in this sitting-room, in a collapsed armchair. As my eyes grew accustomed to the dark and my first inklings developed, I prayed that this was not real life, that I was dreaming. I wanted sleep to move me on again, but a sound disturbed me, a rhythmic, rasping sound that was hard to place. Was someone running a finger to and fro along the fabric of the chair above my head?

Someone in the dark behind me? I scrambled to get up, but at once lost my footing to an empty bottle, and toppled backwards. The bottle roared across uncarpeted boards in a semi-circle, before coming to rest with an oddly delicate clink against something unseen, close to my feet.

Wide awake, I found that it was bitterly cold, and that I was shivering. The chill air bore a rank, foul smell. That strange near-yet-far rhythm sounded now like the steady breathing of someone sleeping, open-mouthed, in a room above. I looked up. Seeing the hole in the ceiling, and, through that, the irregular gap in the roof, I remembered the words of the taxi-driver who had brought me out here the night before, and talked on as though I were sober: 'A mate of mine tried to buy a place out here once, but the building societies wouldn't give him a mortgage. They said it was below sea level.'

It was the sea I was hearing, slapping and sighing, seeming to edge relentlessly away, like the sleep that had deposited, abandoned me here – that I would so much have welcomed back, but would not reclaim me. I was feeling my old injuries then, all right, the wounds were raging as though sleep had indeed been a salty sea. I recalled the events of the previous evening: the police, the mortuary, the publican who had insisted on calling for the taxi, the ride out to the cottage with an overnight bag full of the dead man's belongings.

The bay windows, thick with a layer of grime, admitted only a thin light, but as the sun rose and this thin light became stained with a succession of colours – brown, then red, then amber – bright enough to illumine the squalor and degradation in which I lay, I felt sickened by a sense of betrayal: it was as though Time itself were being peeled back like a dressing to reveal that my legacy, my injuries, my wounds, were

11

open still and festering, and that Time the Great Healer, in twenty years, had healed nothing, nothing at all.

The sea broke softly on the rafters in the loft. Pushing up on my elbows, I saw that the empty bottle had come to rest against a large chipped vase – almost the only object upright and functional amid angles of fracture and decay. The stench seemed to issue from this vase and, peering into it, I found fag-ends and dead leaves afloat on a measure of horrid fluid that looked and stank like stale piss. I gagged and struggled to my feet, to throw open the windows and breathe in the fresh sea air.

On experiencing the view, however, I stopped short. The windows face east and, that morning, the view consisted of two horizontal bands: the lower band, the foreground, was dark and featureless, for the sun had not yet risen over the black horizon of the high sea wall; while above this shone, for all the world like a luminous flame, a wide, intense, brilliant amber sky. And there were figures on the black horizon, dark silhouettes on the sea wall, distorted somewhat by the grimy glass. They were too tall for ordinary people, and motionless. Were they statues? No, there were too many for statues, dozens of them. Was this one of my delusions? But I had not had delusions for a long time, and they used always to accompany a migraine. (I was expecting a migraine to strike at any minute, since that is how alcohol usually pays me off, but just then my head was reasonably clear.) Men on horseback, I decided, with strange, sloping headgear – hoods? Yes, hooded horsemen. I wished very much that it could be a delusion. Dark hooded horsemen, riders out of the fiery void, had mustered on the rampart and were staring down, sternly no doubt, at this derelict cottage and me. Had they heard the news and come to pay their last respects to the owner? Did they blame me, had they come for vengeance? Or, worst of all possibilities, did these spectres know my story, and judge *me* worthy of command? Were these my men now; this hooded host my army? I listened out for calls of summons or salute, but heard no voices, only, above me, the mournful slap and sigh of the ebbing sea. The horsemen simply waited and watched, infinitely patient, uncannily still, their mission evidently timeless.

My sense of betrayal turned to a resigned despair, for I knew how it had been for the owner of this estate, and how it had ended. There had been no escape for him, so how could I have supposed that time would heal *my* injuries. Then, a feeling that had brushed me the night before returned, but stronger and more compelling; a feeling of envy, envy for the dead.

Something stirred, a cold thing, coiled within me, which, on account of its lidless eye, I think of as a snake. He has never let me die, this snake, that is his job, that is why he stirred. Countless times before that morning, I had had thoughts of doing away with myself; usually the snake corrected me with nothing more than an irritable hiss. Finding me marooned on this estate, however, and oppressed by the unearthly hooded host, he stiffened with an icy rage, puffed himself up and exerted his powers to the full. So it was the snake, not I, who advanced defiantly to the window, he who demanded that the hooded host be gone, and lo!, dark clouds raced towards the rising sun like smoke returning to a fire, smothered the amber flame in the sky and transformed the hooded host into a rank of wooden beach huts.

They are still there, those beach huts, even as I write. It was a very conclusive feat.

I gazed out for a long time after that. The pure rage

of the snake had greatly impressed me. It seemed that, while sentimentally I was disposed to accept as inevitable an affinity with the owner of this estate and, therefore, to do away with myself for shame, something had worked to enrage the snake that was very like the mechanism of an allergy. I know about allergies, I have some that are merely physical. I wondered then how many of the afflictions of my adulthood were symptoms of this allergy, and to what extent I had brought them on myself, for I confess that I have cleaved to this estate, kept my knowledge and experience of it a secret, sealed within a dark cave. Suddenly I saw that everything had discernible roots here. But allergies do not remit; how could I rid myself of this one, with its stimulus so radically entrenched? It was my professional connection that gave me an idea. I am not an undertaker, I am a solicitor, and it has fallen to me to act as trustee to this estate, and to deal with its disposal. Now, it was obvious that if I was ever to dispose of it as the law requires, so that nothing of it, not so much as a grain, would remain on my hands, I had first to acknowledge, to explore, that dark cave.

So I moved in. I walked the two miles to St Osyth, collected my car from the forecourt of The Green Dragon, drove home for some belongings, left Monica my address and an inadequate note, and returned here before nightfall.

It is a strange place, a holiday settlement in winter. The lane that runs between the sea wall and the line of cottages is narrow, so I park my car at the end of it, next to a giant ice-cream which guards the locked gates to the amusement park. The ticket-vending booths are boarded up, the caravan park and playgrounds deserted; bare-masted sailboats, packing the boatyard, bump and groan and creak. It may be the foul weather, but all the cottages look run down, except the one on the corner, which has starfish and seashells and a wrought-iron galleon affixed to its bright white wall, and is too twee for anything but the shortest honeymoon. No-one is living in it now, though; I am South Point's only resident, as the postman – obliged to cycle the causeway with a letter from my wife last week – resentfully observed.

Totterdown Lane
Colchester

Mark

What's going on? Was this man a friend of yours? You said he wasn't – is there something you're not telling me? Does Alan know where you are, or are you letting *everybody* down? Can't you see that what you need is proper help? Your behaviour is absolutely GROTESQUE!

Monica

I am not hurt by 'grotesque'. In one of the albums at home, there is a photograph of Monica that is at once grotesque and miraculous. I took it six years ago, before we were married, while she was nursing Mother through her last illness. We were out walking in the woods on Boxing Day. Just as I pressed the shutter, she slipped on ice. The only part of her assembly in contact with the ground is the tip of her scarf: one of her legs is kicked high up in front of her, the other cocked to one side; her arms are outflung; her chin is tipped up to the sky. Her attitude is undoubtedly grotesque, but it is miraculous, too, because here is a picture of Monica *not falling over*. It looks inevitable that she would have crashed painfully to the ground, but in fact she had taken up instinctively the one position from which she was able to save herself. She only looks grotesque because the picture does not show the forces that unbalanced her. If I look grotesque to her now, it is for the same reason; there are forces that she does not see. I have replied to her letter, referring her to the photograph with the assurance that I, too, am miraculously still on my feet, indeed hopeful of achieving a better balance than before. She has not written again, so I assume she is satisfied. She has a car of her own and may visit me here if she wishes, although that is not likely to put her mind at rest.

Alan, I am less worried about. My partner, the Dean of 'Palfreyman, Dean', can cope without me for a while. We have recently accepted an articled clerk who can take on my work-in-progress. I wrote to Alan on my second evening here, explaining my absence – 'A bout of my old trouble . . . may take a week or so' etc. Monica, no doubt, will fill him in on the details.

While writing, I made an important discovery. It was brought on by wondering how Alan would have reacted to waking up here. He would have removed himself as rapidly as possible, I decided, the evidence of poverty would have been far too much. 'That's the way to Carey Street, chummy!' he will exclaim whenever he has spotted something to his pecuniary disadvantage – which happens at least twice a day, because Alan has an unrelenting fear of poverty. He acknowledges this, and puts it down to his childhood, which he tells me was short of cake. I have no views on that. But turning from Alan and subjecting other persons of my acquaintance to the same test, it occurred to me that this estate is rather like a mirror. Anyone looking into it will find a resemblance to some unhappy aspect of his being, in its coldness, remote-

16

ness, loneliness or ruin. And here was my discovery, for, on waking, what image had this mirror presented to me? The image of someone the hooded host might judge worthy of command; a possessor of dark powers, a master of dark forces; the Devil. This is a false image, for I am not the Devil – the snake said so, he insisted. And I say so. Yet I have rubbed along uncomfortably for years with this false image, unnamed. It has been with me since schooldays. It has been with me long enough.

One of the things I brought here from home is a picture of the St Clement's School cricket eleven, 1969. There I am, at the end of the back row, the tallest boy in the frame. I was the scorer. There is no mistaking me, I look very like my late father and several of his line, dark-haired, long-limbed, with a prominent nose well suited to supporting corrective lenses; these are necessary for a short-sightedness that comes as part of the same genetic strain. The only male member of the family who has no need of spectacles, and so no prominence to his nose, is my elder brother, Miles, of whom I do not see as much, these days, as I might. Nature Herself appears to have decided that Miles's perfectly regular features are an unwholesome aberration, for she has restored the familial profile in full to his young son and, unless I am much mistaken, his infant daughter too.

I am smiling in this photograph, and why indeed should I not be? I had every reason to be cheerful: I was in the last days of my final term, I was confident of my exam results, and, behind me, beneath the pavilion's comely thatch, was laid out a very sporting tea. I am struck, however, by the extraordinary wideness of my smile. It is not a face I commonly pull, and I realize it is what I have recently learned to call the smile of a chimpanzee.

MONKEY'S FACIAL EXPRESSIONS
DO NOT MEAN THE SAME AS
HUMAN FACIAL EXPRESSIONS

This was the message on a sign in the pets' corner of a provincial zoo that Monica and I visited earlier this year. Beneath a depiction of a grinning ape, it continued:

SMILING: THE CHIMP IS WORRIED, ANXIOUS.
DO NOT TEASE!

The sign was intended for children, but I can remember how as a child, having but lately come into words, the first language of gesture, grimace and inflection remained the more reliable. Mother, for instance, had a laughing voice which chimed with apparent good humour, but I never supposed that it bubbled up from a light, untroubled heart, for I knew that it was something unhappy in her nature that caused her laughing voice so often to flatten out and harden, long before I understood what her flat, hard words were saying – which was usually how near to her wits' end Miles and I were driving her, and what had she done to deserve us? Knowing, then, from these inflections, that Mother's gaiety was the product of an effort that all of us were duty-bound to support, the simplest ploy was to indicate happiness and gratitude regularly, with gestures of contentment and gimaces of joy.

The smile I presented in 1969 was really a grimace; like the chimp, I was worried, anxious, on no account to be teased. I had to be persuaded to take my place in the photograph, I already had difficulty with my image. I had recently had my last schoolboy encounter with the owner of this estate.

Why did that foist on me the image of the Devil? That is my secret. I shall dispose of it in the way that all secrets should be disposed of when to hold them is poisonous, by making a full disclosure. But to understand anything of my school career, I must first remember an 'incident' that occurred when I was three, or perhaps four, and drove the laughter out of my mother's voice for weeks.

The house in which I was born, and where the family lived for many years, had a large, well-tended garden. A paved veranda gave way to a rockery and then a lawn which ran half the length of the garden, with flowerbeds at its sides, down to a wooden archway, on which was trained a climbing plant with a bright red summer bloom. Beyond the archway, gooseberry, redcurrant and blackberry bushes would snag the incautious explorer of a network of narrow turfed paths, which led through to a vegetable patch and a forgotten pond. Clean-cut, yellow-green hedges flanked the lawn, and where they ended, their lines were picked up by apple, damson and plum trees. Outside the hedges and the fruit trees, around the perimeter of the entire plot, ran a secret path. A greenhouse stood in one corner at the end of the garden; in the other, underneath a cherry tree, an old summerhouse looked out quaintly on to the vegetable patch, and backed on to a thick hedge which separated the property from the wild grasses and ancient stones of the parish churchyard.

This garden was an exciting property for a child. Each season I found new things to wonder at. In winter, every incline became a thrilling slide; rocket-sticks and cartridges from the local firework display would turn up in the bushes, with charred pictures of wizards and volcanoes; sometimes there was the instinct to tiptoe over the frozen ground, as though another world below lay sleeping.

Spring is the time when the child hardly dares step back from one novelty for fear of trampling another, and runs to the house with questions and specimens.

'What's that you've got in your hand, Mark?' called Mother from the kitchen, when she saw me trotting up the lawn one spring day in the year of the 'incident'. It was a dead nestling.

'Birdy,' I replied, holding it out.

Her voice hardened. 'Throw it away, throw it away! Come in and wash your hands. Horrible! Don't bring it into the house!'

Miles, who is six years my senior, swept up on his new two-wheeled bicycle. 'We put dead things in the ground,' he said. 'Four eyes.'

Upset at having distressed Mother, feeling that I had let the side down, I took careful note of his words.

Summer brought the family and all its moods out on to the veranda, but the garden kept faith and hid me in its bloom. Miles would play cricket on the lawn with his friends, using a hard ball which they were forbidden to hit in my direction. I would therefore be sent off to the vegetable patch to search for the tortoise, or despatched with a huge basket to gather windfalls from the secret path.

Autumn was the most beautiful season. When wet leaves gagged my pedal-car, I would set about them with a rake, and turn up many treasures, including some of Miles's lost balls, which I posted through the hedge into the churchyard.

I spent a lot of time in the garden, partly out of respect for Mother's dictum: 'If you're in, you're in, and if you're out, you're out, but don't keep coming in and out, bringing mess into the house.' I would usually elect to stay in, only then to become afflicted by an urgent desire to go out, but, even so, the decision to go out was never taken lightly, and I would leave by the kitchen door, on the understanding that I would not be coming in again until quite a lot later in life, trailing a wooden trolley heaped with toys behind me on a string.

Sometimes, Mother would slip out to the tennis club, or to a friend's for tea, and the role of guardian would pass to Dora, our devout German au pair. Dora was a Salvation Army volunteer who spent most of her time in her room, pressing her uniform, starching her blouse and listening to religious choral dirges. Occasionally, if both Mother and Dora were out, the attendant adult would be Father, who normally commuted to a London office, but sometimes had calls to make in another direction and would work for a few hours in his study at home, behind a locked door. Anything was permitted when Father was in charge, so long as it did not disturb him; he was always saying he had four mouths to feed, an expression that confused me.

The role of guardian was thus passed from grown-up to grown-up, as though one were no better or worse suited to it than another, and when I started at the village school, I supposed this allowed everyone at last to go out. There was, however, one adult whom I knew to be unfit, and one formulation of the adult clues that would fill me with fear and indignation. If the laughing voice was absent from the kitchen and not chiming into the telephone receiver in the hall, and if there was no seepage from Dora's room of the Dresden Assembly of Gothic Voices, and if there was no sound of my father's earnest business voice from the study, my gaze would fall dreadfully on the garden shed, and, sure enough, the padlock would be dangling from its staple, and the door ajar. It meant that I was in the custody of the gardener, Mr Harold, whose little friend I was not, and who smelled like the forgotten pond.

I had been fond of Mr Harold's predecessor, Mr Dick, who had been dismissed in the summer for whistling at Dora. I assumed his mistake had been to whistle a cheerful tune, but Mr Dick would have known only cheerful tunes, whereas Mr Harold, I saw at once, was a subject fit for a lament. He must always have been catching his eyeballs on thorns, from the blood-red punctures in the whites of his eyes. It would ruin my day completely to see him pushing his old bicycle up the front drive, a slight bowing of the rear wheel lending a diseased and limping rhythm to the piece. It was absolutely clear to me from my first view of him, through the breakfast room window one morning, that this old man had come to us to die. So anxious was I to communicate this to the adults, I resorted to tears and a tantrum, and the unprecedented measure of clutching on to Dora's stolid thigh. But my protest went unheeded; Mother invited Mr Harold into the kitchen at lunchtime, to eat his sandwiches, so that he would feel more like one of the family, legitimate members of which made sure to be elsewhere.

Mr Harold collapsed and died on a wet afternoon in early winter. I had taken cover in the summerhouse, with my trolley of toys, and although the rain pitter-pattered on the roof and the washing on the line snapped its fingers in the wind, I heard his moan distinctly. I found him not far from the spot I had already decided should be his burial ground, an area of rich soil near the compost heap, where the carrots and lettuces grew. The rain blurred my glasses, his body swam before me. His eyes were screwed shut and his mouth gaped open, as though he had been expecting a spoonful of horrid medicine.

'We put dead things in the ground,' I recited, and dashed up to the house. The kitchen door was locked. Our boxer dog, Betsy, thumped her nose against the window and growled. I had hoped to find Dora, her arms were built for earth-moving, but then I remembered I had been obliged to kiss her that morning before she left on a daytrip to London. Through the garden gate, I saw that Mother's car was gone from the drive, and that the garage door was open and the garage empty. It was just as I had feared.

I dragged a spade from the shed down to the compost heap and went across to fetch Mr Harold. But, tugging on his foot with all my might, his boot lurched off his heel, and I thought I had broken him. I started to cry. It made it even more important to put him in the ground, now that it was my fault he was broken. I set about digging a hole beside him, but the soil was damp, and when I loosened a clod on to the spade, it was too heavy to lift. I fell to my knees and scraped up the earth, and scattered it over his face and eyes. I mud-packed his neck completely, so that his head looked detached from his body; and over his body, I tossed the withered flowers he had been uprooting for winter storage.

'Stop it, will you? Leave him alone!' yelled the woman who lived next door, from an upstairs window. 'Someone's coming, get away from him, go on!'

The side gate clanged open, and a tall man whom I had never seen before ran on to the lawn and at once fell over. Behind him, Mother clicked in heels across the veranda. The tall man came on, his eyes full of the corpse, his arms widening as if he was about to sweep Mr Harold up and hurl him over the hedge into the churchyard.

'What's happened to him?' he gasped.

Mother was on the scene before I could answer.

When she realized what she was looking at, she closed her eyes in horror; when she opened them again she was staring directly at me, as though I were the enormity.

'You dreadful little boy!' she hissed; then, to the stranger: 'I haven't been out for more than five minutes!'

They did not fetch Miles back from school that evening: he stayed with friends for a few days. I was promised that he would not be told of my part in Mr Harold's death, but somehow enough details leaked out for him, soon after, to roll his eyes at me and say 'weird' in a way that was a vogue with him at the time.

Father came up to my room when I was in bed that night.

'I don't want you to upset yourself over this, old boy. Try and put it out of your mind. It'll be Christmas, soon.' He smiled and shook his head. 'You're a funny little chap, aren't you?' The bedroom light flashed in his glasses. 'Good night.'

There was no reaction at all from Dora, since the episode was withheld from her and she was busy with the housework the next day, when Mr Harold's son came and pushed the bicycle dimly away, but the two women who ran the village school must have been told; every day for a week they greeted me in the special tones usually reserved for the dentist's polio-crippled daughter, and excused me the nature walks, which I had not asked to be excused. I wondered if Mr Dick would be invited back, now there was a vacancy, but he was not. Instead, a team of young professionals poured out of the back of a van once a week and did the work in no time with the aid of electric gadgets.

Mother lay in a darkened room for days. I worried

that her voice might be permanently grounded, but it began to take flight again after a while, in time for Christmas. After Christmas, Miles was sent back to his preparatory school as a boarder. We were implored not to think that this had anything to do with the 'incident', but Miles, for one, was not convinced, and told me so when he came to the playroom to say a resentful goodbye. Dora and my father staggered down the stairs with his trunk, while Mother filled a tuck-box with bottles of Tizer and stacks of his favourite sweets.

At seven, I went to the same preparatory school, a boarder from the outset. Miles had just left to go to St Clement's, and so began a period of ten years when, everywhere, I would find Miles's name, or sometimes just his scratched initials on desktops or in bicycle sheds; among previous owners of textbooks; on rolls of honour; on sports trophies that would never come into my possession – Miles Arthur Palfreyman. When the time came for me to go to St Clement's, I found other evidence of him, too, which I regarded as evidence of a great betrayal.

I had won a scholarship, and Father was very proud of me, not least for the reduction in fees; Father respected economy. In the summer holiday before I went to St Clement's, however, I grew upwards with astonishing, tropical suddenness; it was a prodigal growth, for it meant that I would be unable to get into Miles's old school clothes, which had been kept in mothballs for me, enough to fill a wardrobe.

'Wicked waste,' sighed Mother, as the clothes were piled into sacks and sent off to a charity. Father hummed sadly at the prospect of clothing me from scratch, which would more than account for the saving in fees.

Arriving at the school, overgrown, gangling, the

possessor of a well-known name, but with no outward similarity to the previous example of our line, I expected to attract a certain amount of curiosity, which I hoped my quiet, conforming ways would soon diminish. But Miles had seen to it that I was conspicuous to an intolerable degree. He has always been a gregarious creature and favoured anecdotal conversation of the sort that attracts an informal audience, and grows more fanciful and indiscreet as its material becomes exhausted. I soon discovered that the previous term, his last, he had broadcast a lurid version of the 'incident' with Mr Harold. He had also let it be known, when my scholarship was announced, that I was diabolically clever. This was not so; I had not been considered especially bright at the preparatory school and had come by the scholarship as a result of working hard in order to allay a fear that I might not gain entry to St Clement's at all. It seemed that Miles believed that the existence of a clever brother who had buried and, in all probability, killed the gardener – for such was his anecdote – would reflect well on him. With his all-round sporting prowess and his perfectly regular features, I never understood why he felt the need to do this. Perhaps it was because I had in some way divined his betrayal that I grew so promptly out of his clothes.

The story, of course, placed me squarely under banners of 'celebrity' and 'scandal', where I do not flourish. My remedy was to make a display of my alleged cleverness. When my contemporaries got word of the 'incident' and bothered me with questions about it, I would commend the merits of silence, though observe that, in my view, there was no such thing; that what others called silence, I preferred to think of as a wall of unrealized sound, in which all the great music ever written could be heard, if only one were not so often disturbed.

'I am with Brahms, do you mind?'

Scratching their heads and remembering that I was probably a killer, they would leave me well alone. Inevitably, my nickname was 'The Undertaker'.

It was perhaps not surprising, when even my direst stupidities were accepted as evidence of extreme cleverness, that I came, too much, to inhabit my own pretence. If my French grammatical constructions were prone to collapse, it was because my grasp on the discipline had been loosened by the poetic licence of the Romantics, whom of course I had read and enjoyed. If my basic knowledge of the sciences proved flimsy, it was because I was abstracted by the Truth and Divinity of the Great Theories. Scripture was a good read but I had moved on to Ethics; Economics failed me with its impurities; if I overlooked important facts in my History essays, it was because I, Mark Palfreyman, questioned the probity of such facts. When my exam results at the end of the second year were a shocking disaster, still I was not unveiled, for it was widely put about that I had toppled the short distance from cleverness to unreason, and the word 'breakdown' was murmured. Now, as the owner of a brilliant mind in torment, I was established in a position of detachment where I breathed more easily, and, with hard words from my father to spur me, my academic recovery began at once.

I did not go through my school career untouched by friendship, but I have no friends now from those days. In my address-book, there are a couple of names, Burnett and Idelson, but the addresses beneath them are out of date and have been crossed out. I would cross out their names, too, but who can be sure that by crossing out a name, he does not incite forces of sympathetic magic to strike down the blameless nominee? They are names without addresses, names written large in that cold-store of the memory, the registry of losses there was never time to mourn, which quickens readily at the warm breath of nostalgia. Nostalgia is not agreeable to me, it is enervating, whereas to go all the way back to the first remembered times – to the year of the 'incident' – is quite the reverse: it pushes the blood back into my roots, and invigorates me, and makes me want to paint my own front door.

But I am not behind my own front door. I am on another man's estate. When he rang and called me 'Undertaker', I knew him at once. It was not a pleasant telephone call. He had rung to ask for help, he was in trouble again. The little I did for him seems only to have contributed to his death, but I can say with a clear heart that that was not my intention. He was no more the Devil than I, not really.

I was shocked when we met again. From the look of him, he might well have had a 'dark cave' as his address for the past twenty years. It hurt me to see him like that. I wondered how I could ever have fallen for him, because fall for him I did – he was that powerful, that dangerous, once upon a time. To dispose of all that he has left me – the image of the Devil, the smile of the chimpanzee, the secret that is poisonous to hold – I must risk the enfeebling air of nostalgic recollection. I wish that I could do this as though I were once again a scorer, a bloodless tally-man outside the field of play; had I remained outside the field of play, however, there would be no need to make this record, for I am not, like my brother Miles, a compulsive raconteur.

And what is it really, this 'field of play', this 'derelict estate' which, cold and remote, lonely and ruined, holds up a mirror in which anyone may see a resemblance to his most abysmal aspect? Has it a proper name? Its owner had a name for it, years ago. In one of the packing-cases Mr Bennett's men have brought down from the loft, I recognized a book, a science fiction paperback. Inside its cover I found my name, written in my own hand. A piece of foolscap fell from the pages:

> When I came out of the melting-pot
> I was very, very, very hot.
> They put me on a sill to cool,
> Glowing golden as a jewel,
> But an eagle with a nerveless beak
> Removed me to a snowy peak
> Where, being so hot, I caused a thaw
> Which drowned my folks on the valley floor.
>
> But now, years on, I've cooled a bit
> And seeing my home, could do with it,
> As winter sets, as darkness falls
> I crave the shelter of its walls
> But ghosts inside hold me to blame
> For those murders of my infant flame,
> And so, the Wilderness I must comb
> For the charity that begins at home.

> M.Gabriel. Form: Lower VI (f)

Beneath is written, in a schoolmaster's hand:

> I quite like this one, Gaby—
> can you give it a title please,
> I'd like to use it?
> J.E.

Everyone called him Gaby. To have known him has meant to be uneasy ever after. This verse was published in a school magazine, which was hastily withdrawn from circulation for reasons that will become clear. It appeared under the title 'The Wilderness Song'.

This is my story, from the wilderness.

2

Exile

The thatched pavilion is shuttered and locked, the cricket square is roped off, the boundary line has been washed away by relentless summer rain. St Clement's shimmers in the breathless heat of a golden September afternoon. The weather's attempt to make amends for the downpours of July and August has come too late, alas, for denizens of the school, for it is the first day of the Winter Term, 1968, the beginning of my last school year.

The school stands on a hill at the northern end of a river town midway between London and the Kent coast. A motorist bearing in from the west may not catch the view of the playing-fields available through the Lovat Gate, to his right; half a mile further on, however, having followed a long downhill bend which sweeps the road to the south and aims it at the top of a narrow high-street, he will certainly notice the long, grey neo-Gothic Main School building, parallel to the road but set back from it a hundred feet by grand, untrodden lawns. He may also notice, above the lawns, the inward-looking Founder's Hall, presenting its dignified, stained-glass rear in a manner which gives an impression of the school's relationship with the town that does not mislead. At the point where the low front wall divides, with a graceful inward loop, to admit a drive, two lions on stone pedestals stare blankly in opposite directions. The drive makes a curling passage through the grand lawns to a great arch at the centre of the Main School, through which the playing-fields may again be glimpsed.

At most times of day, the motorist will be brought to a standstill at the top of the High Street, where the white, weatherboard frontages of preserved, historic buildings squeeze the road into a bottleneck. As he waits, he may find himself looking directly into the dark-panelled interior of the Headmaster's study, through the ground-floor windows of the Head-master's house, a fortified winged fist at the end of a pantiled cloister extending towards the road from the Main School's southern extremity.

At the back of the Main School, out of sight from the road, a boy setting out from the great arch on a punishment run around the playing-fields, will cover two-thirds of a mile by completing the circuit. He will run first across a gravelled square to the edge of the Upper Field, which is reserved for cricket and hockey. There, he will turn right, up a gently sloping access road which leads to the Lovat Gate. The Gate, which is always open, displays the school motto, in wrought-iron lettering: FLORET QUI LABORAT. It is set into a neatly compiled stone wall, much higher than the boundary wall at the front. The runner will turn left before the Gate, and proceed alongside this wall, above a patch of ground used for cricket nets or, on open days, as a carpark, until a lime-green hedge bars his route and forces him infield. The hedge confines the garden of Starvecrow Hall, a lodging house for junior masters. At its corner stands the elegant pav-ilion, looking out on the Upper Field; beside that is the scorer's box, a black, wooden construction that looks as though it has suffered a fire, but has not, and sits slightly at a tilt on a set of rusted wheels.

The runner will then turn away from the school and cut through an avenue of mature chestnut trees. Now he will plunge down a steep, two-tiered bank to the Lower Field, and vanish, briefly, from the view of any prefect monitoring his progress through the windows of the prefects' room above the Main School's great arch. This steep bank, dividing the two great fields, makes a natural grandstand for spectators when a match is played on the first fifteen rugby pitch marked out on the Lower Field. If the sharp descent unbalances the runner, a cushion of leaves piled at the corner of the pitch by the groundstaff will soften his fall. Picking himself up, the miscreant will continue along the line of hedges and fences at the field's edge, past the first fifteen goalposts, which soar to a dizzy height, and on to a second, comparatively squat set of goalposts at the top of another rugby pitch. This second pitch is slightly shorter than the first, due to the incursion, at its far corner, of the wild back garden and corrugated bicycle shed of another school building, the Studies. The garden is unfenced, but guarded by a cluster of towering Scots pines, whose spreading canopies look like dark smoke to the prefect, far away in the Main School.

The runner, a remote figure sporadically sighted through the chestnut trees, will traverse the length of the second rugby pitch beside the school's furthest boundary, a spiked railing which cuts off the Lower Field from an apple orchard. Arriving at the other far corner of the field, and resisting the temptation to take a mud-path which leads down to the river and on to a coastal port and a passage to France, the runner will turn and start the long trek back to the school.

To his right the brow of Paddock Hill, on the far side of the valley, may just be glimpsed over the top of a farmer's high hedge. The hedge seals off the first of a series of hopfields, which make a gradual descent to the river's watermeadows. Having crossed the rugby pitches again, the runner, confronted by the steep grassy bank, must now resist a stately flight of steps, which offers an easy ascent. These are the Passchendaele Steps, named in honour of a master who lost a leg on that battlefield in the Great War, but returned to coach the rugby team from their vantage. Members of staff and prefects may avail themselves of the Passchendaele Steps, but if a boy on a punishment run is seen so much as leaning on their mossy balustrade, he can expect to come under very heavy fire indeed.

At the top of the bank, beneath the chestnut trees, the runner, unsteady, perhaps winded, may pause to take in the view. It is a stern, imposing view, likely to drive from his mind any questions he may have about the justice of his punishment. A hundred windows or more look out at him from the Main School, whose towers and turrets and battlements crowd the horizon. Two curiously ill-matched wings reach towards the Upper Field.

To the left, set apart from the gravelled square by a memorial rose garden, the long red-bricked chapel soars above a haphazard jumble of lesser buildings. From its front sprouts an enclosed cloister, through which the congregation enters each morning for assembly, and where, on Sundays, the processional choir forms. On the chapel's sharp-pitched roof, a slim cross stands on top of a pepperpot tower, looking, from a distance, like a wire-doll, dressed in petticoats. The lesser buildings include an L-shaped bungalow with an outsize roof, which is the tuck-shop; the school outfitter's shop, a dingy emporium with a failed patio, forever in the shadow of its neighbour – the old, metal-raftered and always cold Gymnasium, where a medi-cine ball bounces with a cannon's boom. Partly obscured by the Gymnasium is a flimsy, shack-like edifice which is home to the Art and Woodwork Schools, and looks like something the woodwork students have built and the art students declined to paint; nearby is the Music School, trim, two-storied, and built of the same red bricks as the chapel.

To the right of the gravelled square, a new, breeze-block, modernist fantasy, the Beckett Wing – which has perspex pyramids for a roof, and in no way complements the other architectural styles in sight – obtrudes with all the confidence of the crassest parvenu. It houses at ground level an assembly-hall-cum-theatre, and on its upper deck, the school library. Already, rust-stained wash-marks on its bland face show that it is being corroded by a drainage problem.

The runner will now complete his circuit by turning right and following a path around the outskirts of another flap of turf, where the most junior boys play cricket; beyond this, the path will subject him to a winding detour through the fives courts, squash courts, armoury and rifle-range, until at last he will emerge by the snubnosed end of the Beckett Wing and regain the gravelled square, there to be told by his monitoring prefect if his time has been acceptable.

There was no-one out on a punishment run that glorious afternoon; the term would not officially start until six o'clock in the evening. I was sitting on a bench near the Music School, looking out on the Upper Field, not in the best of moods – irritated and still a little shaky. The shakiness was because Father had brought me back to the school immediately after lunch – at my own request, for I had much to do – and driven, as usual, as though pursued by a tidal wave. I did not take offence at this apparent eagerness to be rid of me; although I never knew what caused Father's harebrained driving, I understood that, like a mania, it was involuntary. Even when, at his suggestion, on visits to his mother we took the longer route through Richmond Park in order to admire the deer, Father's speed would steadily build up to the point where the tyres squealed on corners, and his hand would hammer compulsively on the horn to clear the road of equestrians, and any deer we might chance to see would be kicking up dust in wild-eyed flight from our approach. For a long time, I supposed that I was the only member to deplore, or even notice, Father's recklessness. In the old days, Mother would sit in the front, nattering gaily, seemingly oblivious to the fact that her life was part of the stake with which he gambled, while Miles, in the back with me, would shout encouragement and wave V-signs through the back window at those whom we overtook. Latterly, however, I had realized that Father himself was no less dismayed than I by whatever it was that possessed him at the wheel, and I felt rather sorry for him and tried not to flinch. Nonetheless, the journey had been a trying experience; he had picked up a new habit of calling out when about to overtake on corners where his passenger had the more onward view: 'ANYTHING COMING, OR CAN I GO?'

Usually, I could anticipate these corners, so that when the question came, I would be rummaging behind me for something on the back seat, or hiding behind an upheld newspaper, but it still wore on the nerves to know that any moment I might be called on for a split-second, life-or-death decision.

And I was irritated, too, because beside me on the bench were my violin case and a stack of library books. I had been unable to dispose of these, because the school buildings in which they belonged were locked. The small room in the great arch where the porter lodged with his keys was also locked, and I peevishly visualized him tipping back ale on the terrace of The Feathered Oars downtown, or in the beer-garden of The Blue Posts, tucked away behind the orchard at the end of the Lower Field. It was a setback to find St Clement's so soundly asleep, for this was a special day, a day when I hoped to bring order to a new home: I was moving.

The school was made up of nine independent communities – the Houses. A day-boy House convened in common rooms in the basement of the Main School, where the boarders of 'College House' also lived, in dormitories and study-cubicles off the corridor on the top floor. Five other boarding Houses were to be found in a tangle of quiet streets across the London Road to the north of the school; none was more than half a mile from the chapel, on which their members converged each morning by way of the Lovat Gate. The other two Houses, 'Collingwood', which was mine, and 'Clancarty', were sited near to each other down a lane which made a junction with the London Road almost directly opposite the Headmaster's house. The boys of these establishments liked to believe that, due to their proximity to the town, they breathed a more urbane air; their walk to the chapel in the morning took them down the curling drive, through the great arch and up the access road.

Then there was 'the Studies', an additional House, containing the Senior Studies and a dozen or so juniors, new boys for whom no room could be found in their proper Houses. Some were there only for a term, and were able to take their place in House after Christmas, when university candidates and those resitting 'A' levels left; others stayed a full year. Homesick, and intimidated by the manners and rituals of a strange society they had only half-joined, the small boys inhabited the cramped dormitory and communal day-room on the ground floor of the building and rarely disturbed the occupants of the Senior Studies on the floor above.

There were only seven Senior Studies. Their function was to accommodate responsible senior boys and to offer a rehearsal of university life. My unexpected promotion to the rank of prefect half-way through the summer term had qualified me to apply for one of these much-coveted bed-sitting rooms. My Housemaster, Bill Rivers, had warned me not to build my hopes too high; it was most unusual for a boy to be awarded a study for a whole year, and he reckoned that the best I could hope for was to create a good impression at my interview with Mr Ambrose, the Studies' senior tutor, which would stand in my favour should I care to re-apply for the Spring Term, when there would again be vacancies.

I had reported for the interview to Mr Ambrose's flat, on the top floor of the Studies, in the middle of a very hot June afternoon.

'What on earth makes you think that you, of all people, deserve a study?' he began.

I searched his face for a clue to whether his offensive tone was in earnest, or only teasing, but, as usual with Mr Ambrose, his expression was deadpan. I had expected the question, albeit in a more civil edition, and prepared a reply. Just as I was about to deliver it, however, I was checked by a noise from another part of the flat. It sounded like a deep sigh. I wanted to wait and listen for it again but Mr Ambrose was giving me his full, unblinking attention; evidently he had heard nothing, so I began, but nervously, with my timing thrown: 'Well, of course I have important exams at the end of the year, sir. I feel that a less distracting environment will enable me to prepare for them more efficiently, and earn honours for the school. If, on the other hand, the strain proves too much for me, as it did once before in my second year, as I'm sure you know, then obviously from the school's point of view the more discreetly I can be removed to an asylum the better, ha, ha.'

The slight joke, which had sounded so winning in practice, sounded ghastly. Mr Ambrose remained deadpan. I decided to cut the jokes.

'My main subject is History and your junior tutor here, Mr Blake, is my History master, which would be convenient. I'm in Dr Rabbitt's new string quartet, so I'll be spending even more time in the Music School. In fact, if I had a study, I'd hardly be here at all, I'm often in the Music School. I'm already a prefect and have experienced no difficulty in controlling junior boys.'

There was a moment's silence.

'Are you a *complete* queer?'

'Sir?'

'The senior boys here have nothing whatever to do with the juniors.'

'I see.'

A deep rumble came from another room, as though something heavy had shifted an inch or two on rollers. Again the distraction seemed to elude Mr Ambrose.

'Prefects from College House come over in the evening to supervise their prep and "lights out",' he continued, 'otherwise Mrs Binks, the housekeeper, sees to the juniors.'

'Right, sir.'

'Is that perfectly clear?'

'Yes, sir, perfectly.'

'Whatever have you done to upset Marjorie Rivers?'

Another rumbling sound; Mr Ambrose stared on. It was dreadfully close and airless, a prickly heat worried my skin.

'Marjorie Rivers, sir?'

'Yes, your Housemaster's wife – you know the woman, don't you?'

'Yes, of course.'

'Well, what have you done to upset her?'

'Nothing, sir, so far as I know.'

'You must be an absolute creep to have around, then.'

'Why?'

'She's very keen for you to have a study, that's why. Obviously she wants you out of the House. My hard luck, I suppose.'

'Have I got a chance, then, sir?'

'Oh yes, you're in.'

'Thank you, sir!'

'Oh, don't thank me, it's got nothing to do with me.'

Now there was another rumble, but this time louder and obviously human – someone was sleeping in an adjacent room, that much was plain. When the tutor's face was again quite unmoved, I understood at last that, for the purposes of our conversation, these background noises were not happening.

'A lot of very nice boys who it would be a real pleasure to have here have applied this term,' he went on. 'But it's not up to me, is it? I just run the place. If Marjorie Rivers wants a study for one of her boys, well . . .' He shrugged.

'There'll be a meeting of the successful applicants in a week or so,' he said, as he shepherded me out, raising his voice a little to be heard over the snoring, which had grown very loud and regular. 'It's not official yet, so I'd rather you didn't go round telling everyone, but I suppose you will.'

'Thank you very much, sir.'

Thus had the move I was making on that first afternoon of term been settled.

'Are you sure it's what you really want?' Marjorie

had asked, clasping my hand in both of hers, when the news was confirmed. I assured her that it was. We had never been close. Now the way was clear for her favourite, Digby Letts, to be Head of House. A playing-fields hero, to Marjorie, Digby was 'our sportsman'; I was 'our musician friend', or, better still, when orchestra practice made me late, 'our wandering minstrel'. I was quite happy to wander right away, to go into voluntary exile.

Cars delivering boys to College House began to arrive, slipping past me down the access road. Soon there would be bores on fast-moving bicycles, eager for conversation about the summer hols. No-one had come to unlock the Music School or the Beckett Library, so, with an impatient sigh, I gathered up the books and my violin. Hoping that the clear blue sky was auspicious, but perspiring under my heavy load, I crossed the Upper Field, descended the Passchendaele Steps, and made my way over to the Studies.

3

Settling In

Having unpacked my belongings and stowed my trunk
under the bed, I was struck by how spacious my new
quarters were, compared to the cramped booth I had
occupied at Collingwood. The room looked bare, and I
wondered if there was, perhaps, some major item I had
forgotten to bring over. I had supposed that I would
deck the walls, as usual, with record sleeves and posters,
curtain off the shelves with strips of material, and
string up, as a warm ceiling, a wrap of green felt I had
inherited from a leaver. The study unadorned, however,
felt bracingly ascetic, and seemed to imitate perfectly
the clean lines with which I expected to sail the higher
reaches of academe this year. I decided to leave it just
as it was, and so that my concentration would not be
distracted by frivolous titles, I put my science fictions,
novels and musical scores on a high, inconvenient
shelf above the door. I left my record player on the
floor at the end of the bed, and, beside it, my record
collection, in plastic bags, leaning against the wall. My
lightshade I rejected as a luscious decadence, sure to
occlude the clear light of reason with its slight pinkness,
so that, too, was lodged on the high shelf. Having,
now, nothing to do, other than plug in my angle-poise
desklamp and settle down to some work, I went along
the corridor to a small kitchen to make a cup of tea.
Stirrings on the ground floor indicated the arrival of the
juniors. I wandered into the reading-room at the end of
the corridor, which looked out on the front yard.

Fathers and sons were coming and going, ransacking the boots and back seats of family saloons, randomly parked. Beside the cars stood mothers and sisters, in light summer dresses. One boy helped his father wrestle with the strapping of a roof-rack, another, in a crisp, unseasoned straw hat, stood by the gate, his arm round a cake tin, smiling gallantly for a camera held by his younger, gawky sister. Groups formed at empty car-boots for the difficult last moments before a long goodbye; I was glad that I had already arrived and there was no danger of Father swerving in through the gate with me at high speed. A small boy in a Collingwood House hat-band had only the chauffeur who had delivered him to shake hands with, and I felt that his arrival was the easier for this. I remembered how difficult it had been on my own first day to find an adequate response to Mother's final, emphatic reassurance: 'Don't worry, dear, by the end of term you'll be so grown up, we won't know you.'

The kettle boiled. It occurred to me as I poured the hot water that I was probably wasting my time, for it was most unlikely there would be any milk. Opening the fridge, however, I discovered that it was packed with provisions, including a milk bottle. I had poured out some of its contents before I noticed that there was a label stuck to it, bearing the initials A.W.G. All the other items in the fridge carried the same label, and were therefore the property of Andrew Garland. My heart sank.

On learning that he was to be a neighbour, I had made enquiries about Garland, to a classmate, Idelson – known as 'the Wizard' for his practised air of mystic cerebration. The Wizard had delighted in a lurid tale: since the Corps had seen fit to make Garland its senior officer, he had become insufferably officious in the

House; no-one was safe from the jab of his swagger-stick. His peers had deemed him unstable, and rued the lethal weaponry that was at the boy's disposal: as president of the Alpine Club, he held on to its only asset, a presentation ice-axe, which hung from his wall; and nailed up beside it were the effects of the Speleological Society – of which he was also president – a diver's knife and, oddly, a harpoon.

'Blimey. Anything else on this wall?'

'Targets from the rifle range, with all his best groupings, the Corps' ceremonial sword . . .'

'*That's* in the armoury, I've seen it!'

'The armoury? My dear Markus,' said the Wizard, 'what does the school do for a pathological maniac like this but stage a paramilitary rally and present him with the keys to the armoury on a little green cushion?'

He was referring to the Summer Parade, at which there had indeed been such a ceremony. 'Four hundred rifles, pistols, bayonets . . .'

David Burnett, the Upper Sixth's comedian, remarked that Garland sounded the ideal neighbour for an undertaker.

'And watch him with the juniors, too,' the Wizard added.

It had been noted that when the Orienteers, for whom he was pathfinder-in-chief, spent a night under canvas – or the Speleological Society went underground – Garland had a special care for the youngest boys, for whom the guidance of his flashlight was never far away.

'It's all right,' I said, 'the boys in the Senior Studies have nothing whatever to do with the juniors.'

At this, the exchanges had become derisive and unhelpful.

Now I had taken some of his milk. I had, obviously, to tell him about it; anyone who labelled his perishables so meticulously would be sure to notice the slightest depletion of his stock, and since all the other studies were open and empty, I was the only possible thief. When I knocked at his door, it swung open with startling immediacy. Garland was a pink, square-faced boy, with a swinishly open-nostrilled tilt to his nose.

'Hallo, Mark.'

'Hallo, Andrew, how were the hols?'

'Great.'

'May I use a little of your milk for my tea?'

'Couldn't you get some from Mrs Binks?'

'She'll be rather busy at the moment, I've just seen a lot of juniors arriving.'

'Watching the sprogs, eh?'

'Er, no, not specially.'

'How much milk do you want, only I was going to make some cocoa later.'

'Not much.'

'Go on, then. This once.'

As I came back from the kitchen, my mug of tea in hand, his door re-opened.

'All right?' he said.

'Yes. Thanks again.'

'Not at all,' he said. 'My pleasure.'

Entering my study, I thought that the spartan austerity I had imposed on it was a little overdone, and that the short roll of grey carpet in my trunk could be laid without threat to my discipline.

The pockets of muted conversation below had blended into a general hum. I wondered what might be the thoughts of a new boy, gazing out of the day-room window, were he to see, as I did from my study, Mr Ambrose approaching the wild back garden from the Lower Field. Juniors were usually cowed by his appearance. He was a burly figure, whose short legs worked with a fast action to keep up with the momentum of his powerful upper frame. His long torso was not paunched, but padded all around with a layer of sponge, which gathered untidily at his neck into a series of chins. As he walked, his arms, which had been designed on the same insufficient gauge as his legs, hung to his sides without grace or balancing reflex, as though they had yet to be neurally connected. His neck and shoulders seemed to have been hewn from the same block as the head they bore, for when he turned this great head to address a boy, his chest and shoulders would turn also, and he appeared to be squaring up for a fight. His brylcreemed hair was combed back from the high, vertical forehead from which its line of growth was receding. A strong jaw, jutting out over the spongy chins, supported features that were usually set into an expression that would have been stern, had it not been for his eyes. These, like the eyes of a seal, were dark and unblinking, as though tears had frozen in them, and they made his expression seem, not stern, but unflinching before some private hurt.

Remembering how smartly turned-out and available Bill and Marjorie Rivers always were, at Collingwood, on first days or when parents were about, I assumed that Ambrose would now crush underfoot the cigarette clenched in his mouth, enter by the back door, and, forgoing his favourite gambit of opening a conversation with an insult, introduce himself to those delivering their sons into his care. I was therefore surprised when, moments after passing from view, the great head loomed not three feet away, at the corner of my window, as the tutor went by on his way to his flat via the fire-escape.

Familiar music, I thought, would make better company, in the short time before assembly, than the textbook I had laid out. The timing of this idea was fortunate, because I discovered that the plastic bags holding my record collection were touching a pipe which was beginning to heat up. I was squatting on the floor, checking the records individually for warp, when a knock came at the door.

'Hallo, Mark.'

It was the junior tutor, Jonathan Blake.

'Hallo, Jonathan.'

I did not get up – the young man appreciated informality.

'When are you moving your stuff in?'

'I already have. Sir.'

'Oh, sorry. This is it, then?'

I glanced up. He seemed to be poised to throw a dart at my favourite LP, so I snatched it away from his target-line instinctively, before realizing that there was no dart in his hand and that I had been taken in again by his habit of practising sporting techniques. Usually it was cricket. In the middle of a conversation, he would curtsey forward and push the back of his left hand through the line of an imaginary delivery; at other times he would cup his hands and take a fast catch in the region of his groin. Clay-pigeon shooting was another favourite, and I had, on occasion, seen him make a pass or two at a golf-ball, but darts was a new one to me. Now, with the record in my hand, I felt obliged to say something about it.

'Have you heard these? They're great.'

'Goldberg Variations – Bach, eh? I don't know, I may have done.'

'They're very good.'

'I thought you might like to come up later, for a coffee or something. Why don't you bring it along?'

The tutors each had a flat on the top floor; Jonathan's was much the smaller, and situated at the front of the house, above the reading-room.

'OK, thanks.'

'Can you ignore the bell at six, that's just for the juniors. There'll be another one at half-past, for tea, so come down for that.'

He worried over a short putt for a moment, and left.

The meeting that took place downstairs at the first bell was quiet and extremely short. When it had adjourned, there came a single rap on my door, which swung open before I could respond.

'Hallo, Palfreyman,' said Mr Ambrose. 'Thanks for coming to say hallo.'

'Hallo, sir.'

'Catch.' He flicked a copy of the small pocket-book that was issued each term, with lists of the staff and boys and a diary of events. It fell far out of reach and set my fountain-pen rolling towards the edge of the desk. I saved it.

'Thanks.'

'If you're going to smoke this term, would you please do so only in my flat? I can't have this corridor reeking like last term.'

'All right.'

'Do you smoke?'

'No, sir.'

'Good. I won't be seeing much of you then. There'll be another bell soon, for tea. Sit anywhere you like on the top table, but if you're anywhere near me, don't you dare just sit there and eat. I can't stand boys who won't talk. Apart from anything else, I think it's terribly rude. By the way, have you seen Ostler?'

Ostler's name was on the study door next to mine. A classicist, he was reputed to be the cleverest boy in the school. I shook my head.

'I don't think he's come back yet,' said Ambrose. 'Good start, isn't it?' He looked at my bare walls and scant furnishings, and brightened. 'Do you know, we once had a boy who left his study just like this. Extraordinary, eh?'

Although he was the last person a junior would wish to find himself walking beside on the mud-path down to the river fields for games of an afternoon, Ambrose was popular with older boys, particularly those whose unruly behaviour bore the stamp of compulsion. Sometimes, crossing the gravelled square flanked by youths notorious for dissent, his hurry-footed gait would fall in with their swagger, and he looked like the leader of a gang. Since Ambrose himself had been Head Boy at St Clement's some twenty years earlier and had returned to the school as a member of staff immediately after university, some thought it strange that he, of all people, should display an affinity with troublemakers. I saw nothing strange in it at all, it was the key to my theory about him. I thought that his relationship with the school was very like that of my Uncle Fred with my Aunt Joy, and I regarded both Ambrose and Uncle Fred as 'institutionalized', using the word for the connotations that attached to it when I first heard Mother use it.

Not far from home, behind a high wall in thick woodland where we sometimes picked blackberries, stood an RAF establishment, whose gate was always locked. To deter me from climbing the wall, Mother told me that the men who lived behind it were fighter pilots who had suffered terrible burns in crashes, and were so disfigured they could never go out.

'Not even in masks?'

'They wouldn't want to, dear. They'd be lost in the outside world. Most of them have been there for years. They're institutionalized.'

Uncle Fred was no better off than the pilots. Everyone knew that Aunt Joy led him a dog's life.

'Why doesn't he just leave her?' said Miles once,

49

after a family gathering at which Joy had made clear to one and all her particular dissatisfactions with her husband.

'Marriage isn't something you just walk out on, my boy,' said Father.

'It's an institution,' seconded Mother.

This posed the question that if Uncle Fred was stuck in an institution like the pilots, where was his disfigurement, for he was a perfectly agreeable-looking relative? I decided that all the 'putting up with it' – the accommodations and allowances he had made in the interests of compatibility, or at least a quiet life – had chipped away not at Uncle Fred's face, but at some image of himself that only he could see, and had left him with a sense of a disfigurement so gross that, just as the pilots would never emerge from behind the locked gate, so Uncle Fred would never leave Aunt Joy, because he could not believe that anyone else would put up with a man so hideous. He would console himself by revelling in any humiliation that befell his wife. Ambrose, likewise, enjoyed any affront to the dignity of the school, and seemed to glow in conspiracy with the rebel soul who caused it. I understood from this that he, too, regarded himself as inwardly disfigured by the institution in which he had spent so many years. It followed that the more a boy resisted the conformities necessary for a clear passage through the school, the less, in Ambrose's eyes, he was disfigured; the rebel therefore presented to the institutionalized master a flawless and admirable aspect.

The Studies, playing host to a constant traffic of these outlaws while housing the tenderest juniors and most privileged seniors, was seen as a potentially volatile hotbed and stimulated a great deal of gossip. The fact that the gossip was the only dismal produce of this hotbed, which otherwise turned out seniors academically well-endowed, juniors no more or less corrupt than their House-bound contemporaries, and rebels with their protest slightly muted, was attributed to the canny excellence of the tutor, who was said to have a 'way with the boys'. We had an example of his 'way with the boys' at tea that very evening.

'You!' he said horribly, pointing from the dining-room's top table at one of the new boys.

'Me, sir?'

'Yes, you. I'm pointing at you, aren't I? What's your name?'

'Nicholas Binns, sir.'

'Binns?'

'Yes, sir.'

'Do you have to eat like a pig, Binns?'

The boy said nothing, but reddened and looked along the top table as though at a panel of accusers.

'I wouldn't want to sit next to you, eating with your mouth wide open like that,' Ambrose persisted. 'It can't be very nice, can it?'

'No, sir,' said the boy, his eyes beginning to water.

After this, the hush that descended on the juniors, who chewed shut-mouthed in dread of another challenge, quickly spread to the top table, and I racked my brains for some conversational topic I might safely introduce. Garland had sat himself down at Ambrose's right hand, but as the meal progressed, it became clear that he had no idea what was required. Making no attempt at conversation, he instead provided the services of an irritatingly over-attentive steward, passing everything that came within his reach towards the tutor, who was soon beset with condiments and cruets and was beginning to brood darkly.

Suddenly from outside came the strains of an American surfing song. A small open-topped sports car had drawn up in the front yard, its cream bodywork emblazoned with tongues of purple flame. The young man at the wheel silenced the radio, jumped out over the door and pulled an American flag from the luggage rack with the *élan* of a professional conjuror. Ambrose stared out, an unachieved expression wriggling for life at the corner of his mouth.

A Texan businessman, Bosco by name, posted to London and impressed by the ways of the society he found there, had sent his son to St Clement's to finish his schooling and acquire the manners and distinctions of an English gentleman. Since Bosco junior was already aged seventeen when this decision was taken, his compliance was not to be assumed, and it was anyway an impossible mission. Because the school was founded on the customs and principles of the English family it was paid to replace, much was understood by its subjects that failed in explanation to a foreigner who referred to a different grounding, and so the etiquette of repression, the language of denial, and all the other nursery apparatus that found structure in the school's compendium of rules made, for Bosco, an alien code. A naturally courteous boy, he had remained happily unassimilated, indicating as much by going everywhere, even into class, with a camera round his neck and photographing the most mundane school activities with the fascinated air of one who has stumbled on a Lost City. Deeply tanned, chewing vigorously, with crewcut hair, he looked far more American now than he had when he first arrived a year ago. The juniors, watching him through the window, would have thought he was a young master rather than a pupil, had it not been for the Briary House colours displayed on his straw hat; the hat had fallen to the back of his neck and been saved from sailing away as he drove by a length of elastic looping under his chin.

Unaware that he held our attention, he unloaded the car. He seemed not to have packed with the school in mind at all: a surfboard, a guitar, a baseball bat, golf-clubs and lots of photographic equipment were soon heaped up against the sleek suitcase he used instead of a trunk, and when it seemed that the little car could not possibly have held any more, he emerged from its boot bowed under the weight of a crate of Californian beer.

'Garland, would you be kind enough to invite Bosco to join us?' said Ambrose. Garland left at once, with an air of porky importance and a sidelong glance at the juniors.

'Here he is, sir,' he said, on his return.

Bosco strode in. 'Am ah late? Gee, ah'm sorry, sir, ah didn't know there wuz a tea.'

'Well of course there's a tea.'

'Ah'm sorry, sir.' He nodded at the car. 'D'ya like it?'

'As a matter of fact,' said Ambrose, 'I think it's hideous.'

'Aw, c'mon,' said Bosco, chuckling genially.

'Look, would you please take your coat off and sit down? You're setting an appalling example.'

'Oh, excuse me.' As he removed his coat, Bosco caught sight of the dumbfounded juniors. He gave a small wave: 'Howdy.'

He had had the presence of mind, when appre-hended by Garland, to stuff a bottle of beer in his pocket, and now he set it on the table. Ambrose glowered. 'D'ya wanna beer, sir, I gotta stack outside?'

'No, thank you.'

'You guys?'

No-one owned up to wanting a beer.

'You do know that you're not allowed alcohol in your studies, don't you?' said Ambrose. 'When that crate comes into the House, it goes straight into Mrs Binks's kitchen and you're not to touch it. I shouldn't really allow it, it's supposed to be ordered specially. You're allowed one beer at tea, and that's it. It's a crazy rule, I know. It gives you all the excuse you need to reek of alcohol every night, and I have no doubt you will, but if I find drink in a senior study, that's it, you're out. Is that understood by everybody?'

There were six of us at the table with the two masters, Ostler now being the only absentee. We nodded. We understood. Garland, however, did not understand how Bosco had managed to break several important school rules with apparent impunity, and kept looking from the playthings piled in the yard to the young American and back again with a puzzled frown. When no bottle-opener could be found for Bosco's beer, he rallied, and produced a Swiss Army knife. He methodically unfolded its many deadly appendages, and left them on display, until finding at last an opener, he passed it down the table via Jonathan, who handled it reluctantly.

'And you can use that horrible thing to cut the elastic off your boater,' said Ambrose. 'You know that's not the way it's supposed to be worn, we don't have cowboys in this country.'

'No, sir,' said Bosco.

'I've never seen such a travesty.'

'Sir.'

'And I want the keys to the car as soon as you've parked it properly. You won't be going anywhere in that for a few weeks.'

'Sir.'

'If the Headmaster came by now and saw what all these concessions added up to . . .'

Garland, nodding in approval of all this, now made the mistake of adding to the condiments and cruets in front of the tutor by passing along a shallow bowl of jam.

'Oh WILL you stop shoving things in front of me PLEASE! If I want anything, I'll ask for it, all right?'

Five minutes later – and tense, silent minutes they were – Ambrose spoke again: 'The top table here usually calls me Perry, by the way. I prefer it, if you don't mind. Seniors can always manage to make "sir" sound like an insult.'

I lay on my bed after tea, turning through the pages of the term's pocket-book. The lightbulb, unshielded, blazed in my eyes, so I fitted the pink lampshade. In the Collingwood House list, an 'S' appeared by my name, to show that I was resident at the Studies; the same symbol appeared by the name 'P.M. Reed', who must therefore have been the boy I saw shaking hands with his chauffeur. Without the Collingwood colours about his person, I had been unable to pick him out from the other new faces at tea.

It cheered me to think of everyone else on the House list forming a queue at that moment outside Bill Rivers's study door for the inspection with which every term began. The study door would open, the queue of boys would shuffle in, and one by one they would drop their trousers and expose themselves to the House doctor. The doctor, perched on the arm of a chair, would scan each specimen with a pen-torch for signs of an infectious rash, while Bill ticked the register. Sometimes, but rarely, a boy would be held back for a second look and an anointment.

I had always assumed that the ritual was necessary because this was the sort of thing a boy could not be relied on to do for himself. To play fair by the system which had granted me a reprieve from this humili-ation, I decided that it was my responsibility to perform a private inspection of my own. I did this, leaning back against the wall to prevent an untimely intrusion, with the help of a small mirror. Having found myself entire and with no rash, I was hoisting my underpants when a noise outside the window startled me. It sounded like a muffled laugh. It was dark by now and I could see nothing but the reflection of the room's interior in the window, so I flicked off the lightswitch beside me. From that corner of the window where, earlier, Ambrose's head had loomed, a shadow ducked and fled. I had forgotten about the fire-escape.

I could not tell if the voyeur had been going up or down, but later I suspected, from the harsh unfamiliar laughter that could be heard next door while Jonathan and I listened to the Goldberg Variations, that he had been going up, and was greatly enjoying the tale he had for Ambrose. I did not stay long upstairs. I had hoped that Jonathan's girlfriend, the lovely Judy, would be there, but she was not, and the young master, although friendly, was agitated by some aberration in the timetable he had been given for the term. I could see he was anxious to sort it out, so I made my excuses early.

Sitting at my desk, I tried to read, but my eyes were drawn, time and again, to the window, where all I could see was my own reflection. I felt tense and self-conscious, as though someone in the darkness outside was watching me – someone who had already found me ridiculous. Thoroughly unsettled, I thought I would have to undress for bed in the dark, but then remembered the wrap of green felt I had inherited, and pinned it up as a makeshift curtain.

4

Two Sundays

Ambrose informed us at breakfast that Ostler would not be returning to the school; the boy's parents had telephoned to say that he had been unwell during the holidays, was still under the doctor, and had accepted a place offered by a local university, in preference to sitting the Oxbridge entrance exams.

'You're next door, Mark, so keep an eye on his study. He moved all his stuff in at the end of last term. They're coming back for it some time, I don't know when. No doubt as usual I'll be the last to be told.'

As I walked through a heavy dew on the Upper Field towards the chapel for morning assembly, I saw Dr Rabbitt, the music director, stationed at the door of the Music School, scanning the access road up to the Lovat Gate. He whirled round at my approach, and made no effort to conceal his disappointment at seeing me.

'Oh, hallo, Palfreyman. Have you seen Norman Ostler?'

The summer had done Dr Rabbitt no cosmetic good. He appeared to have been staked out under a fierce sun, for his complexion, which was always high, was now a juicy purple, and his massed grey curls were bleached, so that there was no discernible top to his head but instead a white, wispy dissolve.

'He's not coming, sir, he's left. He's gone to university.'

'What! He hasn't, has he? Oh God!'

I had spoken carelessly. A dramatic slump in his

morale caused him to seek support from the door-frame.

'He's supposed to be my assistant in chapel this term!' he wailed. 'Now I won't know where I am!'

'I'm sorry, sir.'

'He promised.'

'He's been very ill.'

It made no difference. He swallowed and shook his head.

'Could you help me out, Mark?' he pleaded, 'just for today?'

Dr Rabbitt was a man too emotionally loose ever to be safely denied, and so, feeling some responsibility, I agreed to make good for the day the damage my news had wrought.

In chapel, a Collingwood House prefect, McGinnie, spotted me first, and waved. He nudged his neighbour, Le Fleming, and pointed me out in the organ loft, high above the Lady Chapel. Le Fleming also waved. Two middle-school boys, alerted by this activity in the row behind, followed suit. Soon, all four rows of the Collingwood block were waving up at me, or aping the flapping gesture with which I urged them to desist.

When Dr Rabbitt saw, in his acutely angled wing mirror, the crocodile of school prefects waiting in the Lady Chapel, he announced the first hymn of the term with a fulsome chord. The school rose from the banked-up stalls which faced each other across the long, flagstoned aisle, and the school prefects, led by Riley, the Head Boy, filed in and disbanded, each to the block accommodating his House. Chandler-Smith, the deputy Head Boy, in whose blood ran an instinct for pageant, nodded his blond head coolly at the cross before departing the aisle, a gesture which our own Digby Letts forgot. The prefects were followed in by a reasonable turnout of masters, wearing black fur-trimmed gowns they had donned in the vestry off the cloister. From my position, I could only assume that the Headmaster and the chaplain had arrived in their elevated pulpits, one on either side at the beginning of the aisle, but when the hymn was done, I leaned cautiously over the parapet, as far as I dared, for a sight of them.

'LET US PRAY.'

The chaplain's voice boomed out of a loudspeaker I had not noticed behind me. My startled jump had me almost out of the loft; Dr Rabbitt's purple colour deepened as he fought to control his mirth.

'HOW REFRESHING', continued the loudspeaker, 'TO HEAR YOU ALL IN SUCH GOOD VOICE ON THE FIRST DAY OF TERM. WELL DONE.'

The chaplain always had his microphone set for maximum amplification, with the result that along with his supplications were broadcast every nasal impediment to his breathing, every watery smack of his lips. At the end of the service, he had to set off from his pulpit at the very start of a three-verse hymn in order to arrive with due pomp at the altar cross as silence fell for the final blessing, and those in the front rows, who had never seen the Reverend Mr Dyson before, stared hard at their hymn books so as not to catch the eye of the tall, athletic, gorgeously berobed figure who sailed slowly by, his face aloft, beaming and winking at no-one in particular as though an angel on his shoulder blew on the back of his neck. Those seated behind, who had experienced his classroom sullenness and spite, knew the chaplain's for a secular radiance, and respect for him was not rife.

Idelson, the Wizard, had seen me in the organ loft and asked me later, in class, how I had come to be there. I passed on the news about Ostler.

'So,' said David Burnett, 'the cleverest boy in the

school is not at the school. Let's face it, you can't get much cleverer than that. You're stuck in that loft for the rest of term, you know that, don't you, Mark?'

He was right. Each morning, with a smile that begged, Dr Rabbitt secured my promise of assistance for the following day. My job was to set in front of him the correct psalms and hymns, to turn the pages of his music, and to answer to his muttered instructions promptly, before he repeated them as shouted instructions, which he was apt to do almost immediately. By the time of the Headmaster's sermon on the first Sunday of term, I had got used to looking down on the school from the level of the stained-glass, whey-faced saints, and had come to feel that, in company with the Reverend Mr Dyson and the purple maestro at the keyboards, rolling his eyes with boredom at the Head's sagacities, I was part of the management.

The boys of the junior and senior Studies lunched at their Houses on Sundays. Returning from Collingwood that first weekend, I came upon Ambrose in the Studies' back garden, seated on a gnarled, initial-carved bench. He was wearing a shocking pink shirt, buttoned almost to his throat. Beside him was a stack of exercise-books, on which he was not working. His eyes were shut and his face was tilted to the sun. I was almost past him when his eyes opened.

'Hallo, Mark.' His lips scarcely moved.

'Hallo, sir.'

'I wish you wouldn't call me that.'

'Sorry.'

'I've had a complaint about you.'

'Me? What?'

'Come up and see me this evening, would you? It's time we got to know each other, anyway.'

'All right. But what sort of complaint?'

'Nothing to worry about. Come about nine.'

He closed his eyes again.

Sunlight streaming into my room had made it stuffy. I opened my window and sat fretting about what manner of complaint my conduct so far could possibly have provoked. Soon, I heard shouts in the garden. Looking out, I saw that Ambrose had been joined by two of his 'rebel' boys, Penney and Dodge, a pair to whom the payment of any attention at all was a resented expense. One of their friends was practising place-kicks out on the Lower Field, and they were yelling discouragement.

In all matters of appearance and dress, Penney and Dodge sought to distinguish themselves from the common run. Most boys went meekly to the school barber when directed, and suffered his drastic work, but not these, who were known to my set as the Lunatic Fringe. They wore their hair far longer and thicker than was approved, and kept it immaculate with metal combs such as we used at home on the dog. Penney was tall and bony, with jet black hair; Dodge, a blond, pudgy and effete. Their shoes were sharp-toed and elastic-sided – Dodge's gave a little elevation. Their trousers tapered in the 'drainpipe' fashion. Where the official uniform required a white shirt with a separate collar affixed by a stud, they wore drip-dry cream-coloured shirts with the collar attached. Each wore an identity bracelet: Penney's was engraved with 'DENNIS', Dodge's with 'LOVE', although his first name was actually Brian.

Ambrose hushed them, but they were not quiet for long. When I looked up at their next commotion, they were engaged in horseplay with the tutor, trying to remove his garish shirt. To have closed my window would have gratified them with the knowledge that they had been noticed, so I put down the science fiction I had indulgently selected from my high shelf, reached for a sterner, syllabus text and stalked off down the corridor to the reading-room.

I reported to Ambrose's flat promptly at nine o'clock, anxious to know the complaint about me.

'Good evening, Perry.'

'What do you want?'

'Um, you suggested I should come up about now?'

'Oh, so I did, you'd better come in. These idiots'll be leaving in a minute.'

He was referring to Penney and Dodge, who were sitting in front of his television, puffing on cigarettes. A suave individual in a pin-striped suit was being interviewed about his chances in an imminent by-election.

'What a smoothy,' sneered Penney, his eyes never leaving the screen.

At the end, the interviewer said: 'Well, thank you very much, and good luck, Mr Penney.'

'That was Dennis's old man, Mark,' said Dodge.

Keen to appear unimpressed, yet having no wish to side with the younger Penney's scorn, I was stumped for a reply, but with time running out, offered: 'I thought he needed a haircut.'

Unexpectedly, they received this as the funniest remark they had ever heard, clapping their hands and howling with laughter. I had made a hit with them. Ambrose looked at me as though I had revealed something promising about myself. The last thing I had intended was to court popularity with this mob; I wished I was back in my study.

'Now come on you two,' said Ambrose, 'I said I'd send you back as soon as you'd seen him, so off you go. You haven't got cigarettes on you, have you? Good. And, Dennis, for God's sake get your hair cut, if that's what your Housemaster wants.'

'Well I don't know, Perry.' A principled look came to

62

Penney's face, which, on account of the blackness of his hair, an Impressionist would have painted yellow. 'This place is, like, a million years out of date, man. I mean, it's nineteen-sixty-eight, yeah?'

When the tutor had seen them out, I said: 'What was this complaint about, then?'

'Eh? Oh, nothing really. Majorie Rivers rang up, moaning because you haven't made yourself known to the Collingwood junior here – what's his name, Reed?'

'Is that all? I suppose I should say "hallo" to him.'

'Don't. I was very pleased that you hadn't. I told her – how many times do I have to say it? – the seniors here don't mix with the juniors. I've already had to speak to Garland about this. God, why do they always send me the queers?'

'Oh, I don't know – I don't think Bosco's a queer, for instance.'

'You'd know, would you?'

'Well . . .'

I stopped short. I realized what he meant. I was offended. The telephone rang.

'Hallo?' Ambrose's face clouded. 'Oh Christ, what do you want? . . . I can't, I'm busy . . . I said I can't . . . I'm sorry, I'm busy . . . I've had a bad day too, go away . . . you're where?' He turned his back to me. 'You really are a bloody cretin, aren't you? . . . you're an absolute fool . . . ha bloody ha, very funny . . . what? . . . all right, well stay there, don't move . . . what? . . . when I feel like it, that's when!'

He slammed the receiver down and sighed so deeply, his spongy torso seemed to shrink.

'Mark, I'm sorry. It seems that I have to go out. A crisis. We'll have to do this some other night.'

On my way back from Collingwood, the next Sunday afternoon, with the heatwave continuing, I sat down under a chestnut tree and read a letter I had found on the mail-board at my old address. It was from Amanda Gough. Amanda and I had met during the last Christmas holiday, on a carol-singing expedition arranged by the parish church, and had written to each other during term-time ever since. She was at a boarding-school in Hastings, and wrote long, confiding letters, grammatically imprecise, from the standpoint of one who, in the face of adversity, has moved cussedly into a good humour.

'Well, here I am under lock and key in the old fortress again, still smelling of sprouts' – this one began. I had not written to her, so far, being unsure if our correspondence was to continue this term. Circumstances had unluckily arrested our relationship. In the Lent holiday, she had gone skiing with her elder sister, and in the summer, her family had departed to Rimini for three weeks on the very day that I had arrived home with my parents from a fortnight in the Canaries. Then, the woman who owned the stables where Amanda's beloved horse was kept had gone off on her holidays, leaving the business in the hands of an incompetent relative who had relied heavily on Amanda for assistance. For some reason, Amanda in person never sounded that confiding note which so encouragingly informed her letters, and on her return from Rimini, she had seemed, more than ever, remote and preoccupied. She had turned up, as my partner, at the Tennis Club dance in a pea-green silk Italian dress whose frank celebration of her female form contrasted startlingly with the stable-girl attire I was used to, and which I had always thought she preferred. It had been flattering to have her on my arm thus decked out, of course, but she had complained of feeling faint all evening and gone home early. The following week she had been mysteriously indisposed, and I had wondered then if it was all over.

The letter signalled a return to form, however, and picked up so unblushingly from where our correspondence had left off that I supposed this coolness must have been imagined. She assured me that she was looking forward to the St Clement's Sixth-Form dance, to which her school had been invited to send a party in November – an event that I anticipated with a niggling dread.

All thoughts of Amanda cleared from my mind a little later, when I encountered, in the Studies' back garden, Jonathan with his girlfriend, Judy. They were seated not on the gnarled, initial-carved bench but on lightweight folding chairs, patterned with blue flowers, which they had brought down from his flat. In Judy's presence, Jonathan's imaginary sporting activities ceased, and it was easy to understand why: her auburn-haired beauty was enough to put anyone off games. A popular visitor to the school, she had earned for Jonathan a nickname: Mr Punch.

It was not, however, her beauty that set Judy apart, it was her voice. Where Mother, for instance, had two voices, one hard, the other hilarious, and some of Miles's girlfriends had three or four – a different one for every member of the family – Judy spoke with only one voice, which was enchanting, warm and expressive, and never exceeded its natural range with gushing swoops, or peals of strident mirth. To my ears, her one, wonderful voice was the resonance of sanity and honesty and a well nature, and made her my Ideal Woman.

'Oh look, it's Mark,' she said, with a friendly smile. 'Hallo, Mark, how have you settled in?'

Had I been free to greet her as I pleased, I would not have shaken her by the hand, neither would I have kissed her; I would have done what I had always wanted to do since first meeting her, reached out my hands and laid them on the top of her head. I told her I had settled in fine. We chatted for a while. They had taken a picnic down to the river, and eaten it by the weir. Then she reached into their picnic basket and found some chocolate biscuits, which she urged me to take in before they melted.

Although the sun streaming in to my study had made it stuffy again, I did not open the window; they might have thought I was spying on them. But it was impossible to work, with Judy in view, and so I lay on my bed and began a letter to Amanda. There was a single rap on my door, which was at once flung open.

'Phew, it's like a furnace in here!' said Ambrose. 'Let's have some air, shall we?'

He went directly to the window and hoisted it noisily. Peering out, he put two fingers in his mouth and wolf-whistled. Then he backed away quickly and looked pleased with himself.

'Can you come up and see me this evening?' he said, helping himself to a chocolate biscuit. 'Perhaps we'll have better luck than last week.'

On the small, top-floor landing that evening, as I knocked on Ambrose's door, I wished very much that instead I was paying a call on the adjacent door, which was Jonathan's. Ambrose let me in and then disappeared into his kitchen for a long time to make us some coffee. I sat in one of his flimsy armchairs, inexpensively upholstered in orange material, and examined a display-frame containing a dozen antique arrowheads. Ambrose's great interest was ancient civilization and its archaeological evidence.

'How's that brother of yours getting on?' he said, coming in and handing me a mug. I told him that due to his involvements with women, sport and beer, Miles had come down from university with an indifferent

degree, and gone into commerce, where his preoccu-
pations were unchanged.

'Ah, drink,' said Ambrose, shaking his head, 'I
suppose you know poor old Vernon Watts had to be
dried out again in the holidays.'

This news of the Clancarty Housemaster did not
astound me, my classmate David Burnett was the Head
of Clancarty House, and kept us up to date on Vernon's
well-known failing; but I could hardly credit that I was
hearing the news from another member of staff.

'Pamela's worried sick about him,' he went on,
referring to the Housemaster's wife. 'Of course, they've
got a difficult lot in the House at the moment, which
doesn't help. That's privileged information, of course.'

'Of course.'

For the next hour, I was treated to a great deal of
privileged information. One by one, Ambrose picked
out his colleagues, and divulged their darkest works.
Here was a fraudster, here an adulterer, a Maths master
had registered as an importer of German wine, such
was his personal consumption. Several were 'almost
certainly queer'. Mr Parmenter had not gone on to
better things, as we had been told, but had left to
undergo treatment for depression – to think we called
him 'Twinkle', on account of his flaxen hair. With a
mass of defamatory data, he left scarcely a one with his
frock on, although the few very old and decrepit
masters who had been on the staff when Ambrose was
a boy at the school he was content to compare
unfavourably with their younger selves, as though
ageing itself were culpable. Had I shown symptoms, I
wondered, of an insatiable, prurient itch? Suddenly
the look of sapient insolence that was common to his
'rebel' boys seemed not so fatuous: an hour with
Ambrose, and one knew all there was to be known.

At ten o'clock he asked me to excuse him for a few

minutes while he went downstairs to check the lock-up and the junior dormitory.

'If the phone rings,' he said, 'don't bother to answer it.'

'I wouldn't dream of it.'

When he was gone, I reproached myself. How shameful to have sat and listened to his perfidious litany. I wished I had been plain-spoken enough to have renounced it at the outset. Gloomily and guiltily, I stared at an electric fire, which stood in front of an unused grate, until mesmerized by the flow of its artificial flame.

I thought I heard a soft knocking out in the hall. It persisted, and quickly became a bare-knuckled rap. I went out to investigate. Ambrose had left his front door open, but the knocking was at a door some way down a passage inside his flat: it was the door to the fire-escape. Its handle turned and rattled.

Bang!

The door lurched in its frame at the impact of a kick, and then shuddered before a flurry of fists.

Bang! Bang! Bang!

I expected its wire-reinforced, frosted window to fall in.

Bang!

The door-handle rattled again. I stepped out of the flat on to the landing, and looked down into the stairwell to see if Ambrose was on his way back. There was no sign of him. Then a really terrible blow threatened to unhinge the fire-escape door. It occurred to me that no-one would dare to inflict such battery on a door unless he was certain he had the right of entry, and that in Ambrose's absence, I was the one denying this right, which I had no authority to do. Perhaps while locking up there had been a mishap and the tutor had locked himself out. There was a key in the door. I realized I must open up. Seeing my shadow through the frosted glass, the visitor withheld his assault. I turned the key nervously and drew open the door. Standing on the platform outside was a Clancarty boy, my most disgraceful contemporary, Martin Gabriel. He flashed me a wicked smile.

'Hallo, Mark.'

'Hallo, Gaby.'

He was wearing a red scarf and a white pleated anorak, into the pockets of which he had plunged his hands, presumably at the last moment for casual effect, unless he had been beating at the door with his head. That would have accounted for the glazed look in his eyes; but the glazed look was already accounted for by the strong smell of alcohol which wafted in with him.

'I shouldn't really be here, you know,' he said. He raked his fair hair carelessly from his brow.

'You made enough noise.'

'Sorry. I thought Perry must be in the front room with something loud on – I don't mean the pink shirt.' He laughed, a high-pitched cackle with a hard top to it, which I recognized at once as the laugh I had heard on the first night of term. 'Where is he, anyway? Kissing the juniors good night?'

'What the hell's going ON?' came a swelling growl behind me. I wheeled round. Ambrose was back in his hallway.

'I'm sorry . . .' I began.

'Oh no, not you!' he thundered at his visitor.

'Shhh!' Gaby put a finger to his lips.

Ambrose squared up belligerently. His jaw jutted, for a moment I thought he was going to charge.

'Was that you banging? Come here!' He slammed the front door and strode into the sitting-room. If I had been Gaby, I would have turned and fled, but he grinned, took a deep breath, and winked at me: 'Here we go.'

I allowed him to lead us in.

'Was that you banging?'

'Well, it wasn't Mark, now, was it?'

'I'm sorry . . .' I began again.

'You just don't care, do you?' yelled Ambrose. 'Waking everybody up! What the hell are you doing here?'

'Well, that's nice, isn't it?' replied Gaby with reciprocal vehemence. 'You said to look in any time. If I'd known you were going to be like this I wouldn't have bothered!'

'I wish you hadn't! Where've you been, anyway?'

'Oh, church, of course, it's Sunday, isn't it?'

'Don't lie! Where?'

'All right, The Blue Posts.'

'The Blue Posts! I thought you were going to start making an effort.'

'I am making an effort. Look.'

He put on a pair of lensless spectacles and pulled his red scarf up to cover his mouth.

'That's supposed to be a disguise, is it?' said Ambrose.

'Not exactly,' came the muffled reply.

'It's pathetic!'

'It's not exactly a disguise,' said Gaby, pulling the scarf away. 'It just means that if I'm seen, no-one has to report me if they don't want to. I have no wish to embarrass my supporters.'

'You haven't got any supporters.'

'So I'm beginning to see.'

'How did you know I didn't have the Headmaster up here tonight?'

'You don't like the fucking Headmaster, Perry.'

'That's not the point!'

70

Gaby turned to me and said quietly: 'How do you like it here? Comfortable?'

'Don't try and change the subject!' cried Ambrose.

'Well, be nice to me, then! Honestly, what a fuss.'

'What do you expect?'

'Oh, you're right, of course, I shouldn't have expected anything different. I should never expect help when I need it.'

'What d'you mean, help?'

'I just wanted you to ring Pamela for me, that's all.'

'You mean, she doesn't know you're out?'

'I got held up, I'm later than I meant to be.'

'You're for it, if you've been missed.'

'Well of course I've been fucking missed.'

'And you want me to ring her up and start lying for you? Well, I'm not going to.'

'I can see that. Never mind, forget it.'

'Well, why should I? You come round here waking everybody up . . .'

'Waking everybody up? It's half-past ten, Perry, not the middle of the night, so who the hell's in bed anyway?' He nodded at the wall: 'Mr Punch in bed with his Judy, is he?' He mimicked a puppeteer's squawk: 'Cor, Mr Punch, that's a lovely sausage!' He gave another burst of the hard-hatted laughter and flopped down into a chair. 'Own up, Mark, go on, own up – that Judy, couldn't you just shag the arse off it? Cor!' He screwed up his face into a look of foolish lust and squirmed on the chair to suggest developments in his underpants.

'Oh Christ!' said Ambrose. 'Don't let him amuse you, Mark, he's only showing off.' •

If I had smirked at Gaby, it was only at the thought of how, inevitably, in real life, worthwhile people like Judy would always elude him.

'Give us a fag, Perry.'

71

Ambrose hurled a packet of cigarettes, which, miraculously, Gaby caught one-handed above his head.

'Ciggy, Mark?'

'I don't, actually.'

He helped himself to one and pulled a face.

'Why can't you buy Embassy like Pamela? You know I collect the coupons?'

'Look, I'm sorry, but I'm not going to ring her,' said Ambrose.

'So you keep saying, forget it, I'm sorry I asked,' said Gaby. 'How would you like me to leave?'

'Very much.'

'No, I mean, do I go down the fire-escape, or . . .'

The telephone rang. We froze. Gaby pushed the spectacles to the tip of his nose and raised his eyebrows expectantly. Ambrose glared at him and, eventually, lifted the receiver. I perched on the edge of my seat.

'Hallo?' said the tutor, quietly. 'Oh, hallo, Pamela, I was just about to call you, actually. Yes, I've just found Gaby in one of the senior studies. He's not sure if you knew he was round here tonight. You didn't? Oh, he's a pest, isn't he? I'll send him straight back. You'll leave the front door open for him? No, no, I shouldn't wait up.' There was a long pause. 'Yes, I'll tell him that. Good night.'

'What d'you mean, I'm a pest?' protested Gaby.

'She was about to ring the police.'

'Rubbish.'

'She was. She's been very worried about you, God knows why.'

'Good thing I looked in on you then, I don't want to worry anyone.'

'Huh.'

'Well, Perry,' said Gaby, 'thanks very much, it looks

like you've saved my bacon again. By the way, I thought you handled that very well, didn't you, Mark? He's really quite a sly-boots, isn't he?'

'Take those bloody glasses off, will you?' said Ambrose. 'They're daft.'

'Why?'

'They're so obviously false, that's why.'

'I couldn't wear ones with real lenses, like Mark's, could I? I wouldn't be able to see a thing, I'd probably end up in the river.'

'Don't excite me,' said Ambrose. 'Anyway, you heard what I said to Pamela, so you'd better get round there, hadn't you?'

'All right.'

Gaby stayed put on the chair. Ambrose got up, and asked him the same question he had put to the Lunatic Fringe: 'Have you got cigarettes on you?'

'Yes thanks, enough for the night.'

'Then leave them here, you fool! What happens if you get stopped?'

'Well, dressed like this, I'd be done for anyway. But you're not going to let that happen, are you, Perry, now that we've got this far? You'll give me a lift home, surely?'

'You must be joking.'

'All right, then I'll have to go back through the hop-fields, I don't care. How about a drink for the journey?'

'No.'

'It's cold in them thar 'opfields?'

'No.'

'Perry?' He cocked his head and pleaded in a petty voice: 'Please.'

'I must be going now, actually,' I said, staring at my watch.

'Cheerio, then, Mark,' said Gaby. 'I expect next time we meet, we'll be neighbours.'

'Eh?'

'Take no notice of him,' said Ambrose quickly. 'He's talking about Ostler's study, but he's not going to get it – no-one is.'

Gaby scowled.

'I'll speak to you tomorrow, Mark,' continued Ambrose. 'I'm sorry about the rude interruption.'

At the door, I said, 'Did you check the lock-up, or do you want me to?'

'No, I did it. But thanks, that's thoughtful. How nice to deal with a thoughtful boy, sometimes. It does make a pleasant change.'

'I'm thoughtful!' said Gaby.

'Yes, but you never think of anyone but yourself,' said Ambrose.

'It's a start!'

Garland threw open his study door when he heard me in the corridor. He looked as though he had just watched a moth land in his cocoa.

'Did you hear all that banging, earlier?' he gasped. 'What was all that noise?'

'I'm sorry,' I said, evenly. 'I've been with Perry all evening, we didn't hear any noise.'

5

Trial By Jury

When I first arrived at St Clement's, the size of the playing fields, and of the pitches marked out on them, astonished me. The preparatory school I had just left was so hemmed in by woodland protected by the National Trust that on Sports Day the sprint was run over eighty yards, rather than a hundred, and even then the swiftest did well to collect himself before the rhododendrons. It was therefore with awe that I observed that the hundred-yard track on the Lower Field gave a runner half that distance again in which to pull up before the farmer's high hedge. Surely only a giant would convert a corner-flag try on rugby pitches drawn so wide? And the long-jump pit was situated so far away from the take-off board, I doubted that my best effort would fly me as far as the sand.

I was awed in the same way now by this scene between Gaby and the tutor. I had felt in Ambrose's flat that a contest had been joined on a wider scale than any I had ever seen. It had been a reckless contest, played out on a full-size pitch, on to which, as yet, I would not dare to venture; a life-size playing-field, perhaps, extending beyond the farmer's high hedge, beyond the confines of the school. I appreciated that a life-size playing-field could have only one boundary, that which divided life from death, but I had been disposed to think of Gaby in extreme terms ever since, years earlier, I found myself at the very edge of his field of drastic activity. I had seen him then treading the same sort of lawless path as tonight, and with the same air – which was always to characterize him – of being too full of motive to suffer regulation or guilt, like one who must kill for a promised land.

This earlier sight of him had taken place in my first summer term. As a member of the choir, still a treble, I was automatically nominated for the chorusline in the Gilbert and Sullivan production, which that year was *Trial By Jury*. I was already more than six feet tall, however, a bespectacled beanpole, and at the dress rehearsal my appearance as a chorus-girl was deemed to be aesthetically a blight. I was stood down. I took this rejection very well – it was a great relief. As compensation, I was offered employment by the stage manager, Mr Edie, the art master, who in those days adopted the semblances of a beatnik. Backstage, I soon discovered that at any malfunction of the electrical equipment, Mr Edie would at once resort to unnecessarily desperate measures, so when I spotted him in the wings, midway through the last performance, poised with a screwdriver over a standing-light, which he was clutching as though by the throat, I moved quickly to stay his hand. The standing-light was crucial to a later scene and had failed. I soon established that the fault lay only with the bulb and set off to the Founder's Hall, where I knew I would find a replacement.

It was a relief to step out into the cool night air. I had been sweating behind the scenes in the Beckett theatre as a result of wearing my jacket underneath my overall. I had done this because Edie had warned us that money had been stolen, the previous night, from the Founder's Hall, where members of the cast changed into their costumes and left their school clothes unattended. The stagehands, too, were meant to leave their jackets there, but I had opted to keep mine on in preference to the risk of a thief's hand rifling my pockets, be they empty or not.

Lights shone from the old Hall, but inside it was deserted. I made my way between two lines of trestle tables cluttered with discarded props and mirrors at which the players had applied their make-up. At the back of the hall, wooden steps gave access to a small stage, which was in darkness. I was rummaging through equipment at the back of the stage for the required lightbulb when I heard the door latch fall. I peered out. The figure of a young girl in a long, pale blue dress stood silent and motionless at the door, which she had closed behind her. Such was the stealth with which she had entered, I fell silent too. She had long blonde hair wound into plaits and wore soft white dancing-shoes. In her hand was a scroll secured by a scarlet ribbon. Slowly she turned her head to survey the hall. Then she took unhurried steps to the centre of the floor, between the trestle tables. The only sound was the rustle of her dress. She set down the scroll behind one of the make-up mirrors, and, catching sight of herself in the glass, gave a slight smile. Suddenly her flat shoes squealed as she spun round quickly to see if anyone was behind her. For a slow count to ten she was perfectly still, before turning again towards the stage. Her eyes narrowed, to pierce the darkness. I thought she must have seen me, for she called out: 'Hallo?'

I was about to call back, but in a large hall even the immediate response pays a moment's tribute to the acoustic, and in that moment I realized that she had not seen me at all, and that here was the thief, trying to convince herself that she was alone. I knew also that 'she' was Martin Gabriel, a boy who looked so fetching in a chorus-girl's costume that his appearance on the first night, when the audience had been the school, had been met with whoops and whistles remarkable for their lack of irony. I would have made my presence known before he approached the benches at the walls, on which were strewn the school clothes, for I had no wish to witness a squalid act of theft, but just then the great door swung open to admit the show's producer, the Right Honourable Geoffrey Treat, a huge-bellied giant.

'Palfreyman!' he roared, with epic sonority.

I waited a second before answering.

'Yes, sir?'

The chorus-girl, feigning a search through bric-à-brac on one of the tables, stiffened at the sound of my voice but did not look round.

'Have you found this doo-dah for Mr Edie yet?'

'The lightbulb? Yes, sir, I'm just coming.'

'Well, hurry up, darling. Tempus fugit.'

The Right Honourable Treat, the head of the English Department, was known to parents, staff and boys as Gorgeous Geoff, on account of his high effeminacy. At the time of his theatrical productions, like a flightless bird afflicted by an instinct to soar, he became both pathetically grand and flapping. His bulging eye now fell approvingly on Gaby.

'Hallo, boy.' He worked his lips through a series of little pouts and smiles like a wine-bibber savouring a delight. 'What are you doing here?'

'Oh, sir, I've lost my scroll,' said Gaby sadly. 'Can you see it anywhere? I'm on soon.'

'I'm sorry, darling,' said the producer, suddenly pettish, 'I can't stop to help you, I've got a show to run.'

'I must have put it down somewhere,' said Gaby, seemingly on the verge of tears.

'Oh God, spare me the amateur stage!' cried Gorgeous Geoff. 'Come on then, try to think of everywhere you've been.'

'Everywhere I've been?' Gaby arched his eyebrows; a grin played at the corner of his mouth. Gorgeous Geoff, delighted, murmured: 'Don't be filthy, child.'

But although he presented himself as a queenly buffoon, the producer was by no means unobservant and when he located the scroll almost at once, on a table which Gaby was purposely ignoring, he stopped short, as at a handclap of suspicion, and his eyes became beady.

'Well, here it is, boy.'

'Oh, thank goodness for that!' cried Gaby. Receiving the scroll, he curtsied and said sweetly: 'Thank you, kind sir.'

His confidence was misplaced now, however, for the queenly buffoon had given way to a waspish inquisitor.

'Funny I should find it on this table here,' said Gorgeous Geoff, 'because I thought I saw you girls getting ready over there.'

'That's right, sir, we were over there, you're quite right.'

'How did it get on this table over here then, I wonder?'

'Don't know, sir.'

'Hmmm?'

'Perhaps someone's tried to hide it from me, sir.'

'Don't be ridiculous, boy, who'd want to do a thing like that?'

'Oh, I know who, sir.'

'Well?'

'Come off it, sir, you wouldn't expect me to sneak, would you?'

The Right Honourable Treat deliberated briefly, and then fell for it.

'All right, then, off you go. You shouldn't be in here at all, you know that.'

'Yes, sir. Thank you, sir.'

Gaby left the hall with the bearing of a brave young thing who is protecting the name of an oppressor. Only then was I remembered.

'Palfreyman?'

Perspiring in my many layers, I stepped down from the stage, lightbulb in hand. 'Yes sir, here it is, I've got it. I'd better run.'

The producer called after me: 'And don't crash in, backstage, darling – it's a theatre of art, not a theatre of war!'

If any doubts about Gaby had lingered in Gorgeous Geoff's mind, they would surely have been allayed at the celebration party after the performance. Still in the costume of a chorus-girl, he sat on the edge of a table with his hands under his haunches, swinging his legs, flirting with everyone, quaffing shandy from a silver goblet regularly replenished by an attentive baritone judge. Even when he threw off the blonde wig he lost none of his popularity. A crowd gathered round him, vying for his attention and his smile, the latter a handsome gift; no-one could have suspected that here, charming the company, was the company's thief. He cast not a single glance in my direction, which I felt was at least consistent, because if, for Gaby, the incident had never existed, as so it seemed, how then could it have had a witness?

I had had no dealings with him prior to *Trial By Jury* and knew only, from gossip overheard in the tuck-shop, that he was generally considered a tart. I would not have despised him for that: a pretty boy rarely escaped entanglements and a poor reputation, and I was glad no prefect made a diary-note of my bath night, or offered to hold my spectacles while disciplining me with a cold shower. The next morning, however, when I saw Gaby again, he was trudging into the cloisters, disconsolately, for the Sunday service, scowling and slovenly, entirely without lustre. A piece had been torn out of his straw hat, and it looked as though one of the stone lions at the front gate had found life enough to take a swipe at him as he passed. Seeing him like that, making no account of himself, I felt a sharp twist of resentment, and wished I had exposed him.

Half an hour after I left Ambrose's flat, footfalls on the fire-escape signalled Gaby's departure. I waited a few minutes before turning off the angle-poise lamp and pushing aside my makeshift curtain. It may only have been a light from one of the homesteads across the valley on Paddock Hill, but I fancied I saw the flare of a match in one of the hopfields he must cross on his way back to Clancarty. More than three years had passed since *Trial By Jury*, and nothing had occurred in that time to improve this first impression of him. The boys of Collingwood and Clancarty would often see him ducking through a hedge into the cemetery which lay between the two Houses; it was known that he stored his cigarettes there, and smoked them in a crumbling mausoleum, in defiance of the warning on a council sign: 'Unsafe structure. Keep out.'

It may have been during the time he spent in the cemetery that he wrote the dispirited, doggerel verse which would crop up in any publication that allocated space to its readers' creative endeavours. A typical offering had appeared in the latest issue of the Clancarty House magazine, beneath a happy photograph of Pamela Watts' Bring-and-Buy stall at the Summer Fête. It was entitled 'Gangrene':

> I buried candles in the earth
> And marked the place with stones.

> I turned them up today and wept
> To find my infant bones . . .

From this sort of thing I understood that introspection must be a melancholy characteristic for a thief. The poet was championed by the 'polo-neck brigade' — those younger masters who attended all society and discussion-group meetings of an artistic nature. One by one they took Gaby up, not scandalously but in a spirit of amity which, when the relationships evaporated — as they always did — with a whiff of rancour, somehow made the masters, rather than the boy, look naive.

It was extraordinary that he had never been expelled; he had been rusticated more than once, and on those occasions I had wondered if his father had received a refund of fees for the weeks of schooling he had missed. Mine would certainly have claimed one.

The high cost of my education was impressed on me at home. When the school bill arrived, Father, whose profession was accountancy, would pore over it for hours, working through the debits item by item, trying to neuter the menace of the inconveniently large figure at the end. It was hard, sometimes, not to feel that the inconveniently large figure was, in fact, me, and that from an accountant's point of view, I was an unjustified expense, a prodigality: had he not paid these accounts once before, for Miles? If I wasted time at the school, therefore, or applied my efforts frugally, I would feel, with a clutch of anxiety, that I was wasting Father's money, as good as stealing it, and so, even if I had not seen Gaby in the Founder's Hall that night, I could never have enjoyed, as some did, the spectacle of his disgraceful career, for in its wastefulness I would anyway have detected the signature of a thief.

Was he now to be my neighbour? Ambrose could

not deny him; the more I thought about it, and I lay awake for a long time, the more I was convinced that the Life-Size Playing Field was Gaby's territory, on to which the tutor had merely strayed in search of that consolation he obtained from rebel souls. In any contest played out on it, Gaby would inevitably prevail. Fortunately, though, it was not up to Ambrose which boys were awarded a study; as he liked to point out grumpily, he just ran the place. Gaby would discover this, soon enough, and then, I supposed, the liaison would end and he would allow himself to be taken up by some other benefactor, some other fool. Until then, keeping a hand on my wallet, I had only to stay out of his way.

6

In Harmony

For a long time, Dr Rabbitt's head was invisible, buried beneath his arms as he slumped on top of the grand piano. The string quartet practice had gone badly. We dared not look at each other. Elwyn-Jones, our first violin, was glad of the respite, I could sense him pulling himself together. A fine player, beside whom I ran a pedestrian bow, he was also a chronic giggler. We had kept getting stuck at the same place, where the piece we were practising made a sudden transition from a slow dirge to a gay dance: to remind us to play happily at this point, a manic, open-mouthed smile would fly to Dr Rabbitt's face, where-upon our cellist, David Burnett, would play a couple of wrong notes, to signal that the manic smile had put him in difficulties, at which Elwyn-Jones's playing would completely fall apart and the quartet grind to a halt. It had happened four times; as the music director had become more irate, so had his manic smile grown more ludicrous. Now his rage was spent. Eventually restoring himself to a free-standing position, puce in the face, with oxygen-starved eyes, he announced that he wanted to go home. We called after him to come back, we were sorry, but he lurched inconsolably from the room.

At the door to the Music School, we found that, as though in sympathy with Dr Rabbitt, the weather at last had broken; it was teeming with rain. Burnett remarked that this was only to be expected, on the very night he had planned a fire-drill for his House. I hurried back to the Studies along the London Road. Lights shone from the masters' residence, Starvecrow Hall, which I had always thought of as an ivory tower, until privileged enough to learn from Ambrose that, most nights, it housed a card-school. Elwyn-Jones, a day-boy, rang his bell and waved as he sped homeward on his drop-handled bicycle.

At eleven-thirty that night, having just gone to bed, I heard Gaby leaving by the fire-escape again. He must have missed the Clancarty fire-drill, at which there would have been a roll-call. Surely he would be in serious trouble? I hoped so.

While we waited in a classroom the next morning for Jonathan to arrive to take a history lesson, I asked Burnett if the fire-drill had gone ahead as planned.

'Oh, yes,' he said. 'We all trooped out into the yard, and got a bit wet. I called the roll and we trooped back in again. Mind you, the pre's had to work jolly hard on the fire-rattles to persuade everyone it really was a drill, and not just Gaby coming in for the night.' The class laughed.

'And was he there for the roll-call?'

'Gaby? Good lord, you don't think I called his name out, do you? I'm not looking for trouble, you know.'

'How the hell do you put up with him?' said the Wizard.

'Put up with him? It's an honour to have him with us,' said Burnett, insincerely.

'I've told the pre's to treat him as though he's the Head Boy. That's the best strategy. Nothing's going to stop him breaking all the rules so we may as well pretend that he's above them – he seems to think he is, anyway. In any case, he is a sort of Head Boy.'

'Wrong-in-the-head boy, if you ask me,' said the Wizard. 'I'd report everything he did straight to the

Headmaster if I was his Head of House, indeed I would.'

'I can't do that, he'd be expelled!' said Burnett. 'Then where would we be? Pamela would just *die* – she's absolutely besotted with him, you know. Then Vernon would start boozing again and *he*'d die, and guess who's next in line to be a Housemaster?' He spread his arms and took on the expression of one descrying a miracle: 'HOW REFRESHING!'

There was a knock, and Jonathan put his head round the door, puzzled.

'Ah,' he said, 'we are in here, I'm sorry.' He came in, sketched a cover drive and grinned. 'I thought I heard the chaplain.'

When he took the register, there was only one absentee: Elwyn-Jones. The day-boy was away from the school for two days. Then, in the organ loft before morning assembly, Dr Rabbitt spotted something in his acutely angled wing-mirror which caused him to hit and sustain an inaccurate chord.

He hissed over his shoulder: 'What's happened to Elwyn-Jones?'

Peering over the parapet, I saw our premier violinist emerge into the aisle with his left arm in plaster, supported by a sling.

'It looks like he's had an accident, sir.'

'He won't be able to play like that!' wailed Dr Rabbitt. 'It's his fingering arm!'

A moment later: 'The quartet! Just as it was going so well.'

This was, of course, simply incoherent, but Dr Rabbitt always made much of anything that was lost – he doted on composers who had died young.

'Perhaps it's just a sprain,' I offered gently, trying to give him heart enough for the hymn he must soon accompany.

But in the cloisters afterwards, Elwyn-Jones gave us bad news.

'It's my thumb,' he said, 'I'm afraid I've broken it.'

'How long will you be in plaster?' I asked.

'Six to eight weeks.'

'How could you?' sobbed Dr Rabbitt.

'Well, I'm sorry, sir, I fell off my bicycle in the rain.'

'Bicycles! God, I'd ban them, so I would! That's the quartet done for, then.' He turned to me. 'Mark, you'll have to lead the orchestra at the Carol Service. God knows, you're not up to it!'

My violin mistress, Miss English, took the news of my elevation as an excuse for a hearty scold: 'Well, heavens, whatever next? Leader of the orchestra. First violin, ho, ho, ho.'

Miss English only scolded when she was pleased. She had borne the excruciation of my early struggles with the violin doughtily, like an unembarrassable nurse, and only in the past year, when my playing had shown a marked improvement, had she thought it worthwhile to find fault with me – and to ask me occasionally to tea on her houseboat, moored beneath the arches of the redstone bridge in the High Street.

'Mark Palfreyman, you know darn well you haven't been practising your fiddle. What the mad Doctor's going to say when he hears you at your pieces, I just don't know. If you don't start taking your practice seriously, I'll have to have a go at you like my rats.'

'Rats?'

'Rats. They always come aboard when it rains.'

'Ugh. What do you do about them?'

'Well, I don't lay them a place at the table, that's for sure. What d'you think I do? I whack 'em on the head with the big stick. Woof, woof.' She beat the floor with her bow, and nodded: 'So there.'

At the end of the lesson she reached into a cupboard

and brought out an old violin-case. Inside, wrapped in a midnight blue scarf, was an ancient, dark-grained instrument.

'Now you're such a grand fellow, perhaps you'd care to take a turn on this? You could prepare a piece on it for next week. That's if you can find the time.'

The violin had a well-loved, well-used aura, and was obviously a treasure. Miss English saw that I handled it cautiously.

'It won't bite, you know.'

'No, it's lovely. Thank you.'

'There's nothing wrong with your own violin, but this'll give you a better tone. I'll leave it on the shelf here. It doesn't matter if you don't get on with it.'

'I'm sure I will.'

Inside the battered case, and seemingly an original feature of it, was a metal nameplate. Assuming it carried the maker's name, I read out its curly inscription.

'Eileen Logan?'

'Oh, she's just one of its ghosts.'

'Did she play it well?'

'She certainly did. You're looking at her.'

'Oh, I'm sorry,' I said, feeling clumsy.

Miss English was not put out; she sat with her hands clasped in her lap, wearing a smile full of secrets.

'Why should you be sorry?' she said. 'It's not a crime for you to know my married name.'

'I didn't know you'd ever been married.'

'And I still am, don't have me for a widow!' she protested. 'Mr Logan and I have taken our happiness in separate ways for a long time now. He goes his way and I go mine. Isn't that what we call a study in harmony?'

She clapped her hands and leant forward: 'You know, Mark, a lot of people think they're trying to live in harmony, but they're not – they're trying to live in *unison*, and as you and I know, *that*'s not the same thing at all.'

Late that night, the fire-escape door opened and closed very quietly. There was no sound of footsteps, but soon I could hear a low, monotonous drone outside; Gaby's stealthy tread had left the metal stairs humming. I took down the makeshift curtain at my window and stared out. Moonlight bathed the wild back garden, and out on the Lower Field, his shadow moved between the long straight shadows of the towering pines. Then dark clouds shut out the moon, and finding that I was staring into nothing but darkness, with my nose almost pressed up against the window, I was forced to acknowledge that here were the beginnings of a fascination, the sort of fascination that had snared Ambrose and Pamela Watts and many others; a dark fascination, that always ended badly.

Suddenly, I felt disgusted and ashamed, for I saw myself through Judy's eyes; her image was always with me, an image of beauty and honesty and reason. How I hated Gaby at that moment, for his power to bring me into discord with this image. But Miss English's words came to mind: to live in harmony with Judy, that was my ideal. And so, out of ignominy I yet drew strength, for I resolved henceforth to refer everything to Judy, and where there was harmony would be sanity and truth, and where discord, madness and lies. I was certain, then, that I would resist Gaby: his long, cold, dark, lonely walk through the hopfields – I dismissed it from my mind.

7

Brighton

Dear Mark,

I'm afraid that Mummy and I will not be able to see you on Exeat Sunday after all. Our plane back from the Paris convention is not scheduled to land at Heathrow until 1.53 p.m. We're sorry about this, but never mind – your Aunt Lucy has *very* kindly offered to look after you for the day. I enclose twenty-five shillings. Your return ticket to Brighton will cost 14/6d – use the change to buy her a nice box of chocolates. You know where she lives; her address is: 35, Hanswick Square. Her flat's on the third floor. *Remember*: your Aunt Lucy is, of course, very fond of you, but she's used to living alone quietly and it's *your* responsibility to ensure that the day is not too much for her.

Take the *12.18* to Redhill and *change* there for Brighton. You will probably have to *change platforms*, so keep your wits about you; you should be in plenty of time for the *12.55*, which gets in at Brighton at about 1.30 . . .

With such detailed instructions, it was perhaps excusable that, on arriving in Brighton and finding my aunt not at home, I felt like the victim of an elaborate set-up. I sat on the stairs outside her flat for an hour, hugging a large box of chocolate liqueurs wrapped in a brown paper bag, for which I had just laid out ten shillings.

Before making the purchase, I had dithered, not because of the cost, but because I wondered if it was sensible to buy Aunt Lucy liqueurs. She was a tall, handsome woman, who made a living as an artist, painting scenes of the Sussex coastline. She would arrive last at family gatherings, distracted, frantic with apology, usually in a flowing outfit adorned in some quarter with feathers. Having communicated her nervous intensity to the party, so that upsets and spills began to occur and certain uncles, notably Uncle Fred, to drink more than was acceptable to their watching wives, Aunt Lucy would then be the first to leave; dogs and infants had often to be restrained from leaving with her. To the adult world, however, her departure was always a relief. At her going, everyone would agree how nice it had been to see her, and how brave it had been of her to come, in view of her 'trouble'. Whatever Aunt Lucy's trouble was, it occasionally landed her in a local nursing-home.

'It's a loony bin,' Miles would say.

'It's *not* a loony bin,' Mother would insist. 'Don't let your father hear you say that. It's just a place for her to go when things get, you know, too much for her.'

'What things?'

'Oh, she's had a terrible life, you'll have to ask your father.'

Father, when asked, would screw up his nose and plead: 'Let's not talk about that now.'

The time had never been right for talking about Aunt Lucy's 'trouble'.

When hesitating over the liqueurs, in a tobacconist's near the station – the only shop I could find open – my problem had been that I could not recall if Aunt Lucy took alcohol. As Father had made clear, it was my responsibility to ensure that, today, she was not overtaxed, and it would assuredly be my fault if the liqueurs brought on this mysterious 'trouble'. I had plumped for them in the end because the only alternative was a two-and-sixpenny carton of marshmallows that looked to have been sat on and was simply unpresentable. Now, having only sixpence left in my pocket, I eyed the chocolates hungrily. But surely eating them would make me drunk? What if I fell asleep on the journey home and missed Redhill and woke up at Charing Cross, penniless? There would be nothing for it then but to join the tramps on the Embankment – not that I had ever seen the tramps on the Embankment, but Father often cited their existence when impressing on me the need for diligence, industry and 'A' levels.

At half-past two I left the building, and walked down the square to the seafront and along to the Palace Pier, where my last sixpence bought me a bag of mints and a postcard. Sucking on a mint, I considered the view. The sea looked like an undulating, panelled floor. Its panels were of many colours: inshore, jade and emerald, slate and stone and a hundred other shades of green and grey; beyond the end of the pier, abruptly, all the panels took a blue-rinse; far out, a school of silvery panels cartwheeled away to the indigo-rimmed horizon; to the east, where the sun streaked through a broken sky, gold and turquoise panels splintered into white shards on the rocks off Rottingdean. The smudged outline of a cargo ship, with a crane on its deck, lurked, as sombre as a gallows, on the horizon.

Suddenly the wind got up, bringing with it a fast, slanting rain. Gulls wheeled hectically in the upper air as though surprised by the pull of a new gravity. I put on my raincoat, which I had discovered only that morning to be far too small for me; if I buttoned it up, it grew wings at the hips and preferred me not to breathe, so I left it undone, which I knew looked slovenly. Averting my face from the rain, I set off back to the square.

I had not got far when I caught sight of a group on the other side of the road emerging on to the steps of the Hotel Metropole. Instantly, I recognized a St Clement's Sunday suit. It was Gaby and his parents. Oblivious to the wind and rain, they were moving slowly and prosperously, as though they had just negotiated the purchase of the hotel over a sumptuous lunch. I ducked into a shelter. It was lucky I had seen them, for had I taken a few paces more, I would have been in plain view, and with the brown paper bag now soggy and torn, and the belt of the shabby raincoat drooping at my sides, to the party on the hotel steps I would have looked little more than a vagrant or a beggar. Through the shelter's storm-window, I received a blurred impression of them strolling idly down the hotel's steps, Gaby arm-in-arm with his mother. When they disappeared down a side street, I ran back to my aunt's as fast as possible, although the raincloud by then had travelled on.

Twenty minutes had elapsed. I rang the doorbell. No-one answered so I rang again. There was a brass knocker on the door and I rapped on it firmly. Still there was no reply. Then, another door across the landing half-opened and a very old woman, with white, ringleted hair and goggling rheumy eyes, cried: 'Uh-huh!'; and laughed and waved.

'Would you happen to know . . .' I began. She closed her door again. I slumped back on the stairs.

In the hope of finding a forgotten pound note, I emptied out the contents of my wallet, but I have always been accurate with money, so it was no surprise to find none. It pained me to think of the five-pound note tucked in my writing-case back at the school. It was my budget for the second quarter of term, and I had thought myself prudent in leaving it behind lest, while elated by the strong sea air, some trinket should charm it out of me.

The search of my wallet did turn up a postage stamp, and for that I had a use. The postcard I had bought carried a view of the Regency front on a fine summer's day; I got out my fountain pen, aimed an arrow at Aunt Lucy's window and printed across the clear blue sky: WE ARE HERE. On the back of the postcard I affixed the stamp, and wrote, at arm's length so that raindrops did not fall from my sleeve on to the ink.

> Dear Amanda,
> Having a lovely time in Brighton
> with my aunt. Will write in full soon.
> Love, Mark

By half-past three, I was beginning to view Aunt Lucy's absence in a sinister light. What was her 'trouble', exactly? Could it be 'troubling' her inside the flat? At lurid conjectures of my aunt lying helpless, perhaps paralysed, perhaps dying, behind the door, I wanted to hammer on the knocker, yell through the letter-box and raise the house, but the weird old woman across the way had unnerved me. I was loth to disturb her again, she looked mad. Was Aunt Lucy mad, too? Was that her 'trouble'? Was this, then, the nursing-home – the loony bin, as Miles had it? There was no plaque on the front door, but perhaps it was an annexe. Would there be a warden along in a minute to protest at my bothering the inmates?

Wary, now, of my surroundings, I noticed, for the first time, evidence of genteel dereliction: on the wall, the fingers of a white, sculpted hand bearing a torch, in the art deco style, were nicotine stained; through a yellow-glazed porthole on the landing, a stale shaft of daylight swam with columns of airborne dust; and, cast into relief on Aunt Lucy's painted door, was a caucus of blisters like the diagram of a germ. A thin reek of disinfectant laced the air, and from a floor above came the dry, mortal cadences of a persistent, frail-chested cough.

A sudden need for fresh air propelled me down the stairs and out into the street, where at once another influence constrained me, for might I not, round any corner, bump into the strolling Gabriels? At least the sun had come out and so, turning no corners, I found for myself an unoccupied bench by the lawn in the centre of the square. I sat with my back to the road, and hoisted the collar of my raincoat. I discovered I was running low on mints.

There came irresistibly to mind the means by which, had this trip not been arranged for me, I might have made a carefree disposal of the day. With all my homework completed at leisure, I could have spent an hour on Miss English's violin, another with a novel from my high shelf; then, perhaps, a ride along the towpath as far as The Olde Oast House for tea and macaroons; after that, a long soak in a hot bath; and, with everybody else out, an evening of Bach, played loud. It rankled. When a mobile snackbar drew up on the square and released a cloud of appetizing aromas, it was too much to bear, having not even tuppence for a cup of tea. I resolved to make one last call on my aunt's spooked chambers, and if that failed, to get back to the station.

This time, when no-one answered the door I moved off at once. I left the box of chocolates on the mat to show Aunt Lucy that I had not departed her door in rage, but the composition of an accompanying note defeated me – every message, every phrase I could think of seemed to contain at least the possibility of sarcasm or reproach.

I would have liked to return to the station by way of The Lanes, where Aunt Lucy's paintings were sometimes exhibited in private galleries, but at teatime on a blustery day, that warren of narrow pavements was just the sort of place a daytripping family might visit; there would be no escaping the Gabriels if I ran into them there, so I walked back along the promenade. The wind had stirred up the sea and out beyond the pier, where there had been the blue-rinsed panels, now were swollen crested waves that tossed up spray like the plumes of smoke from a hundred primitive fires. Over the last furlong to the shore the rollers chased and tumbled, crashing at last on the pebbled beach with a maledictory hiss. The seascape was dazzling, a prospect of chaos that made the promenade seem truly a frontier, and as I gazed out on the ferment, reflecting that it was my avoidance of Gaby that had brought me to this edge of the world where the wind boomed in my ears, I felt righteous, stern and just. The gallows-ship had drifted far to the east and now lay charred and smouldering in the flames of an inferno where the sea and sunlight fused.

And behind me, the town. I had never been especially fond of Brighton, and if I was looking for a serious objection to the place, I found one over the letter-box into which I dropped the card to Amanda. There was a poster advertising The Aquarium, and it struck me as very queer that, at the seaside, one should have to visit a building in order to see fish. This prompted the observation that nowhere along the town's considerable span was there to be found a fish-market, or the reek of nets and fresh catches. It seemed a reprehensible omission, and to indicate a flaccid lack of application on the part of the townspeople. And it further occurred to me that the town itself had no intercourse with the sea. It neither gave nor received;

nowhere did it throw out arms to harbour and tame the waves, neither did the high-collared frills of its frontal façades give way at any point to the thrust of a great river, whose existence would have made the town's position natural. I decided that Brighton was a genderless fraud, an impotent swindler I would gladly leave behind.

By the time I handed in my return ticket and set off towards the school, it was dark. There had been rain, and seeing how the road, lit by streetlamps, streamed like a golden carpet up through the town, a lightheadedness, which had set in for lack of food, transformed into something more exalted. As I crossed the redstone bridge and passed The Feathered Oars, I felt lean, spare, euphoric, as though I returned not feeble from a day of deprivation, but cleansed and elevated by a day of fast. Once again I felt righteous, at a moral advantage to everyone, and my progress up the High Street was a triumph. The wind funnelling through the bottleneck at the top of the town roared the Hosannas of an ecstatic choir. I had intended to follow the road all the way to the Studies, but the lions on their pedestals at the front of the school hinted too much at grandeur to be passed. The curling drive led me to the great arch, and having crossed the gravelled square, I strode with dreadnought confidence into the darkness of the playing-fields. The rain had unlocked from the piles of autumn leaves a perfume of decay as powerful and abounding as an essential energy. At the top of the Passchendaele Steps, I paused for the invigoration of a fresh breeze, which scamped across the Lower Field and roared in the chestnut trees. I breathed in hugely, spread my arms, and experiencing a moment of unprecedented liberty, howled; then I laughed, because no-one could see me in the darkness; then I howled again.

At the corner of the Studies' back garden, a rude shock brought me down to earth. The only light shining in the house came greenly through the makeshift curtain in my study. It was not the main light, which I might have left on by mistake, but my desklamp, which I used only to work by. Was someone working, then, in my study? Evidently not; as I approached the house, the jangle of a pop song reached my ears, which although not to be found in my record collection, was nonetheless emanating from my room. From my record player! Who dared? I had only one name in mind, of course – Gaby. What was he up to? Why had he returned early from Brighton? I thought of the five-pound note, was it safe in my writing-case? My writing case! My letters! I burst into the house, dashed up the stairs, and flung open my study door.

'You BASTARD!'

Dennis Penney lay sprawled across my bed, in shirtsleeves, his knee in the groin of a girl spreadeagled beneath him. My shout had been drowned by the pop song, but when the door struck the edge of the bed, he looked up and gave a puzzled frown as he tried to focus on the doorway. It was as well that the noise made speech impossible, I was dumbstruck. To manufacture a quick exit, I stabbed a finger angrily at my wristwatch, as though to indicate that his time was up, and slammed the door.

I did not turn on the light in the reading-room; I had no wish for Penney to come and find me with apologies. Soon, the music stopped and they hurried off down the corridor, whispering. From the window, I watched as they mooched across the front yard, arm-in-arm, Penney clutching his LPs in his free hand.

My room stank of cigarettes and perfume. I took down the curtain, pushed the window up and emptied out the lid of my pencil box, which they had upturned and used as an ashtray. Nothing was broken or missing, but every amenity was slightly awry – the chair, the record player, the lamp, the bed – and everywhere I sensed fingerprints of disdain.

I decided to go over to Collingwood for the evening. First, I would go up and tell Ambrose what I was doing. I would tell him why, too – if this made me a sneak, it was too bad. If I said nothing on the matter, to what further abuse might the Lunatic Fringe subject me? I wondered if, at university, which the Studies were supposed to imitate, students had locks on their doors; and would Ambrose allow me to fit one?

I knocked on the tutor's door. There was no reply. I knocked again, much louder. Still nothing. Confronted once more by a locked, unanswered door, in an outburst of accumulated frustration I banged on it and flapped the letter-box.

'Perry?' I hollered.

The other door on the landing half-opened, and a voice from the dark hall within said: 'I'm afraid Mr Ambrose is out.'

It was Judy. She sounded a bit nervous, but when I stepped back from Ambrose's door and she saw who I was, she switched on the hall light and opened up.

'Oh, hallo, Mark, it's you.' She called into the flat: 'It's all right, Jonathan, it's only Mark.'

'Yes,' I said, 'it's only me.'

'You're back early, have you had a nice day?'

'Yes, thanks, I've been to Brighton.'

'I love Brighton,' she said.

'So do I.'

'Is that where you live, then?'

'No, I went down there to see an aunt. She was out, as it happened.'

'That sounds like a spot of luck, there's tons to do in Brighton.'

'Oh yes, tons.'

She smiled; the hallowed region at the top of her head glowed from the light directly above her. Jonathan loomed.

'Evening, Mark. Good Lord! You look a bit of a fright.'

'Jonathan!' said Judy.

With dismay, I realized that I had done nothing to smarten my appearance since returning, and that I stood before them in my shameful raincoat.

'I'm just going off to Collingwood for a couple of hours,' I said, backing away. 'I thought I'd better report in first.'

'Right ho,' said Jonathan. 'I'll tell Perry you're back, when he gets in.'

'Good night, Mark,' said Judy, looking directly at me, and not at the raincoat at all. I saw in her eyes that she had understood there had been no 'spot of luck' in Brighton. I was glad that she knew; it sustained me.

'Good night,' I said gratefully. I wondered if she also knew how much I wanted to reach out and touch her, and if it frightened her.

After the nine o'clock roll-call at Collingwood, there was a prefects' meeting which I was supposed to attend, but before it began, a junior found me, with a message: there was a telephone call for me, on the private side.

Marjorie Rivers awaited, her hand covering the telephone receiver: 'Lucy Willis?'

'Oh, yes, that's my aunt,' I said.

Aunt Lucy sounded very upset. 'Whatever must you think of me? What a dreadful thing to happen!'

Her distress was tempered, however, by a measure of indignation which seemed justified, for she had received a letter from Mother bidding her to expect me

on 'Sunday week', which had arrived only the previous Monday, and so misled her.

'It's my fault, though,' she went on. 'I really should
have checked. And those lovely chocolates, I take it
they were from you?'

'They've got alcohol in, is that all right?'

'I love them, I've had several. I wondered who on
earth could have left them. I thought I must have an
admirer. It was only when your mother rang to ask
how the day went that I realized they must be from
you.'

'She's back from Paris, then?'

'Back and hopping, dear. You haven't spoken to her,
she hasn't rung?'

'She may have done, but she'd ring on a different
number. I've moved, you see. I'm in a special place
now, for seniors.'

'And is it nice?'

The Rivers's living-room door had been left open,
like a giant ear. I raised my voice. 'Yes, I get a lot more
privacy there. It's a bit of a fluke you've caught me
here.'

'Well, I'm glad I have. I wanted to apologize
personally. But please don't tell your mother I've rung,
will you? For some reason she didn't want me to. I'm
in disgrace with your folks, I'm afraid. What a shame
you didn't manage to find me, though. I was only
round the corner, in The Lanes.'

When I rang off, Marjorie Rivers appeared at the
living-room door.

'Are you all right, Mark? Has the day gone horribly
wrong?'

'I'm fine, thanks. I went down to Brighton to see my
aunt, but when I got there she was out, that's all. A
misunderstanding.'

'Oh, poor you!'

'Not really. There's tons to do in Brighton.'

Out of view, in the living-room, the Housemaster gave a delighted chuckle. 'An aunt in Brighton, you say, Mark?' he called. 'I haven't heard that one for years!'

'But did you have lunch, anywhere?' said Marjorie, ignoring him. 'Were you all on your own?'

'I had a lovely lunch, thanks, I've rather enjoyed the day.'

More chuckling.

'Oh, Bill, don't laugh. Mark's had a wasted journey, his aunt was out.'

'Out, was she? You don't say? Aunts in Brighton are usually hard to trace, when it comes down to it.' He came to the door. 'Survive the ordeal, did we, Mark?'

'Yes, thank you, sir.'

'We'll have to watch out for this one, my dear, I think he's growing wings.'

There was a note on my study door when I returned. 'Report to me as soon as you get in, your mother has rung twice. P.A.'

Gaby reclined on Ambrose's settee in lordly fashion; he seemed to have the prosperous mood of the Metropole on him still.

'Your mother's called three times, now,' Ambrose was saying, 'she sounds worried about you.'

Gaby arched an eyebrow: 'Hallo, Mark. Mother calls?'

'Come on, you,' said Ambrose, 'let Mark sit there, he's got to make a phone call.'

'All right, Perry, all right. I expect Mark would like a drink, I know I would. Mark?'

'No, I just want to ring my mum, actually.'

'Yes, of course you'll want to get that over with.' He stood up and stretched. 'Mine's a scotch, Perry.'

'Well, you can bloody well get it yourself, can't you? You know where it is, unfortunately.'

Gaby shrugged and sauntered from the room. I dialled home. Mother answered.

'Mark? Are you all right?'

'Fine, thanks.'

'Did you go to Brighton?'

'Yes, of course.'

'Oh no! You went all the way down there?'

'Yes. All the way. Aunt Lucy was out.'

'Yes, I know she was, darling. I'm so sorry, I'm afraid she's had a bit of a relapse. More of her "trouble", you know. It was very sudden.'

'Really?'

'Yes, she was taken in first thing this morning. I *am* sorry, dear, what a waste of your day. I expect you wondered where she'd got to, didn't you?'

'But is . . . but . . . is Aunt Lucy . . ?'

'Now don't start worrying about her, dear, it's just her usual thing. She can't help it, poor old duck. Actually, I've spoken to her tonight; she's terribly upset about it all, of course – quite honestly, I shouldn't be telling you this, you know what she's like with her "trouble", never wants anyone to know. I promised her we'd tell you there'd been a mix-up over the dates or something, so you won't forget, will you?'

'No, I won't.'

'You won't go blurting anything out when you see her at Christmas or anything?'

'No.'

'Now, look here, I've had a word with your master – Mr Ambrose, isn't it? What a nice man he sounds. I think you're better off with him than with old Marjorie, don't you?'

Gaby entered the room, grinning broadly. In his hand was a huge drink, poured to the brim of a good-size, cut-glass vase. Ambrose hissed and rushed across the room, grabbed Gaby by the wrist and applied a

Chinese burn until he was forced to put the vase down. Ambrose seized it and made off towards the kitchen with Gaby in pursuit.

'Mark?' said Mother.

'What?'

'I said, what a nice man Mr Ambrose is.'

'Yes.'

'He says it's perfectly all right if we come down next Sunday and take you out to lunch – you know, to make up for today.'

'Oh, no, don't do that.'

'But, darling, he's given us permission now. What time shall we come?'

'But there's an orchestra practice next week after chapel.'

'It'll stop for lunch, though, won't it? Don't be silly, dear, we don't mind. We'll be outside the chapel at twelve-thirty, how's that?'

Breathing heavily, flushed and giggling, Gaby came back into the room, this time with a glass in his hand. Ambrose followed, glowering. They settled in armchairs, lit cigarettes and waited for my conversation to end.

'Mark? Half-past twelve, then?'

'Oh, yes, all right.'

'We've brought you back something from Paris.'

'Thanks.'

'I won't tell you what it is, it'll be a surprise for next weekend. By the way, that's marvellous news about the orchestra. What are you now, the captain.'

'Leader, it's called.'

'Leader, that's right. Your father's very proud. So, we'll have that to celebrate next week, won't we? That'll be lovely. Quite the little Mozart, aren't we? See you at twelve-thirty, then – we'll be there!'

She rang off. I rounded on Ambrose. 'She says

104

you've given them permission to take me out next week.'

He stared at me, nonplussed. 'What do you mean, I've given them permission? They're parents, they don't have to ask my permission for anything.'

'Well, that's what she said.'

Gaby laughed: 'Oh, aren't parents sweet?'

'If I've given anyone permission,' said Ambrose, 'it's *you*, to go out with them. Most boys would be pleased. What's been the problem today, then?'

'No problem, really. I went down to Brighton to see an aunt, and when I got there she wasn't in. For one reason or another. It wasn't the end of the world.'

'I was in Brighton today,' said Gaby. 'You should have come round to the Grand. We had lunch there, you could have joined us.'

'Oh.'

'Did Clare come down?' said Ambrose.

'Of course,' said Gaby, adding for my benefit: 'That's my girlfriend.'

'That's nice,' I said, baffled; there had only been three of them, and it had definitely been the Metropole.

'Mmm.' He sipped his drink, closed his eyes and nestled back in the chair. 'It was wonderful.'

As I left, with Ambrose accompanying me to the door, Gaby called out: 'Mark?'

I turned. He raised his glass: 'I'm sorry you've had such a bloody awful day.'

The stink of tobacco and perfume had almost dispelled by the time I went to bed but my study felt violated, and I wondered again about a lock. And what was the truth about Aunt Lucy? Why did Mother have to tell so many little white lies? And howling on the Passchendaele Steps – what was I, some sort of ape? It had been, as Gaby said, an awful day; and that was what troubled me the most, that he had said it, and also, the way he had said it, as though he knew it for a certainty. It seemed that he had read my feelings. The only other person to have done that was Judy – how strange that they should have that in common.

One morning the following week, there was a package for me amid the spread of mail on the dining-room piano. I opened it in my study. It contained a miniature oil painting of Brighton at twilight, with two moons, one in the sky and one in the sea. There was a note:

A token from your very guilty aunt,
Love
Aunt Lucy

I hid it in a drawer, under socks.

8

Shadow Over The Blessed

Early on Sunday morning I was making essay notes on the poems of George Herbert and, for an atmosphere conducive to metaphysical contemplation, had switched off the main light, drawn the curtains and put on a record of organ music at a discreet, background level. Outside, there came the approach of a familiar heavy tread. There was a single knock and at once my door swung open.

'Blimey, what's this, a funeral parlour?'

I blinked as the main light came on.

'Hallo, Perry.'

'What the hell's going on?'

He peered behind the door to see if anyone was hiding.

'Nothing, I'm just reading.'

The tutor wore a cricket sweater which hugged his unathletic frame and had ridden some distance up his midriff. Beneath it was his shocking pink shirt. His trousers had worked their way down to the level of his hips and looked set for further descent. The ghost of a wounded grin possessed his features.

'Do you realize you've made me look a complete fool?' he began.

I removed my feet smartly from my desk.

He nodded at the gramophone, playing almost inaudibly. 'Would you mind turning that down when I'm talking?'

I pressed 'reject'.

'Have you got no sense of responsibility whatever?'

'How do you mean?'

He closed the door behind him.

'Dennis Penney came to see me today, and apologized for being caught here last Sunday.'

'Ah.'

I had avoided Penney since the weekend.

'In your study.'

'Yes.'

'But, of course, I didn't know what he was talking about, did I?

'Sorry.'

'And do you know why he came to apologize?'

'No.'

'Because he assumed that someone in a position of trust, like you, would have felt duty-bound to report the matter to me. But oh no!'

'I was going to.'

'Well, why didn't you?'

I faltered for a moment.

'You wouldn't expect me to sneak, would you?'

'Yes! Don't be so stupid. I simply have to be able to rely on you seniors to keep me informed, particularly if you find people on the premises. For God's sake, quite apart from the question of property, there are some very junior boys here.'

'I don't have anything to do with them.'

'Don't try to get clever with me, that's not the point, is it? In any case, don't you care about someone trespassing in your study?'

'Of course I do, very much. In fact, I was wondering if I could fit a lock, to stop it happening again.'

The wounded grin widened, the dark eyes streamed.

'Oh you were, were you? Well, no, you can't fit a lock on your door, that is absolutely forbidden. What d'you think I'm running here, a hotel? The best way to make sure something doesn't happen again is to report it when it *does* happen, I should have thought that was obvious.'

'Yes, I suppose so.'

'I'm extremely disappointed.'

On leaving, he switched off the main light again. As his heavy tread receded, the desklamp, which had been insecure since Penney's intrusion, nosedived slowly to the surface of the desk, where it folded at the neck and shone up at itself, like a mantis inspecting its own backside. A moment later, the bulb failed. I restored the overhead light and, thoroughly distracted, put George Herbert away and wrote a full account of the exeat for Amanda, which the postcard had promised and which, being entirely false, was tedious to compose.

Outside, it was another blustery Sunday. I wrapped Miss English's violin in the midnight blue scarf and laid it in its case. There was half an hour before my parents were due to collect me for lunch, so I could have continued, but for some reason the practice had exhausted me. It had something to do with this violin. I regarded it, thoughtfully. The first time I had drawn the bow across its open strings, I had almost dropped the instrument for shame and surprise at the immediate dark intimacy to which it gave voice. I soon discovered that, although I delivered it unevenly, this new voice articulated all the pieces in my repertoire with a fresh emotional potency. I recalled how, once before, I had acquired a new voice, which I had also delivered unevenly at first, and how that new voice had announced to the world, more frankly than I might have wished, the arrival of another sort of potency, as well as other personal changes. There were changes taking place in me now, awakenings, fresh stirrings, but it was all very well for Miss English to complain, as she had during our session earlier in the week: 'You're going at it too preciously, Mark, it's not going to play the piece for you.'

She did not know that the reason I played coyly was that, although this new deep resonance expressed quite accurately these latest stirrings, I was not sure that I yet knew their nature well enough myself to start proclaiming them out loud, while to exhibit their potency to the good mistress would have felt simply immodest. When she grabbed the violin and sawed out the piece with brazen confidence and gusto, I had blushed. Playing on it alone, however, gave me an almost guilty delight, but now, I felt drained.

Burnett and the Wizard had passed the window earlier, heading in the direction of the Art School. I went to see what they were up to, and found them in conversation with Mr Edie. The art master had shed his beatnik image a year since: black-rimmed glasses had given way to contact lenses, long lank hair to a severe, cannon-ball crop. This new exterior disguised no better than the old his amiable nature.

'Hallo, stranger.' He smiled shyly.

He and Burnett were listening, sceptically, to the Wizard's defence of an abstract eyesore to which he was putting what he claimed were the final touches. As we stood making jokes at the Wizard's expense, I saw Gaby enter the Art School. Pale and dishevelled, he had evidently been caught out in the worst of the weather. He scowled at us, as though our good humour was a personal offence, and then selected from a peg the most paint-splashed overall available.

'Oh-oh,' muttered the Wizard.

There were twenty or so boys at work in the Art School, and very soon all were aware of the newcomer and his mood. Having collected a tray of powder paints, a stick of charcoal and a water jug, and plonked them down with a crash at a station in the corner, he lodged a sheet of white paper on the upright board, and produced from his pocket a packet of Embassy cigarettes.

'Hoy, Gaby,' protested Burnett.

'Don't worry, David, it's empty,' he said over his shoulder, in a scornfully appeasing voice. 'It's *cigarettes* that are illegal, you know, you can't smoke the packet.'

Edie, exchanging a disquieted glance with us, went off to attend the pottery section, screened off at the far end of the room.

Copying from a pattern sketched on the cigarette packet, Gaby drew an apparently meaningless, asymmetrical grid. He used such decided strokes that the stick of charcoal snapped twice under the pressure; with a great show of bother, he bent down to pick up the pieces that broke off, and slung them at a wastebin, missing on both occasions. When the grid was completed to his satisfaction, the cigarette packet flew in the same direction, and also missed. A loud curse announced that the tray of paints did not include a colour he wanted; having fetched a large tin of the required powder, and discovered with more curses that its lid was jammed fast, he suddenly brought to hand a savage-looking sheath knife and went at it with that. He prised the lid from the tin with such force that it spun into the air and crashed like a cymbal on the window-sill.

'Oh, no,' groaned Burnett.

The Wizard was whistling, irritatingly. 'Head Boy's playing up a bit today,' he remarked.

Before going after the lid, Gaby stabbed his knife into the upright board like a dagger. A boy at the next station began quietly packing up his things. I doubted it would be possible, in this frame of mind, for Gaby actually to paint anything, but it was time to find my parents, so, with a word of farewell to Burnett, who was looking strained, and the Wizard, who was still whistling, I left them to it.

My parents had already arrived. The car was outside the chapel, at the end of two long furrowed scars in the gravel; Father was at the wheel.

Lunch at The Feathered Oars was a slow affair. My parents had had one of their rows. Although there were tables with a river view available, for there were few people dining, Father asked for a position over-looking the carpark. He had had to park next to the gate, where the car made a hazard for others coming in and out, and he spent the meal gazing out on it, worried. After a thin soup, an elderly waiter whose legs splayed at the knees served us with roast meat so reverently, it might have been the flesh of a dead relative; Mother cooed, and learned his name was Robert.

The conversation turned, mainly, on a racehorse, Mister Moonshine, in which Father had recently purchased a half-share, and which Mother described as 'honest' – an expression she must have picked up in the paddock. During a long silence, I visualized a 'dishonest' racehorse, dipping his trotters in the stable takings and leering at fillies in a forbidden field through long, amorous lashes.

'Don't smile to yourself like that, darling, Robert will think you're a bit simple.'

The meal over, as we left the dining-room, the old unsprightly waiter gave dogged chase with Mother's coat and gloves; Father tipped him with a gesture so slippery, he might have been knifing him. At the door, he knifed the head waiter, and then me, to the tune of five pounds, while Mother was in the powder-room.

'Jolly good show, this orchestra thing.' He shook his head. 'Your mother's very proud. How's the work coming on?'

'Fine, thanks.'

'Keep your mind on it, won't you? It's an important year.'

'Don't worry, I will. I promise.'

As we crawled up the traffic-bound High Street, Father drumming impatiently on the wheel, Mother presented me with a small plastic bag.

'Here you are, dear, this is what we brought you back from Paris.'

The bag contained a pair of soft leather, yellow-brown gloves. Getting into them was a squeeze.

'Will they be useful?'

Unless I deliberately extended my fingers, my hands – under pressure from the stretched leather – curled like claws.

'Very useful, thank you.'

Then, dreaded words from the driver: 'ANYTHING COMING, OR CAN I GO?'

'Oh, I don't know!' said Mother. 'Go on, then, quickly though.'

I shrank lower in the back seat. I had assumed that Father would drop me off at the Studies, so having taken my eyes off the road, I was too late to correct him when he swerved in through the Lovat Gate, followed the access road down to the gravelled square, turned a complete circle, sped back up to the chapel and brought the car to a halt at the very place he had earlier picked me up. There was a light rain, and, in view of the walk I must now take, I put on my ill-fitting raincoat. Mother was appalled, and it was agreed I should buy a new one on account at the school shop. With smiles all round, and a spatter of small stones, my parents were gone.

As I walked along the London Road, a sad figure emerged from the Studies' front gate and started, very slowly, towards me. It was Gaby. Even at a distance it was clear that, since my last sight of him, his condition had deteriorated. His head was bowed, his shoulders were stooped, his hands plunged deep in his pockets. He stopped and watched from the kerbside while a convoy of gravel-filled lorries churned by, as though considering the final relief to be had beneath their wheels. He appeared to wipe tears from his face with the back of his hand, and then to be sucking on his wrist, as at a wound. As we approached one another, I saw that he had indeed been crying.

'Hallo, Mark,' he choked. His mouth sagged open, to allow for shallow breathing.

'Hallo, Gaby. Everything all right?'

'Oh yeah, everything's just great,' he said, and sniffed. 'You won't be seeing me around the Studies any more, I expect that's a relief, isn't it?'

It was the best news for weeks, but I said nothing.

'Perry's banned me, hasn't he? He's told me not to come round any more.' He glanced back at the house. 'Bastard!'

'Oh dear.'

'Yeah. Another one with my best interests at heart. Slob! He told me this morning, now he's gone out. You wouldn't give him this for me, would you?'

He thrust an envelope at me; on seeing my gloved hand, however, he recoiled. 'Ugh! You got eczema, or something?'

'No?'

'Only they gave me gloves like that when I had eczema, to stop it spreading.'

'No, my mother's just given them to me, as a matter of fact, they're from Paris.'

114

'Oh, sorry. I never said I didn't like them, they just reminded me.'

I almost recoiled myself when I took the envelope, for I saw, from a set of livid indentations on his wrist, that he had not been sucking on it, but biting, obviously very hard. I stood quite a lot taller than Gaby, and looking down on his blotched, tearstained face, his intemperate distress gave me no cause for elation; in this mood he seemed very young and precarious. He must have sensed that something in me relented.

'You couldn't lend me ten bob, I suppose?' he said quickly.

I lent him a pound, I had no ten-shilling note. It cheered him up a bit and speeded him on his way, but when I turned in at the Studies I looked back down the road and saw that he had stopped and was leaning against the neatly compiled stone wall, with his wrist back to his mouth.

I tried to deliver the letter at once, but got no reply from Ambrose's flat. Judy was spending the weekend with Jonathan again, and, mindful of the disturbance I had caused them on my return from Brighton, I made sure that my knocking did not suggest an emergency. I tried again, half an hour later, after which my possession of the letter began to unnerve me. The envelope, which had not been sealed, was addressed simply to 'AMBROSE', in the scrawling hand of one who, fading fast, has attempted to nominate his assassin. Did the letter contain an ultimatum? Had he pledged himself to some drastic deed, was a fatal deadline imminent?

The letter was written in a clearer hand than the envelope.

Dear Perry,
      I'm sorry about the whisky and the money,

115

and your attitude. I'll pay you back as soon as I can. I've written a poem, you know it keeps me cheerful. It's called 'Shadows Over The Blessed' — here's the last verse:

> I saw the end from the beginning,
> A fate from which I'll not digress
> For if I take the long way home
> I cast my shadow over the blessed.

Hope you don't like it. I'm sorry I darkened your door, it won't happen again. Try not to die of boredom.

Goodbye.

Gaby.

What a strange boy. Outside in the corridor, Bosco and his friend, Hammond, were flogging a reel of Sellotape at each other with hockey sticks; Garland was in the back garden, supervising punishment gardeners; the other two Studies boys were playing chess in the reading-room. And Gaby, what would be his afternoon's recreation? I imagined he would hole up in the cemetery's crumbling mausoleum, smoke a packet of cigarettes, gnaw at his wrists and turn out some more of the doomstruck poetry. A shadow over the blessed, indeed. But what a subject was this to preoccupy me, on the same day I had promised my father I would keep my mind on my work! I licked the envelope and sealed it down. When I knocked again at Ambrose's door, he answered.

'Ah, you're back,' I said.

'What d'you mean, I'm back?'

'I knocked earlier.'

'Well, you couldn't have knocked loudly enough, I've been here all afternoon.'

Mystified, I suggested that perhaps he had fallen asleep, at which he became cheerfully indignant.

'I have not been asleep. I've been in my study, marking, if you must know. As it happens, one of the things that's kept me awake is a complaint, or should I say yet another complaint, about you.'

'Me?'

I glanced nervously at Jonathan's door; whatever the complaint, I hoped Judy would not overhear it.

'Yes, you. Marjorie Rivers rang to ask where you were at lunchtime.'

This was easy. I spoke up in a loud, clear voice.

'I was with my parents for lunch, Perry. You gave us permission last week, don't you remember?'

In an equally loud voice, the tutor replied: 'Do you think I am in my dotage or something? Why are you shouting, I am not deaf? Of course I remember, but why didn't you tell them that at Collingwood, they were expecting you.'

'Sorry,' I muttered.

'I must say, Mark,' he raised his eyebrows and actually smiled, 'I didn't expect to have all this trouble with you.'

I handed him the letter. 'I bumped into Gaby earlier. He asked me to give you this.'

'Oh.' He did a doubletake at the dramatic scripting of his name on the envelope. 'How was he?'

'He was a bit upset. He says you've banned him from the Studies.'

'Huh! He said that, did he? I haven't banned him at all, he's just gone off in a huff. Oh well.' He stuffed the letter in his pocket and said, with a certainty that depressed me: 'He'll be back.'

Rumour had it that he was often to be found in the Art School, but in the two weeks to half-term, I hardly saw

Gaby at all, and never at the Studies. Lending him the pound turned out to be an excellent investment, for when our paths might have crossed, he changed direction to avoid me. I hoped he would never pay me back, I hoped we had seen the last of him.

Amanda wrote, with the news that one of her best friends was receiving anonymous letters, the latest of which – addressed 'slut' and full of vicious lies – had been pinned to her locker door with a pair of geometric dividers. The story worried me, because Amanda did not name her friend and this was unlike her; usually her letters were peppered with names and, to understand them fully, I had to read through the entire body of her correspondence to identify every-one. By withholding the name, of course, Amanda left open the possibility that she herself had been the unlucky recipient, so I wrote back deploring anony-mous letters, and sympathizing with the victim. Pri-vately, I congratulated myself; had I panicked when Gaby was around and threatening to move in, I might have resorted to an anonymous letter – a telling weapon, but despicable.

In the light of Ambrose's remark that Gaby had merely gone off in a huff, the boy's continued absence began to look as though it was intended as a punish-ment for the tutor. Ambrose took it stoically: in fact, he seemed so insensible, I suspected this was a punish-ment that failed completely in transaction and existed only in Gaby's head.

Having no late-night visitors, the tutor invited me up to his rooms once or twice, after lock-up. On the first occasion, he offered me a whisky; half an hour later, I accepted a second. I went to bed dizzy that night, and later, when a train passed clangorously through the valley, I hopped on it with Judy and we blissfully eloped. In the morning, however, such was the throbbing in my head, it felt as though Jonathan had caught up with us as we slept and clobbered me with his invisible cricket bat. Thereafter I declined the nightcap. Sometimes as I sat with Ambrose in those late hours, he would fall silent and stare into the artificial flames of his electric fire. I would pity him then, for I knew that his thoughts had turned to Gaby and it was as though something hung over him that was indeed very like a shadow.

The day before half-term, Burnett came to class with dreadful news. Having not received a black mark all term, Gaby was to be made a prefect.

This caused a furore, the Wizard was incensed. 'Of course he hasn't received a black mark; how could he, if you pretend he's above all the rules?'

'Exactly.'

'So how does that make him fit to be a prefect?'

'It doesn't.'

'So why are you doing it?'

I knew why, I had tumbled to it at once – it was the same ploy Marjorie had used to get rid of me. Burnett explained: 'There's going to be no less than five Senior Studies available next term – Mark, here, and Garland are the only two staying on. Since only prefects can apply for a study, we thought we'd give Gaby a chance. Pamela should clinch it for him.' He looked over: 'Sorry, Mark.'

'It's corruption, that's what it is,' said the Wizard. 'Hypocrisy!'

'What are you getting so excited about, Wiz?' said Burnett. 'Were you going to put in for a study yourself?'

'What, and live with Garland again? No thanks, we've only just got rid of him.'

'Precisely.'

'There is one slight problem, David,' I said. 'Gaby's

119

not speaking to Ambrose at the moment, they seem to have fallen out.'

'Expect a short campaign, Mark,' he grinned, 'and a reconciliation.'

At seven o'clock that evening, I heard footsteps ascend to the top floor, followed by knocking at Ambrose's door. The knocking quickly became a bare-knuckled rap. Ambrose was out; it was his night for the Archaeological Society and he would not be back before roll-call. The visitor departed. At eight o'clock he came back and repeated the performance, and again at ten to nine. I assumed the 'campaign' had begun. About five seconds after the door slammed in the front lobby for the last time, the back door opened; Ambrose was home. After roll-call, I went out for a walk. It was a long walk. It ended in a telephone booth across the road from the Lovat Gate. I dialled the Headmaster.

'Hallo?' His dry, patrician voice was remote.

''Allo, is that the St Clement's 'eadmarster?' My yokel accent sounded awful.

'Yes?'

'Oy'm jest callin' to tell yer . . .'

'Excuse me, who is this?'

'It don't matter oo oy am, oy've just seen one of yaw boys drinkin' in The Blue . . .'

'I'm sorry, I don't receive anonymous telephone calls.'

He rang off.

When I reported in, a minute or two later, Ambrose said: 'Oh, hallo, Mark, come in. Do you know, I'm so angry I can hardly speak.'

'Nothing to do with me, I hope.'

'No, no. Go in and sit down, I'll make the coffee.'

I expected it was news of Gaby's promotion that had angered Ambrose, but when he entered with coffee and biscuits on a tray, he said: 'Do you know what bloody Marjorie Rivers has done now? She's arranged a move for young Reed, he's going over to Collingwood for the rest of term, she's made room in the junior dormitory.'

'Why?'

'Well, I suppose you know there's been trouble for him at home?'

Bill Rivers had mentioned this at the last Sunday lunch, and had asked me to keep an eye on the boy for signs of distress; my answer to Ambrose was therefore: 'Yes.'

'Really?' He stopped short and thought for a moment, and then turned on me a questioning stare: 'How do you know?'

I had made a mistake, a careless mistake. My stomach lurched.

'Didn't *you* tell me?' I tried.

'No, I didn't, how could I have done? I didn't know anything about it myself until tonight. So who told you? Come on, you must know.'

'Bill Rivers, actually, but only a couple of days ago, honestly.'

He shook his head; I had let him down, again.

'I wish you'd told me, I really do.'

'I haven't seen you since then. He only asked how he was getting on.'

'And what did you tell him?'

'Nothing! I just said he appeared to have settled in very well.'

'He *had* settled in very well, perfectly well. God, I wish you'd told me, I had no idea this was brewing.'

There was an awkward silence.

'So, why's he going to Collingwood, then?' I said breezily, hoping to move the conversation on. 'What's the point of that?'

He told me, but with none of the scurrilous detail

with which he usually dressed a tale, that Reed's father had quit the family home since the beginning of term, and that Marjorie and the boy's mother had agreed between them that it would be a good idea if he were transferred to the House where Marjorie could keep a closer eye on him.

'It's a dreadful mistake,' said Ambrose, bitterly. 'Moving the boy away from his friends at a time like this, it's cruel.'

He glared into the flames of the electric fire. The biscuits lay untouched on the tray. There was nothing else for it – I gulped back my coffee and got up to leave. He came with me, he was going to lock up. In the hallway, he had just opened the front door when we heard, down the passage, soft knocking on the fire-escape door. Ambrose swung round, but before he could react further, the telephone started ringing in the sitting-room. The knocking became a bare-knuckled rap.

'You go on down,' he said wearily.

The fire-escape door crashed and shuddered.

9

Under The Eye

I awoke early the next morning, before daybreak. The
wind in the trees at the end of the garden breathed a
song of complaint as soft as a vein. Confronted by my
horrible cowardly offence – the anonymous telephone
call – I lay in bed, paralysed by shame and isolation.
And what a day, too, to wake up paralysed, for it was
half-term, and at lunchtime I would be going home,
where I always needed to be at my most pliable!
Solitary and base, a sorry wretch, there was yet one
avenue of investigation open to me, on which I ventured, having first set the condition that no conclusion
I might reach could be valid unless it made me feel
better.

It had to do with a recurring dream. I had two
recurring dreams, and it was the second of them, the
more lately arrived, that was the subject of my inquiry.
The direction of the inquiry, however, was predicted
by a conclusion I had drawn from the first dream, an
unhoped-for visitor since childhood.

The first dream was a terrifying coda which, posing
as a didactic moral, would append itself to any
morphic narrative, regardless of its temper or plot. I
would be crossing a road, alone, in no particular
hurry, when a truck, or some such vehicle, would
appear over a distant brow and bear down on me at
speed. In trying to get off the road, every movement
would mock the enormous effort it required of me by
occurring in slow motion. At the last moment before

impact and annihilation, I would always, abruptly, wake up.

How lucky, I used to think, how providential, that I have again woken up just in time – or is it impossible to die in dreams, perhaps it can never happen? At about the age of fifteen, however – a time when Big Ideas on The Meaning of Life became my favourite toys – I decided that the opposite was true, that I always died at the end of this dream and that my sudden waking up represented my sudden death. After all, waking up was the end of the dream-life, a disconnection from the unconscious world of the dream, and what was death but exclusion from the Unconscious? I accorded this conclusion – that waking up suddenly from a nightmare represented sudden death – that special, inviolable status we reserve for ideas we have had for ourselves. And I applied it to my analysis of my second dream: It is a warm, sunny day. Someone is walking along a pavement beneath me. It is me. I am not overjoyed to see myself, neither does it depress me. I am merely an observer. I observe that I am wearing far too many clothes for the fine weather. At a corner of the street stands a red telephone booth, beside a flowerbed filled with yellow flowers. I enter the telephone booth. Quite a long time elapses, I must be very hot in there. I swoop to investigate. I observe that, inside the booth, I am agitated and trying to look out in all directions at once. I move closer. The receiver is in my hand and I am dialling; I observe that I dial 999. Someone must answer, for I hear myself say, quietly and urgently as though anxious not to be overheard: 'Can you give me the police?'

Pressed up against the glass, the better to see inside, I observe that I am not looking out in all directions any more; I am tensed over the apparatus, with the receiver to one ear and a hand to the other as though expecting an explosion. Now, in a voice that is noticeably trembling, I say: 'Police? Can you help me? I'm being followed.'

This is odd, the street is deserted. Now I say something too quietly to be heard by the person receiving the call, and I have to repeat it. It is still hard to make out but it sounds like: 'An owee.'

My shoulders slump in despair; I have been asked to repeat it again.

'An owee,' I sob.

I observe that, inside the booth, I have begun to sink to my knees and to cower, as though a blow is threatened from behind; I am cracking up. In an instant, I pass through the glass and take possession of myself.

It is stifling. A prickly heat chafes my skin; I have on *far* too many clothes. It is airless, too, my chest feels tight; my hands are slimy with sweat, my teeth, clamped and grinding. I have taken possession of a terrified being, close to panic, but, being newly arrived, I do not know what it is that I fear. Neither do I know the cause of my sorrow, but sorrowful I am; the bright yellow flowers outside fill me with sadness, as though for some reason I will never again enjoy the world to which they belong.

'I'm sorry, sir,' says a voice through the receiver, 'can you just tell me calmly who's following you, I'm afraid I still didn't catch that?'

My mouth opens. I do not know what I am going to say; suddenly I am braying like an ass: 'An owee! An owee! An owee!'

My body rocks back and forth with the words; I crack my head against a sharp edge; a spot of blood splashes on my shoe. Then, I turn, and there it is, the cause of my distress, pressed up against the window, throbbing slightly, hysterically fixated, cold, perfectly round.

'UN ŒIL!'

I can hear the word tailing away, like the distant shriek of an unnatural death, as I awake.

This was the complete edition of the dream, which had visited me only once, at the beginning of the year. Subsequent versions had been cut short at the first sound of the word 'œil', which had woken me up. The use of the foreign word was not the only thing to mystify me about the dream, but I had never examined it closely because the conclusion I had drawn from the first dream had convinced me that if I delved too much in the world of the Unconscious, I might one day 'wake up' to something that was beneficial to me, and by raising it to consciousness, kill it. Now, however, paralysed by the shame of the anonymous telephone call – an act uncannily reminiscent of the dream – I decided that where a dream recurs, it must contain something the Unconscious wishes urgently to impart, and that I had therefore been remiss in declining to interpret this one. I ran through it again. The only thing I could be sure about, unless I wanted to challenge my earlier, inviolable conclusion – which I did not – was that here was another dream that ended with my death, or waking up, or exclusion from the Unconscious. What was it that had killed me this time? Obviously, it was the eye; I had been scared to death by the cold eye, with which I had been observing myself. So observing myself had the same effect as being run down by a truck? So self-observation, self-consciousness – here was a new toy – meant death? Self-consciousness meant exclusion from the Unconscious? Delighted by this promising notion, and little doubting I was on the brink of founding a new religion, I launched into my inquiry confidently.

— What is my new toy, Self-consciousness?

— Consciousness of the self, obviously.

— Should I think of self with a capital letter, is it also a new toy?

— Yes.

— OK, Self, then. What is it?

— All I know is that consciousness of it seems to exclude me from the Unconscious.

— And what is that?

— The Unconscious? Oh, the Immortal Spirit, the Immanent, the Holy Ghost; God, perhaps?

— I much prefer 'the Unconscious'.

— OK. Now, I think it's reasonable to propose that this horrible dream warns against too much Self-consciousness, and that, having ignored its warning, I have now gone and done something which is quite unlike me . . .

— The telephone call?

— *Most* unlike me.

— And which is presumably something I have done in the interests of my Self, whatever that is. Now I am feeling remorse. What is it that makes me feel remorse?

— My Conscience.

— That old toy! So my Conscience deplores something I have done in the interests of my Self. Conscience must therefore belong to the world of the Unconscious, and not to the world of the Self. Surely though, I must have known that what I was doing would offend my Conscience?

— Yes, but I didn't really think about it.

— Ah! And if I had thought about it?

— I would never have done it.

— So thinking about it, or Contemplation, joins Conscience on the side of the Unconscious. What made me do it then?

— Impulse?

— All right, Impulse. So Impulse is on the side of the Self. In fact, the Self, having no Conscience or Contemplation – they being in the world of the Unconscious – cannot resist Impulse. The Self is starting to look a bit like a criminal, isn't it? This inquiry is not a moment too soon.

— Yes, but it's getting out of hand as usual. Far too many new toys, and they don't seem to be leading anywhere. Let's just look at this particular Impulse. What brought it on?

— Seeing Gaby through the windows of The Blue Posts, I suppose.

— So that's it, is it? I see the disgraceful boy drinking and that impels me to make an anonymous telephone call to the Headmaster, so that he doesn't get made a prefect and therefore can't have a study next term?

— I think that that would suit my Self, little though I know it.

— Yes, but it's rubbish, isn't it? I get impulses like that every day, but I don't go through with them. I think I need another explanation for this Impulse. Let's try to recreate it. If it came when I saw Gaby through the window, let me try to imagine him as best I can, let me visualize him. There. There he is. Now, what is it about him? There must be something particular about him, so what is it?

— It's his head.

— His head? What about his head?

— I don't know exactly, but look at it, it's a good head, isn't it? You'd think he'd be intelligent with a head like that, it's sort of well-made. I've noticed this before, it's really quite . . . a . . . noble . . .

— Why am I crying?

— He's just sitting there, all on his own, all by himSelf, pouring drink into his well-made head as though it were an empty vessel.

— But why am I crying, I never cry?

— It's because he's dead, that's why, he's dead! It's obvious, isn't it? Never mind that it's a well-made head, it might just as well be a skull! Oh, I don't want to go on with this, I understand it now.

— Do I?

— Well, no, not exactly, but it's all this talk of the Unconscious . . .

— You know, I think I prefer God.

— Well, whatever it is, without it you're dead, and that's what's happened to Gaby, somehow he's got disconnected, and whatever the Self is, it's all he's got left.

— Poor Gaby.

— I thought the Self looked like a criminal, and Gaby is a criminal, isn't he? Why, the first time he came to my attention was as a criminal, in the Founder's Hall . . .

— And it's terrible, because if the Self *is* all he's got, he must feel like I did, in the dream, but all the time. In a constant emergency, a perpetual nightmare, under the eye! Every minute of his life he must feel like screaming!

— Poor Gaby.

— And that's his motivation, that's why he always looks as though he's doing something important, even when he's just off somewhere for a smoke. Self-important! That's how he looked and that's how he is, always at the mercy of the Self . . .

— But mercy is surely on the side of the Unconscious? God is merciful.

— So he is always at the mercy of the merciless Self, and it never gives him any peace. Poor Gaby!

— Poor little Gaby. And what a sensitive boy I am to be crying for him.

— Yes, it's more than he could do for anyone, of

course, but that's not his fault, he can't help it, he's innocent, in a way.

— But what can I do for him? It looks like he'll be here next term, should I try to save him from him-Self?

— No, everyone tries to do that, I shouldn't think it's possible.

— Perhaps I should kill him?

— It would be a kindness, certainly, but misunderstood. They'd take *me* for the criminal then!

— So there's nothing to be done for him.

— Poor Gaby, I must say a prayer for him.

— And I will. Soon. As soon as I feel better. Right now, I can't face it.

But I was already feeling better, much better, and before the tears on my face were dry, I had fallen back to sleep.

Later that morning in class, Burnett told us to forget what he had said yesterday: Gaby had refused to be made a House prefect. The very suggestion had wounded him, for some reason, and he had stormed off in a rage. Burnett declared it a mystery.

'Ha!' crowed the Wizard. 'It's obvious, isn't it? You're treating him like the Head Boy already, so what's in it for him? It'd be a demotion! Serves you right, David, indeed it does. Now you'll have to go on turning a blind eye to him for the rest of the year.'

So the visits of the previous night had not been the start of Gaby's campaign – what a fool I had been! I decided to take the Wizard's perfectly apt expression for the resolution of the morning's inquiry: I, too, would turn a blind eye to Gaby, as I should always have done. This resolution lasted less than an hour.

There was to be a week-long book fair in the

Founder's Hall, and, as an added attraction, an art exhibition. We had seen Mr Edie unloading the art exhibits from the boot of his ill-sprung Morris Minor and so, after the last lesson, as self-appointed arbiters of artistic taste, Burnett, the Wizard and I went to make a critical inspection. Continuing round the Hall while the other two fell into argument in front of the Wizard's contribution – the abstract eyesore, a surprising inclusion – I found myself looking at a painting which, with no blended outlines, no subtle shading, had the economy of a cartoon. It depicted a bright red wall made up of two rows of large black-edged bricks; the wall was set in a flat yellow desert dotted with two-fingered cacti under a deep blue sky. Its title:

THE BRICK WALL
by M. GABRIEL (17)
Form: LOWER VI(f)

I recognized from the pattern made by the bricks, some showing a short side, some a long, that this had been the grid he had copied from the cigarette packet. As a member of the Signals, in the Corps, I was quick to detect that the picture made a statement. It was a very clear statement, too, for in Morse Code, the bricks spelled:

FUCK
OFF

I said nothing; before the book fair was over, others would have made the decipherment, and I had no doubt that *The Brick Wall* was destined for popular fame. But, every minute of his life, my inquiry had decided, he must feel like screaming, and for one

131

perpetually 'under the eye', the picture's slogan seemed perfectly legitimate. What integrity! Gaby's metamorphosis was complete: the disgraceful boy had become a tragic hero.

10

Half-Term

'At last!' cried Miles, as his ball landed on the distant green and rolled towards the flag. 'I'm in birdie-land!'

'Shot,' grunted the assistant professional, from the other side of the fairway.

'What d'you reckon, bro? Ten feet away?' said Miles, sliding the club into his golf-bag, which I was carrying.

'Less than that,' I proposed. What an ill-bred little moustache my brother was sporting these days!

We were on the eighth hole of the Country Club's nine-hole golf-course, and nothing had gone right for Miles since the first tee. There, driving off into the sun, he had sliced his shot out of bounds into a private garden. Having lost sight of the ball, on being told of its fate he had made the surprising decision that, since his golf-swing had been specifically designed to eliminate any possibility of a slice, a gale-force wind must exist in the upper air. There was not a breath of wind at ground level, and the treetops were motionless, but he had clung to this belief, and had aimed off-line to allow for the wind ever since. As a result, he and I had spent much of the afternoon foraging for his ball in undergrowth, and his mood had grown steadily uglier. The assistant professional, a Scot no older than myself whom Miles had cajoled into playing, had become understandably tightlipped and dour.

I had not been especially keen for the exercise myself. It would have been far more enjoyable, on this fine Sunday afternoon, to have taken Princess for a walk. The excitable little dog had disgraced herself, however, when Miles arrived for lunch; vaulting in welcome from the stairs, she had soiled his tangerine cardigan. Her expulsion by way of the back door had been so forceful that, after lunch, she could not be persuaded back to the house, even when I waved to her with the lead.

'How's the ankle, now?' asked Miles, referring to a minor injury he had inflicted when hurling aside a club in rage.

'Just a bruise,' I said; I was limping only slightly.

He missed the putt for a birdie – treadmarks round the hole allegedly threw the ball off-line.

The ninth hole led back to the clubhouse, a grand pink-walled mansion with a blue-gabled roof which, a quarter of a mile from the tee, looked like the doll's house of every child's dream, too perfect and precious for play. Miles's second shot, over a small lake to an elevated green protected by sheer-faced bunkers agleam with ivory sand, looked, to a non-player in love with the view, impossible and irrelevant. While we waited for golfers up ahead of us to play out, I daydreamed that this entire estate was mine – its well-ordered woodland, black-water lakes, patches of wilderness, free-roaming deer – all mine; that the Country Club's flag on the gabled roof was my flag; and that inside the fabulous doll's house, with her auburn hair loose and tumbling over a simple dress, Judy was watching out for me through one of the sun-burst windows.

I smiled broadly up to the house, just in case it were true.

'What is it, bro? Seen someone we know?'

'No, no. Just taking in the view.'

When the green was clear, Miles made excellent

contact with his ball, which flew long and true and, since he had aimed off yet again for the non-existent crosswind, far to the left of his target, over a row of box-hedges into an ornamental garden. I stepped smartly behind a tree in case he hurled his club again, but, now in sight of the members' lounge, he contained himself. He hit a second ball more accurately, so I handed him his bag and set off to retrieve the first.

All the paths in the ornamental garden, which was circular, led to a green-domed aviary at its centre. The aviary was unlocked and empty. I sat on a bench beside it and massaged my ankle. What a tedious fellow was Miles! Whatever was I going to do with the bullfight posters he had brought back from Tarragona as a gift for my study? Hide them in my bedroom cupboard, I supposed, behind my telescope. They were no more edifying than the pack of pornographic playing-cards he had sent to Collingwood House from Amsterdam earlier in the year, which had fallen into Digby Lett's permanent possession. I was certainly not going to search very diligently for his ball, but, scouting around from the bench, by chance I caught sight of it in the middle of a path. I got to my feet and was about to fetch it when, sensing movement beyond the ball, I looked further down the path. At once I let out a cry of fright, for I saw that I was watched, from the perimeter hedge, by a dozen or more restless eyes, dark blue, dark green and lustreless gold, wobbling a little as though on the end of strings. For a moment I stood dumbstruck in their unswerving gaze. Then, they fell to earth, as though the strings had been cut, and I saw, on the path, the pinheaded peacock who had fanned his tail. He glared at me, and then strutted away, dragging his tail behind him like a failed entertainer.

I sank back queasily on to the bench. Dark suspicions grew in my mind; that there were peacocks waiting at the end of every path, their unspeakable galleries erect; that I was, therefore, surrounded by a wide-eyed host; and that, even as I thought of it, those at my back were starting an inward advance. I jumped up and spun round. There were no birds stalking me, but as I looked down each of the radial paths, I felt the pressure of spying eyes from the paths I left newly unguarded behind me. There was never enough time to convince myself that the way was clear in one direction before fear tugged me round in another. Where had the failed entertainer gone? Had he mustered a chorusline of staring reinforcements? I danced in a circle and, with panic mounting, jumped into the aviary and clanged shut the door. Realizing that I was trying to look out in all directions at once, I wondered if this was a variation on my dream, my nightmare. I tried the password.

'Un œil! Un œil!' I hissed. I did not wake up. 'Yeux! Yeux!' I tried.

Then, above the perimeter hedge, a casement window scintillated in the sunlight and brought me to my senses. What if Judy were watching out for me from the upper floor of the doll's house? I knew she was not, but what would she think, to see me cavorting in circles and hurling myself into a cage and barking out of it like a baboon? She would think I was mad. Judy, the exemplar of sanity, would think that I was mad! Would she have seen enough to be repelled for ever?

No, I could hear her one, wonderful, reasonable voice soothing: 'But they're only artificial eyes, silly,' and ending with an indulgent laugh because she knew this behaviour was not typical of me. But then quite unwilled and unexpected, the same imagined voice continued: 'Gaby's the one who's under the eye, not you. Think of Gaby. Weren't you going to say a prayer for him?'

I looked up at the scintillating window and made a promise that at the parish church that evening, which I would be attending with my parents, I would remember Gaby in my prayers. Then I was able to step out of the aviary and trot from the garden.

Joining the players as they quit the green, I reported to Miles that his ball was lost. He shrugged and announced that he was, anyway, giving up the game.

Mother had laid out a huge tea in the lounge: fishpaste sandwiches, chocolate cupcakes, a Swiss roll, a ginger cake, jam, cream, honey, scones, an orange jelly mined with mandarins. She had used her best china.

'Gosh, Mumsy, what a spread!' said Miles.

'Tuck in, boys, we'll only be having a light supper,' said Mother. 'How are your new corduroys, Mark? Comfy? Do they fit?'

'Yes, thanks. What shall I put on for church, my school suit?'

'Oh, we've decided to let you off church this evening,' she said. 'I should think you get enough of all that at school, don't you? We go most weeks, of course, but old man Saunders, he gets more doddery every time we see him, doesn't he, Dad?'

'What's that? Ouch!' Father was preoccupied with lighting a coalfire; he had burned himself with a match.

'Oh, do leave the fire and come and have some tea,' said Mother. 'I was just telling Mark about the vicar. The last few times, the service has run well over the hour, it never used to take so long.'

'There's some firelighters in the scullery, aren't there?' said Father. Mother said she had no idea. He wandered out, poker still in hand; Princess bolted in from the hall and made a pass at the fishpaste sandwiches.

137

'Bloody hell, 'cess, OUT!' yelled Miles, springing up.

'Mind the china!' cried Mother.

Miles shooed the dog from the room and slammed the door after her; almost at once it opened again as Father returned with the firelighters.

'Shut the door!' we chorused.

'Sorry.'

'Eat up, Mark. Can I help you to something? You've got nothing on your plate.'

'I'm doing fine thanks, Mum.'

'I don't suppose you get much in the way of tea at school, do you?'

'The food's not bad, actually.'

'Oh.' Mother seemed hurt. 'Good.'

'From what I remember of St Clement's grub, it was absolutely beastly,' said Miles, loyally wolfing a cupcake.

'It's a bloody scandal, when you think of the fees,' muttered Father.

'It's better at the Studies than it was at Collingwood,' I said. 'Mind you, it's not that good.'

'Piece of Swiss roll?' said Mother.

'All right, then.'

'And how d'you like it at the Studies, really?' she asked. 'We haven't met Mr Ambrose, yet, but he sounds awfully nice.'

'He's a good man, Ambrose,' said Miles. 'He was Head Boy, in his day, you know.'

'What, at St Clement's? Really?' said Mother. 'Obviously a very good type. I think you're far better off with him than with old Marjorie, don't you, Mark?'

'Probably.'

'It must have been a bit of a blow at exeat, wasn't it, bro? Getting all the way down to Brighton for nothing?'

'Oh, I knew there was something I meant to tell you!'

Mother exclaimed. 'We've seen your Aunt Lucy, she turned up for Uncle Fred and Aunt Joy's anniversary "do" – late, of course, the usual hoo-hah. But guess what? She had her latest boyfriend with her. Sammy. My dear, you should see him. A tiny little man! We said – didn't we, Dad? – half her size and twice her age. Your father thinks he's Jewish.'

'Oh, he is Jewish,' said Father, at last giving up on the fire.

'I didn't think he looked as Jewish as all that,' said Mother.

'No, he's certainly Jewish,' Father insisted. 'An art dealer in Brighton? He's Jewish all right. Not that it matters, of course.'

'Why didn't you just ask Aunt Lucy, she'd have told you, wouldn't she?' I said.

'Oh, you can't do that!' said Mother.

'Perhaps she doesn't know, herself,' suggested Miles.

'I expect she does, dear,' said Mother, starting to giggle. 'I gather they've been going out for quite some time. I'm sure she knows all his little secrets by now.'

After tea, my parents gave me a violin. Naturally, I made a show of gratitude for this expensive gift, which was of far higher quality than the one they had given me when I started taking lessons, but even as I plucked on its strings, I felt that I was being unfaithful to Miss English's violin, its ghosts, its impassioned voice. So far as violins were concerned, I was spoken for. All that impressed about this new, glossy piece was how closely its yellow-brown colour matched that of the gloves from Paris, which I had disappointed Mother by leaving behind at school.

'Come on, Yehudi, give us a tune,' said Miles.

I explained that before it could be played, it needed proper tuning at a piano.

'You'll be playing it at the Carol Service though, won't you, dear?' said Mother. 'Miles is coming this year, aren't you, Miles?'

'You bet.'

'So there you are, Mark, we'll all be there to see you play your new violin, it'll be absolutely lovely!'

Feeling that, as a gift, the instrument came with more strings attached than the average violin, I took it to my room, where regarding it with flat dislike, I noticed a key sellotaped to the inside of the case. It has always characterized me that where a lock and key exist, I will use them, and so there and then I locked the case and put the key in my pocket.

The next morning on the common, Princess scampered down a path we had not followed for years, which led, through a gate that was usually locked, to farmland and a small secluded lake. The lake was known as Benjamin's Water, after the son of a lord of the manor who, according to legend, had fallen through the ice and drowned. The legend held that the poor little lake was haunted and infernal, but I accorded more weight to the unprejudiced authority of Princess's instincts, which acquitted the lake of its evil repute and judged it fit for a swim. After a while, she collected a stick and begged for it to be thrown. Then, retrieving the stick from the water's edge and catching sight of her image, she yelped and sprang back, so that her ears clapped above her head. She charged off into a thicket. It was my turn to introduce a game, so I climbed quite high up a tree whose branches came invitingly to hand. 'Prin-cess,' I called in a spooky voice. 'Prin-cess.'

She bounded eagerly back into the glade, but finding no-one to greet her, her excitement quickly died; she sank to her stomach and laid her head on her paws. I was going to float my handkerchief down, as a clue to my whereabouts, but when I pulled it from my pocket, something else fell out. A silver flash caught my eye, and I watched, appalled, as the key to my new violin dropped into the lake, which the branch I was straddling overhung.

I said nothing of this to my parents. On the way back to school that evening, as Father raced down the country lanes in his customary fashion, I carried the violin-case on my lap, not out of prideful ownership but to buffer me from the dashboard in the event of an accident. On the back seat were the bullfight posters, which Mother had run out to the car with, just before we left – I had very nearly left them behind.

I was the first one back to the Studies. A letter had arrived, over the weekend, from Amanda. It ended with 'sensational news'; the unnamed friend who had been plagued by abusive, anonymous letters had owned up to sending them to herself. Reading this, I felt one of my inquiries coming on, but the direction in which it pointed felt unsafe, so I quashed it. No nonsense of this sort, I vowed, was going to mar the second half of term.

11

Revelations

In the days after half-term, every turn of the wind brought dark clouds, and downpour followed downpour with a hopeless sort of passion. The deluge spat to extinction the dance of withered leaves around the dustbins at the side of the Studies; a lake formed beneath the Main School's great arch, like a rude mirror; buckets catching leaks in the Beckett library needed emptying twice a day; Miss English reported that her houseboat was riding alarmingly high on the swollen river; and buses were re-routed to avoid the redstone bridge in the High Street. I was still wearing my old raincoat. A new one had been ordered by the school outfitter's shop, which had stocked none in my size, but the delivery had fallen overdue.

One morning during a study period, as the pine trees heaved and sighed in the weeping wind and the fire-escape outside my window hummed at the fall of heavy raindrops from the roof, I became aware of a repetitive clicking sound, too faint at first to betray its source. Removing my glasses and shutting my eyes, I listened for it harder. It was coming from upstairs, from Ambrose's flat. This was strange, for I had seen the tutor not ten minutes earlier, hurrying across the gravelled square in the direction of his classroom. Who could be in his flat? It sounded like a blind thief, tapping around the furniture with his stick. Then the tapping became more distinct and took on a shape, a percussive figure, constantly reiterated. Soon it swelled to a fulminating march, mechanical and obsessive, its unremitting figure unmistakeable: someone was playing 'Bolero' on Ambrose's gramophone. When the piece thundered to its climax, there was scarcely a moment's quiet before it started up again, but this time the visitor had decided that of Ravel's famous seventeen minutes, only the last, hectic five were worth hearing, and they, a little louder. 'Bolero' sounds like the approach of a promiscuous war-machine to me, and when the visitor launched this war machine on a third advance into Ambrose's living quarters and the floor began to shudder, I knew there could be only one explanation: Gaby, who since half-term had made the Studies his daily haunt, must have accepted a key to the tutor's flat.

Not only did the uproar disturb my work, but it distressed me too, because as it continued I began to hear echoes of his fervent banging, weeks before, on the fire-escape, when I had let him in. Poor Gaby, I thought, he may have a key, but he is still knocking to get in. I was having nothing to do with affairs on the top floor now, but as 'Bolero' climaxed hideously for a fourth time, I wished that I could open a door for him again.

I had said no prayer for Gaby, though. I was saying no prayers at all. Finding that I had lost the habit of prayer while serving in the organ loft, where Dr Rabbitt's antics militated against devotion, I decided that, rather than make good this dereliction by attending early Communion or other voluntary services, I would treat it as an experiment, the purpose of which would be to evaluate the worth of the habit I had lost. When the loudspeaker boomed 'LET US PRAY', and Dr Rabbitt stretched and yawned and fidgeted with his music until he lost his place and panicked, I would gaze down on the rows of bowed heads and ponder the significance of what they were about. Since prayer was addressed to the world of the Unconscious, where time obeyed different, inscrutable laws, I doubted that it could ever be untimely and thought that, if I postponed it until my experiment was over, my prayer for Gaby would still not be too late.

A dull afternoon was in prospect. The rain had not let up all week. Miss English had abandoned her houseboat and checked in at The Feathered Oars; there was still no sign of my new raincoat; and in one of the buckets in the Beckett Wing, a frog had been found – the work of a prankster, of course, but I have an aversion to frogs which kept me from the library. Suddenly there was a single knock, and my door flew open.

'Hallo, Perry.'

It was to be our first conversation since half-term.

'Thanks for brutalizing the juniors,' he began, referring to the bullfight posters, which I had donated to the junior common-room.

'Haven't you got games today?'

I explained that the authorities had been forced to give up the pretence that the River Fields were fit for play, now that the fire-brigade had been sighted rescuing livestock from fields on the other bank.

'You can come up and watch the Varsity match on the telly if you like, unless you prefer to be anti-social.'

On entering the tutor's flat, I could see from the hall that the curtains were drawn in the lounge, which was in darkness save for the red, fitful glow of artificial flames and a muffled light from a table-lamp by the wall next to the settee. Gaby was stretched out on the settee, with cushions nestling his head and a newly lit cigarette protruding from his mouth at an absurdly rakish angle. Behind him, the lamp was muffled by his straw hat, which he had placed on top of the shade.

From the centre of the hat rose a thin column of smoke. Ambrose rushed in and rescued it.

'For God's sake, do you want to start a fire?' he cried, beating the hat against his trousers.

'I love fires.'

'Look! You've scorched it!'

'It was like that before.'

'No, it wasn't!'

'Oh well, people will just have to think I'm a hothead.'

'Ha bloody ha. When did you get here?'

''Bout half an hour ago.'

'Do we have to have the curtains drawn?'

'We do, unless we want daylight, Perry.'

'What's wrong with daylight?'

'I've got a bit of a headache.'

'You won't be wanting this then,' said Ambrose, reaching cumbersomely for a glass of beer on the coffee-table. Gaby whisked it away.

'Now you come to mention it, I suppose a scotch would be better for me.'

'You're not having whisky, I've told you.'

'I'll just have to make do with this then, won't I?'

He was wearing, over an open shirt, Ambrose's cricket sweater. The garment looked a tired old weave on the tutor's barrelled torso, but on Gaby, it romped and tumbled, creamily effulgent like the product of a magic loom.

'Mark!' he pretended to have just noticed me in the doorway, and fired off a blazing smile. 'Do come in!'

The removal of the straw hat had released more light on the scene. On the floor at the end of the settee, Gaby's shoes, shabby, with knotted laces, lay where he had kicked them off, one stamping on the other. He had taken off his belt and slung it over the back of the settee, like a lifeless snake run through by the sheath-knife affixed to it. His jacket, collar and tie were screwed up in a refugee's bundle at his feet. The sunglasses he had taken to wearing now that the weather was so awful stared out from beneath the table-lamp, one lens contradicting the other's reflection of the room. A novelty lighter in the form of a handgun nuzzled a packet of ten cigarettes on the coffee-table, where deposits of ash encircled a large seashell, which served as a useless ashtray. On the floor within easy reach were a half-consumed packet of chocolate biscuits, a newspaper open at the sports page, a book lying face down – *The Master Builder and Other Plays* – and a battered *Mad* magazine. Under the coffee-table, two bottles of beer stood in reserve, as yet undetected by Ambrose. Records and record-sleeves were strewn recklessly on the floor beneath the tutor's rudimentary gramophone. From the gramophone came the strains of a washed-up jazz band. *The Brick Wall* hurled its coded abuse from the mantelpiece above the electric fire. It had earned the expected popular fame, and with the authorities preferring to ignore it, had hung in the Founder's Hall for the duration of the book fair, which had enjoyed a bumper year.

'Hallo, Gaby,' I said, 'have you been rained off, too?'

'Nope, I'm off games.'

'Oh dear. Nothing serious, I hope.'

'I've got a twisted knee.'

'Liar,' said Ambrose on his hands and knees, restoring the records to their sleeves.

'I've got a note from my doctor at home!' retorted Gaby.

'Yes, but you forged that,' Ambrose reminded him.

'Oh, all right then, I haven't got a twisted knee. It was a lie, Mark, an affectation, an untruth. I'm so sorry. I have not got a twisted knee. Now I suppose you're dying to know what's really the matter with me?'

'Aren't we all?' said Ambrose.

'Not if it's personal,' I said.

There was a quick burst of the hard-hatted laughter.

'Oh no, it's not personal, I haven't over-exercised my crutch sadly, if that's what you're implying. The truth is, an extraordinary thing's happened to me, which I can't explain, so don't ask me to.'

'Another affectation.'

'Oh, shut up, Perry, it's not an affectation. The fact is, Mark, I simply can't bear to be touched any more – you know, casually. It happens all the time, doesn't it? People run into you in the corridors, in the House, in the tuck-shop – barge, barge, sorry, sorry – I just can't stand it any more. It makes me feel ill.'

'Oh dear.'

'It completely rules out games, of course. I don't suppose I'll ever play rugger again. I'll probably be like this for the rest of my life.'

'Only a short illness, then,' put in Ambrose.

'Yes, thank you, Perry, would you like to get on and count my Embassy coupons now, please?'

'I counted them yesterday, you've got a hundred and sixty-five.'

'One hundred and seventy!' said Gaby, producing a blue card from his back pocket.

'Where did you get that from?'

'Pamela.'

Ambrose tutted. He took a carved musical-box from a cabinet and slipped the coupon into a stack of identical coupons secured by an elastic band; the musical-box tinkled a few bars of 'Träumerei'.

'What are you saving up for?' I asked.

Gaby blew a smoke ring and shrugged: 'It depends how many fags we all get through. Pamela's going like a train at the moment, at least forty a day, I'd say, which is jolly helpful. Perry's useless, of course. It takes him the best part of a week to get through a packet, just to annoy me, so far as I can see. I do what I can.'

'You're smoking at least twenty a day,' said Ambrose.

'Well, there you are, that's not bad, is it, considering my time is not my own? I need eleven hundred for an air-rifle, but I don't expect we'll ever get there. I'll probably cash them in at the end of term, you can get a snazzy hip-flask for four hundred and fifty. Do you want to contribute?'

'I'm afraid I don't smoke.'

'No, I know, I wasn't suggesting you should. Don't let me corrupt you. I was thinking of that greasy middle-school boy round at Collingwood – Summers, isn't it? I say greasy because that's the way he looks to me, I may be quite wrong. You probably know him better, perhaps you're sleeping with him, who knows?'

'No, no. Greasy is right.'

'Anyway, someone told me he smokes Embassy too, and apparently the little squirt's boasting he's got five hundred coupons. If you could see your way to confiscating them, they'd be very welcome.'

'I don't see how I can, really. I'm never on duty round at Collingwood these days.'

Gaby shrugged. 'Well, bear it in mind.'

The washed-up jazz band gave out, severally.

'Turn on the telly, Perry, it'll be starting soon. Who do you support, Mark? Oxford or Cambridge?'

'I don't mind, really.'

'Nor me, I couldn't care less. Perry supports Cambridge, he was there as a lad, bless him. I've bet him a thousand pounds they lose. You'll have to pay me if they do, Perry, you realize that, don't you?'

'Oh yes? And you'll pay me a thousand pounds if they win, will you?'

'Of course.'

'And where are you going to get a thousand pounds from?'

'That should be my commission from the book fair, if you ask me.'

'Huh!'

'Did you see it when it was up, Mark?' He indicated *The Brick Wall* and glowed with pride. I nodded and congratulated him. (In this, his sanctum, it felt treacherous to recall Burnett's response to the work, which had been to say that if, as the maxim had it, a picture painted a thousand words, how come Gaby's had only managed two and did this not indicate poverty?) There was a knock at the door. Ambrose cursed. Gaby crossed his arms behind his head and sank back into the cushions.

'Let's hope it's someone frightfully important,' he said.

'Thanks a lot!' said Ambrose. 'Just pipe down while I answer it, will you?'

He came back with Dennis Penney.

'Hey! Everyone looks very comfortable in here!'

In the half-light, the swarthy boy's footling grin looked more artful and yellow-fleshed than ever.

'Hallo, Dennis,' said Gaby, frigidly, pocketing his cigarettes.

'I thought the "fifteen" had a match this afternoon, Dennis,' said Ambrose. 'Been cancelled, has it?'

Penney explained that the match, an 'away' fixture, had not been cancelled, but Captain Mills, the sports master, had thrown him off the team coach before it departed for being improperly dressed. He flapped his tie at us. It was a shiny black patent tie, and he was wearing it out of respect for a rock-and-roll star of whose sudden unsurprising death he had learned from his transistor radio at lunchtime.

Ambrose groaned. 'You really are determined to make a balls-up of this term, aren't you?'

'I'm sorry, Perry, but it's a matter of principle with me – this was one of my gods, man, one of my heroes. We'd all have to wear a black tie if the Queen died, wouldn't we? It'd be a different story then, right?'

Gaby caught my eye and gave a faint snort.

Penney elaborated on his set-to with Captain Mills. 'Do you know what he said? "I'm not having you on my coach dressed like that," he said, so I said, "But it's not your coach, is it? It's not even the school's coach, it's the *Weald of Kent Coach Company*'s coach – it says so on the side – so you don't even know what you're talking about, man, 'cos it's not even your coach to throw me off."'

'What did he say to that?' said Ambrose dully.

'Nothing. He smacked me round the face, so I split.'

There was another snort from the settee.

'I'm not standing for that, Perry,' the boy went on, 'I'm bloody well going to report him.' He frowned at us all. 'I mean, what is it with this place? Don't people realize you can't go round doing that sort of thing any more? Like, hasn't anybody heard, it's nineteen-sixty-eight, man!'

Gaby reacted to this by glancing at his watch. Seeing that I giggled, he started giggling too.

When the Varsity match started, Penney declared himself on the side of Oxford because a very good friend of his was studying there, who, when he came to think about it, was probably his best friend, or if not his best friend, then very nearly. Gumming a metal comb, he gawped intently. 'Brilliant' saluted a muffed kick, 'magic' a fumbled pass. Ambrose kept an interested eye on the match while marking exercise-books. Gaby paid it virtually no attention at all. He glanced at the newspaper, tried the book of plays, and

150

eventually settled for the *Mad* magazine. From time to time, when boredom pressed, he lowered the magazine and had a dig at Dennis Penney.

A heaving scrum appeared on the screen: 'Which one's your friend, Dennis?'

'Oh, he's not actually playing.'

'Oh, I see.'

Later: 'Where's Brian?'

'Brian?'

'Yes, Brian Dodge, you know the chap.'

'I dunno, why?'

'No reason. You're so often together, I hadn't realized he was capable of independent life, that's all.' He accompanied this remark with the sort of beaming smile that condemns its recipient to silent umbrage. Then, to an outburst of rebuke from Ambrose, Penney produced a packet of cigarettes, as he was obliged to do if he wanted to smoke, since none was on offer. Gaby deplored the cigarettes too, because they were not Embassy and there were no coupons. He managed to accept one, though, and with the cigarette packet in his hands, set to work on an anagram of the brand name: Penney's brand was PERFECTOS, the anagram Gaby came up with, SOFT CREEP, which he announced as he handed the packet back to its owner with another beaming smile. The magic sweater thrilled to a host of little shrugs and adjustments as he snuggled back into the cushions with his magazine.

Ambrose tried to draw Gaby's attention several times to the seashell which was full to overflowing, and spilling copiously every time he stubbed out a cigarette. In the end the tutor gave up and stomped out to the kitchen to empty it himself. He stomped back in again and sent the shell spinning on to the coffee-table.

'Thanks,' said Gaby, not looking up from his magazine.

'You could have done that, couldn't you?' grumbled Ambrose.

'But never with your grace,' came the reply, as marvellously prompt as ever.

He dazzled me that afternoon. As he posed, trashily supreme, on the settee, with every imaginable comfort to hand, his hair unkempt, his manner indomitable, there was yet something about him, something vital and vivid and, impossibly, innocent, that transcended the hubristic façade and gave him what a pose can never give anyone, a natural glamour, undeniable allure.

Penney bunked off as soon as the rugby match was over – driven away by Gaby's incontestable jibes. I should have left at the same time, but by then I was captivated, and dared to hang on until an incontestable jibe instructed me to go. But the instruction never came. It seemed that, for some reason, Gaby approved of me. Furthermore, in the presence of Penney, the bickering skirmishes between him and Ambrose had ceased, or at least been conducted in an idiom less disparaging and libidinous than that to which they reverted as soon as Penney left. I wondered at my status, that they should be so unguarded in front of me. Gaby kept drawing me into the conversation, albeit in ways that invited a short contribution. Then, for no particular reason, he asked me how I came to be known as the Undertaker. Flattered by his interest, I told of my attempt to bury the disgusting old gardener, Mr Harold, whose death I had foreseen. In order to receive full credit, I inserted a sly inaccuracy: I advanced my age at the time of the incident from three or four, to twelve.

'Were his eyes open?' asked Gaby.

'Staring horribly,' I replied.

He paid me the accolade of sitting up, for the first

time that afternoon, and resting his well-made head attentively on the heel of his hand, so I invented for his further amusement a bid to set fire to the corpse with lawn-mower fuel, which had failed only for want of a match. Wide-eyed, he shook his head.

'You're obviously a monster. Perry, Mark's a monster! And will you be an undertaker when you grow up, do you think?'

'Oh, I expect so.'

'I want to be cremated.'

'Right-oh.' His scorched straw hat was to hand, and I picked it up and showed it to him. 'With or without your hat?'

He laughed – a genuine laugh, not the hard-hatted cackle – and with the artificial flames twinkling in his eye and playing on his cheek, held me for a moment with a look of the warmest, most generous favour. No-one could be immune to such a look. It was exciting to be regarded with such approval. I felt that, if I was dazzled, it was by a kindly light; and the revelation made by the kindly light was that this boy who, for reasons unknown, was rare and remote, solitary, precarious and excluded, was also, as a consequence, exclusive. If he accepted me, it would mean that I was accepted into an exclusive club. I had never been a member of an exclusive club before. I wondered what the subscription would be: love, I supposed, which at that moment felt not beyond my means. But before I had made any such outlay, there came another revelation.

Oxford had won the Varsity match, and it occurred to Gaby that Ambrose owed him a thousand pounds. Ambrose replied that this was not a convenient sum and declined to sign an i.o.u. Then, to my outrage – but no-one is such a stickler for decorum as the newly elected member of an exclusive club – Ambrose turned on Gaby and began to offend what I assumed to be the club's first principle by deliberately upsetting him.

'Do you know, you haven't got off your backside all afternoon?'

'I shouldn't let him speak to you like that, if I were you, Mark.'

'I'm not speaking to Mark, I'm speaking to you.'

'Well, how very rude. You've obviously forgotten about my headache and my bad knee.'

'You haven't got a bad knee. Why don't you go and make us all some tea?'

'I don't know how.'

'God, you're hopeless, aren't you? I don't think I've ever met such an absolutely useless individual – go on, make the tea.'

Gaby closed his eyes; his long lashes seemed to take a long while to settle, and from his hard-faced expression it looked as though it would be quite a time before he bothered to open them again.

'Go on!' persisted Ambrose.

'No, I don't want one.'

'Well, I do, and I expect Mark does, don't be so selfish.'

'I told you, I don't know how.'

'Well, learn.'

'Why don't you ask Mark, you're always picking on me?'

'Yes, I don't mind,' I said, getting up. I could see no point to Ambrose's nagging. The lashes opened, my reward was a lovely smile.

While I was in the kitchen waiting for the kettle to boil, I heard a 'snap' from the sitting-room. Puzzled, I went to the door. In the hallway, there was a gilt-framed, upright mirror on the wall by the front door, which gave a view into the darkened sitting-room. I could see Gaby's upper half recumbent on the settee.

He had an unlit cigarette in his mouth. As I watched, he raised his hand and snapped his fingers. Ambrose's arm came into the frame. He gave the boy a light with the handgun. The arm withdrew. Gaby sucked on the cigarette and then extended his hand, as though reaching for something, and snapped his fingers again. Ambrose stepped fully into the mirror's eye and, with a quick look over his shoulder, dropped on one knee and took the proffered hand, and kissed it. He pressed it to his cheek, and then kissed it again, holding it in both his hands as though it were the thing he most cherished in the world. Gaby looked on with detachment, perhaps merely to assure himself that he was not being touched casually, as he so abhorred. He was not. With another snap of his fingers, he brought the wordless routine to an end. Ambrose obediently rose to his feet and shuffled out of view. Then, as I was about to retreat, Gaby turned his head towards the door. Just as his eyes were about to meet mine, he blew out a large cloud of smoke, which baffled his image. I stepped back into the kitchen, where the kettle was boiling rapidly.

12

Emancipation

Before I left that afternoon, I let drop to Gaby and the tutor that I knew of the pass to which their relationship had come; not in straightforward terms, of course, but obliquely: 'Well, it's been an interesting afternoon,' I said, getting to my feet, having not lingered over my tea. 'I'll leave you two to your own devices.' Gaby picked up the aspersion at once.

'Our own devices, eh?' he said lightly; the sheath knife, with which he was stirring his tea, gleamed. 'That will be fun for us.' He gave me a knowing, half-faced grin. Ambrose's deadpan expression remained set, and he may have taken the remark for no more than a figure of speech, although I felt as I left that his gaze impended heavily on my back.

The next evening, reporting back late, I left him in no doubt.

'Hallo, Mark,' he said, answering his door, 'I was wondering where you'd got to.'

'Sorry I'm late, I did my prep down at the school,' I replied. Then, peering over his shoulder into the flat, I added, in a tone that was even more arch and pointed than I intended: 'I do hope I'm not disturbing anything?'

Suddenly his eyes looked peeled and full of dark wonder, as though reading from a point just in front of his nose the date of his death and finding it imminent.

'Of course you're not disturbing anything, what a strange thing to say,' he said quickly, and, as if to prove it: 'Come in.'

Gaby lay on the settee, in a bit of a sulk.

'Hallo, Undertaker.' He managed a lukewarm smile. 'I'm glad you've arrived, we're having a terrible row.'

The terrible row concerned his hair, and whether or not it was blond. Ambrose called it mousey, and said that Chandler-Smith was a good example of a blond.

'Yes,' said Gaby, 'but that's because he tints his hair, everyone knows that.'

The very idea of the haughty Chandler-Smith, a model of correctness, stooping to such a deed made me laugh. It was the first thing to have amused me all day. I realized that I had been longing to see him.

'At least I'm a natural blond – not platinum, of course, but there must be a word for it. Ash blond, is it? Honey blond?' He fluttered his lashes.

'Mousey,' insisted Ambrose.

'Mousey blond? No, that's not a colour, Perry, that's an insult.'

'Vermin blond?' I put in nervously.

'Vermin blond!' Gaby seized on it. 'Brilliant! I love it! It's so me!' His lukewarm smile caught fire. He winked at me. It was nice to feel exclusive again.

When Ambrose went to fetch him a drink, Gaby handed me a pound note. 'Sorry to have kept you waiting so long for this,' he said quietly.

I was quite overwhelmed.

The next evening, when I again reported in late, Ambrose grumbled: 'Why aren't you working in your study these days?'

'I'm using reference books in the Beckett Library, I'm not allowed to take them out.'

This was untrue. I had stayed out merely to give myself an excuse for knocking at his door, and had spent the evening rehearsing things to say that I hoped would amuse Gaby. I had also been lifting an English essay almost verbatim from a textbook, the first of many such departures from my usual diligence. Once I would have called these departures 'lapses', but so completely did Gaby's image now eclipse the lights of my former code, I felt not delinquent, but emancipated.

My emancipation brought about many changes. Burnett and the Wizard no longer seemed bright and clever, but self-appointed élitists whose credentials I had seen bettered; they bored me, and, in their turn, complained that I was moody. Father, in a letter, supposed that it must be pressure of work that had prevented me from writing home since half-term. It had worried Mother, he said, noting also that it was the first time he had ever had to complain about this.

In Gaby's service, I cornered Summers in the Collingwood bicycle shed at the weekend, and relieved the unlovely youth of his cigarettes, which gratifyingly proved to be Embassy.

'I won't report you, just this once,' I said. 'You can write out the first psalm for me twice – neatly, mind.'

'Gosh, thanks, Palfreyman!'

It was an imposition I had once been set myself. Gaby was delighted when I presented him with the cigarettes, complete with coupon.

'I think the air-rifle would be better for you than the hip-flask,' I said.

'But mightn't I decide to shoot myself with it?'

'Well, man, that's your privilege, I mean, it's your life, like, it's nineteen-sixty-eight, man.'

He laughed. I was becoming quite a clown. Ambrose dumped the coupon unceremoniously in the musical-box, without bothering to slip it into the elastic band. Sometimes Ambrose forgot how lucky he was. There was nothing I wanted from him, except access to Gaby, so though I could have demanded much for my discretion, I charged him lightly. To square the account, I chastised him a little. When his television went out of service, I found Gaby twitching with boredom on the settee and belabouring the tutor for the shortcomings of his record collection, on which they had fallen back for entertainment. He demanded to hear something new. Among the records I fetched for him, I included one that had long been in my collection, of Dukas's 'The Sorcerer's Apprentice', whose programme was completed by another of the same composer's works, the lesser-known 'La Péri'. Gaby, learning from the sleeve-notes that 'La Péri' translated into 'The Fairy', made a connection I purported not to have made myself.

'Oh, Perry, your name means "fairy", how sweet!'

The look of dark wonder sought me out.

'Fairy!' Gaby went on. 'Grant me a wish, fairy, I wish I could have an ickle whisky.'

'Well, you're not getting one.'

'I don't believe in fairies, I don't believe in fairies, I don't believe in fairies! An ickle fairy dies every time I say that, Perry, don't you care?'

'Oh, shut up.'

When we played the record, he urged the tutor to dance.

'Come on, fairy footsteps, they're playing your tune!'

In the end a deal was done. Ambrose poured him a whisky on the understanding that the name would be dropped.

We cheated: 'Undertaker, are any of the juniors worth interfering with, or don't you bother? I know La Péri prefers you not to sleep together.'

'I must say, I don't bother.'

'I'll have to take a look at them some time.'

'You dare,' rumbled Ambrose, always touchy on this subject.

Soon, there was no need to find an excuse for calling on Ambrose; my attendance upstairs would be expected each evening. Sometimes it was after midnight when we left by the two doors, Gaby's giving on to the humming metal flight, mine, more prosaically, to the stairs. Never had I been so amused and enthralled, never had I been so amusing, and as the days passed, with each day having as the measure of its fulfilment the amount of time I spent in his company, I fell willingly under his spell. Yet my surrender was not unconditional. All the while, even as a rapport developed between us of the sort by which friends may enlighten each other while leaving outsiders in the dark, there was something in my mind on which I was careful not to enlighten Gaby, a view which, had he known of it, he would have thought duplicitous, a betrayal.

It was the view in the mirror. It had come like a second sight of him, and was all the more powerful for corresponding with my own second sight, my intuition. I was not untrue to him, not really. I did seek his company and revel in his favour, I was entertained and dazzled, but I only allowed this to happen because I knew that my second sight could never be dazzled, nor could it turn a blind eye, nor could he corrupt its judgement, because, like the mirror, my second sight was not a judge; it was merely an observer. It observed that, for Gaby, all the world was not a stage; for Gaby, the world was an unbearable place, and so he drew the curtains and shut out the light and the outward views, and created a world for himself. It observed that this world of his own creation, this heroic contention of his will that cost all his time and talents to sustain, was a cold, hopeless, tenebrous place, a place of false worship, an abyss. He was God, of course, in this abysmal place, but my second sight observed its essential poverty, the poverty that Burnett had pointed to in *The Brick Wall*, the poverty that had made him a thief.

I had abandoned my experiment regarding prayer and decided simply that I was never going down on my knees for anything ever again, so I said no prayer for Gaby, but it was unnerving that he took so readily to calling me the Undertaker, because if I had prayed for him with the exercise of any humanity, I would have prayed for him to die. Having this second sight for a restraint, I was never going to be more than a half-member of his exclusive club. This was the condition under which I surrendered, because it made it possible to be of his world and at the same time outside it, dazzled and yet not dazzled, with him and without. How could I have accepted his warmth, had my second sight not pierced the façade and found him as cold as the dead? How could I have borne to see the trust that lit up his blue eyes when he mistook me for a disciple, had my second sight not advised me that there was no place for trust in Gaby's world, and no such thing as friendship, either. It was not a true friendship, it was more like an adventure – an adventure which I felt I had under my control, and would never have to pay for; a bargain. Once, a bargain would have filled me with suspicion, but that was the sort of scruple that belonged to my former code – now in total eclipse.

13

The Sixth-Form Dance

'Testing, testing, one-two—' wheeeeEEEEEE phut!

Deafening electronic feedback filled the Founder's Hall as technical difficulties continued to dog The Vendettas. A long-haired foursome of recent old boys, I worried a little for their safety when I saw, behind the stacked amplifiers that made the old stage look very small, the crop-haired Mr Edie, peeping up like a theatre cat to see if his latest connection had done the trick.

'Test—' wheeeeEEEE phut!

In the usual way I would have offered assistance, but Amanda was due at any minute, and I had taken trouble over my appearance. In any case, the more offensively the band created, the sooner I might reasonably propose that we find somewhere quieter and more comfortable. My study was a suitable resort, having undergone some changes. I had turned my desklamp to a corner like a dunce, and fitted an orange bulb. On a raid next door, I had found the absent Ostler's study swathed in rugs and littered with cheerful cushions, a nest of warm furnishings beside which my own study bared a martyr's ribs. His curtains now fell plushly at my window, a pair of his cheerful cushions adorned my bed. Aunt Lucy's two-mooned picture of Brighton hung from a hook. Mindful of the tactics of David Burnett, who reckoned that, where girls were concerned, nature took its course more readily for the accompaniment of a 'cello,

I had hoped, while sorting through the 'cello concertos in my collection, that by ten o'clock or thereabouts, its high emotional charge would not disqualify the Boccherini; I had placed it on the turntable. Under the bed was a less subtle stimulant, a bottle of Sauterne, already opened with Garland's gadget-packed Swiss Army knife, which I had borrowed on a pretext. Having cycled out to buy it at a nearby village, I had wrapped the bottle in my shrinking raincoat and smuggled it in like a gangster nursing a hidden gun. Breaking one of the school's cardinal rules had been exciting, a novelty. And to think, once I would have considered the alterations to my study and the presence of the wine to be sly, dishonourable measures — what a hidebound fellow I had been! Perhaps my new emancipation would bring me better luck with girls.

Hanging about in the Founder's Hall, however, on the fringes of the Collingwood set, my optimism ebbed. Gaby was topping up at The Blue Posts, where it was skittles night, before coming on to the dance. I had not told him about Amanda, partly in case everything went wrong and she ended the evening in the arms of Chandler-Smith, but mainly because I wanted him to believe, as I escorted her from the Hall having apparently only just met her, that I had made a conquest of my own. I had wanted to impress him. In his absence, my plans seemed wildly ambitious, and the changes I had made to my study, sordid. And now, a shadow on the wall showed me that my hair had sprung an unruly lock, like a question-mark, at the side of my head. Bosco's hair dryer, in my inexpert grip, had blasted a series of unnatural curls which, to suppress, had required a heavy application of water. Now they were drying out, and just as I succeeded in trapping the question-mark with the frame of my glasses, another one winged out on the other side. Had any of the first party of girls, which trooped in at this moment, been looking in my direction they would have seen me apparently tearing at my hair. This first party, which I saw with relief was not Amanda's, entered vibrant with team spirit, and endured our all-male scrutiny with a marked absence of modesty, as though emboldened by a vulgar singsong on the coach. Having left their coats with Andrew Garland who, with two volunteers, was standing to attention behind a trestle table with a reel of numbered tickets, the girls moved on to another table, where a feeble young master, Mr Heston, dispensed soft drinks, sweet bottled cider, and pale ale bled by a leaking tap from a large inexhaustible can.

When a second coach party edged into the hall – convent girls under the eye of a nun – The Vendettas launched without warning into 'Wild Thing', at a volume which caused Mr Edie to flee from the back of the stage. Bosco broke the ice; he moved in on a leggy brunette and ushered her to the centre of the hall. His friend, Hammond, a stammerer, whose impediment under The Vendettas' din was no impediment at all, naturally took possession of the brunette's friend, and the dancing got underway. Penney and Dodge, the air about them shimmering with aftershave, conspired with their eyes over a pair of pretty blondes, who may have been twins. Elwyn-Jones, who had earlier flashed a packet of contraceptives at me, picked up a real beauty – but lost her after one dance to Forest-Nicholls, an athletics hero. Elwyn-Jones retired to a chair by the wall, where his face lengthened as Forest-Nicholls and the beauty jubilantly hit it off.

By the time the hall door opened again to admit the last batch of guests – Amanda's party, which I had begun to hope might never arrive – the centre of the floor was a crowded mêlée. The Vendetta's lead singer, cocksure after half an hour on stage, breathed huskily into the microphone: 'Hi, girls.'

Those at the head of the incoming party pulled faces and looked ready to withdraw, but pressure from behind pushed them in. In order not to be smotheringly expectant of Amanda, I drifted away from the door. Garland's voluntary helpers had deserted him, so there was quite a delay while he coped, singlehanded, with the coats. When, in the corner of my eye, I saw the door close on the last of the newcomers, I turned casually for a first sight of my partner. She was not immediately to be seen. I strolled over to the bar, where Mr Heston was having trouble with a new assistant, a bossy girl from the convent with an aggressive crush on him, who kept trying to push her bosom into his hands. Amanda, though, was not there, nor was she dancing, nor, on a circuit of the hall, was she anywhere to be found.

Someone tapped me on the arm, a girl from Amanda's school.

'Are you Mark?' she shouted over the music. 'Mark Palfreyman?' She had a round, pretty face, and a torrent of dark, wavy hair past her waist.

'Yes?'

She handed me an envelope. 'Amanda asked me to give you this. She says she's . . .'

Her last words were lost to a flourish from the drummer.

'She's what?'

'Very sorry.'

She smiled and turned away. I opened the envelope.

Dear Mark,
    I'm so sorry I haven't been able to make it tonight, but I'm afraid I've got myself into a spot

of trouble, I'll write in full as soon as poss. I've
given this to a girl called Cheryl, she's one of
my best friends. Please be nice and ask her
to dance – she's *terribly shy*.

       Sorry again,
           Love,
             Amanda

At first, considering all the trouble I had taken for her
visit, I was peeved, but this soon gave way to concern.
What sort of trouble could Amanda have got herself
into? I had always thought of her as dependable. At
home, the riding school trusted her to lead out the
weekend hacks, and to collect the money; she never
rode without a hard hat. There was a strain of
moodiness in her nature, perhaps, but I knew that all
girls had bad days, and if she had not been at her best
at the Tennis Club dance, that was because she had
been unwell, and uncomfortable with her dress. It was
a puzzle. Perhaps Cheryl could enlarge on the unsatis-
factory note, but I would allow a decent period to
elapse before asking her to dance, so that a report
would not go back to Amanda describing me as fast or
unfeelingly versatile.

The Vendettas took a break.

'Hallo and good evening.'

The Head Boy, using a microphone, addressed the
hall from a table in front of the stage.

'Can we have a jolly good hand, please, for our
group tonight, The Vendettas!'

He was answered by a salvo of good-natured abuse.

'First of all,' Riley went on, 'on behalf of St Clement's,
I'd like to welcome our guests. It's very nice to see you,
and I do hope you enjoy your evening with us. School,
three cheers for the girls. Hip hip . . .'

'Ray!'

'Hip hip!'

'Ray!'

'Hip hip!'

'Ray!'

'The ladies' cloakroom, by the way, for those of you who have not already found it, is in the Main School building, which is directly ahead of you as you leave the Hall. There is a sign. My name is Andrew Riley, and while our musicians . . .'

Another salvo of abuse.

'Ha, ha, thank you, settle down. As I was saying, while our musicians take their well-earned rest, I shall be playing some records.'

With that, he set the needle down on a Rolling Stones LP, starting with '19th Nervous Breakdown' at the wrong speed.

Now that the volume of noise was modest enough to allow for conversation, some of the new relationships fell apart under the strain, but not that of Dennis Penney and his catch – one of the blonde twins; they were already locked in a passionate clinch on a wall-side bench. I looked for Cheryl. She was standing in a corner of the hall, near the door, with two friends, staring in on the proceedings with an air of cool indifference. A symptom of her terrible shyness, no doubt, I thought, as I approached.

'Would you like to dance?' I said.

She smiled at me very sweetly.

'No thanks.'

I flapped at my unruly locks.

'Perhaps I can get you a drink?'

'I've got one, thanks.'

I tried a breezy approach.

'Well, well, well, what's old Amanda been up to, then?'

Her two friends, who were very plain, muttered to

each other and eyed me as though I was topical for some reason.

'She's asked me not to talk about it, actually,' said Cheryl.

'Oh?'

'She wanted to tell you herself.'

'Ah.'

Suddenly, the Hall's great door, only a few paces away, suffered a violent impact. The girls spun round. The iron door-handle dipped and the door swung inwards. With one hand clutching the outside handle and his back hard up against the panels of the door, as though he had been pasted to it, it was at once clear that, on skittles night at The Blue Posts, Gaby had topped up to excess. With a cigarette sticking from his mouth, his tie loose, his face flushed, he took in the view with benign incomprehension, as though the goings-on in the Hall came as a wonderful surprise. This first appearance was very brief. It was like a peep-show on the pier: having swung open to reveal him, the door swung closed again, still with Gaby pasted to its panels. Ignoring him, I tried to pick up the conversation with Cheryl.

'Nothing serious, this business with Amanda, is it?'

The door swung open again: this time there was no-one attached to it. A moment or two later, Gaby lurched in, lifting his feet unnecessarily high as though stepping through glue. He had ditched the cigarette. Steadying himself, his eye fell on the bar. Someone turned up the gramophone: *These boots were made for walking. And that's just what they'll do, One of these days these boots are gonna walk all over you* . . .

Clicking his fingers and moving in a way that was perhaps intended to be rhythmic, Gaby set off. Then he spotted me: 'Unnertaker!'

He threw up his arms in a gesture of greeting that

would have had him on the floor had it not been for an astonishing, rubber-legged recovery that left him further from the bar than he had been when he came in. Frowning with concentration, he renewed his aim, having forgotten what it was that had just distracted him.

'Friend of yours?' said Cheryl.

'No, not specially.'

One of Cheryl's friends let her opinion of my continued presence be known by putting her hands on her hips and glaring fiercely.

'Well, send Amanda my love, won't you?' I said, which according to the reaction of the hostile by-standers, was a simply outrageous remark. I retreated.

All too soon, Riley announced the return of The Vendettas. In their absence, a slight edge of formality had returned, but they soon had the top off everyone's behaviour again with their version of 'Can't Buy Me Love'. The hall teemed with jiving couples; someone turned off half the lights. Suddenly, something at the centre of the gyrating mass caused a wave effect, as people stepped aside. At the eye of the disturbance, Andrew Riley danced woodenly, as though warming up for a rugby match; around him, his extravagant partner writhed and cavorted, windmilling her arms, her streaming dark hair almost sweeping the floor. It was Cheryl. Amanda was going to hear about this! Terribly shy? A thought occurred: was Cheryl the wretched girl who had written herself letters addressed to a slut? The deed seemed within her range, and since the idea compensated me, I made up my mind that it was so.

I was beginning to feel conspicuously marginal, when my fortunes changed. On the outskirts, among a group of girls dancing together, was a very tall, very slender girl — the sort who finds herself in the high-jump final without being really an athlete. Other than myself, there were not many tall enough for her; when I asked her to dance, she looked agreeably surprised. Her name was Heather. We stayed together, and even danced closely when The Vendettas' rendition of 'Yesterday' put everyone in need of support. Gaby sighted us from a chair in which he was slumped. Hopelessly drunk, he grinned at me blearily, screwed up his face in his look of foolish lust, thrust an elbow into his crutch and made a giant phallus of his forearm. I steered Heather gently away from him.

After that, everything went wrong very quickly. The Vendettas followed 'Yesterday' with more slow numbers, during which I saw, over my partner's shoulder, the Hall's great door open and Brian Dodge slip out with his blonde; Forest-Nicholls and the beauty, and then others, went the same way. I turned with foreboding to the wall-side bench – no Dennis Penney, no blonde, they too had slipped off. Where could all these couples have been going? A classroom would have suited for a kiss and a cuddle, but Penney, for one, would have had more thoroughgoing activity in mind. The Gymnasium might be broken into, where there were springboards and tumbling-mats, but not for nothing was it known as the Grim, being cold, draughty and echoing. To make matters worse, I saw that none of the Senior Study boys had left. If Penney or his like had ventured to the Studies, he would have found the door open and the senior corridor deserted. Would he dare to use my study? Yes, I decided. He had done it once, he would do it again. Remembering the reek of perfume and tobacco, and the fingerprints of disdain left by his last violation, I knew that I must go home at once.

'I have to leave now, I've got to get back to my study, I'm afraid,' I said.

Heather's face started to drop, so in an attempt to replace bad news with good, I added, without thinking: 'Would you like to come, too?'

Her face continued to drop. 'Oh, no, thank you.'

She recoiled, shocked, brushed at her skirt, and hurried to rejoin her friends. That was that. Before leaving the Hall I glanced across at Gaby; he was fast asleep.

Half an hour later, having found no intruders on my return, I drained my toothmug with a reckless swig, and shivered with revulsion. The hot pipe under the bed had warmed the sweet Sauterne. The Boccherini 'cello concerto was playing rapturously. I poured another drink, I was beginning to feel tipsy. The door burst open.

'What the hell's going on?'

Ambrose glared at me, and then the toothmug, and then the bottle. He peered behind the door to see if anyone was hiding. I reached out to the gramophone and turned the volume up.

'What the hell d'you think you're doing?'

I grinned. He strode in and pulled the plug from the wall.

'I said what the hell d'you think you're doing?'

I kicked off my shoes, lay back on one of Ostler's cheerful cushions and stared up at him.

'Well?'

'Just having a little nightcap.' I could hear my voice slurring. 'What are you going to do about it, Perry?'

He clenched his teeth, his jaw squared. Thrilled by my insolence, I curled my lip: 'Pass me my drink, would you?'

When he made no move to obey, I reached out my hand and snapped my fingers.

'Come on, my drink!' I ordered.

After a long pause, he handed me the toothmug, but held on to the bottle, which was three-quarters empty.

'I'm going to take this,' he said, very quietly. 'I'll speak to you in the morning.'

'No, I wanna talk to you now,' I said. It had occurred to me that there was, after all, something I wanted from him.

'You're drunk.'

'Course I'm drunk. So what? I shouldn't really be here, should I? I should be down at the dance, shouldn't I? But I'm not. Do you know why I'm not, Perry?'

'Go on.'

'We're supposed to act like grown-ups here, aren't we? According to you, it's supposed to be a rehearsal for university, isn't it? But do you know what, Perry, I bet they have locks on their doors at university, I bet they do. In fact, Perry, I'm not sure I can be quite as grown up as you'd like me to be, without a lock on my door, without some fucking privacy, Perry, and let's face it, let's face it, Perry, you're rather counting on me being grown up about things, aren't you?'

There was no dark wonder in the expression with which he regarded me, only hate.

'All right, I'll see what I can do,' he said. 'Now I suggest you go to bed.'

I felt very full of myself when he had gone. I began a letter:

My dear Amanda,
I was so sorry not to see you tonight. I didn't stay to the end – I expect Cheryl's told you. I want you to know that whatever trouble you are in, it will not affect the way I feel about you. I wonder if you know how very fond of you I

am – in fact, I'm in love with you, Amanda, and I've never told anyone that before . . .

My eyes felt heavy, I would finish the letter in the morning.

14

A Place Of My Own

Amanda was pregnant. It was not I who was responsible – I have reserved nothing. I heard the news on the Friday morning following the dance, which had been held on a Wednesday. Jonathan caught up with me on the stairs down to breakfast.

'Mark, can you go up to Perry's flat?' He rocked back and fended off a long hop. 'He's got your mother on the phone.'

Ambrose was waiting for me on the top landing. We had not spoken since the night of the dance and he was still avoiding my eyes.

'I'm going down to breakfast. Will you shut my door on your way out?'

'Sure.'

'Is that you, Mark? How are you, dear?' said Mother in a whimpering voice that gave cause for immediate concern.

'Fine. What is it?'

'I hope you're not going to be too upset about this.'

'About what?'

'It's Amanda Gough, dear. I'm afraid someone's got her into trouble.'

'Oh I knew she was in a spot of trouble, she didn't turn up for the dance the other night. What is it exactly?'

'No, dear, you don't understand, someone's got her into trouble. You know, in the family way. She's pregnant.'

'Pregnant?'

'Yes, dear. Her mother's just rung me.'

'Gosh.'

There was a pause.

'We are sorry.'

'Well, it wasn't me.'

'Oh don't worry, dear, everyone knows that,' said Mother with a little laugh. 'No-one's suggesting it was you. Quite honestly, this is the sort of scrape I'm always afraid Miles will get himself into, one day.'

'Oh it wasn't *him*, was it?' I said, thoroughly disheartened.

'No, dear, of course not, he hardly knows the girl. Mind you . . .' Mother's voice warmed up, 'I understand it wasn't anyone Amanda was very close to.'

I reflected that, in the circumstances, this would seem to rule out only her pony.

'It was someone she met on that holiday of theirs in Italy,' Mother went on. 'An Italian, of all things. Very sudden.'

Ostler's curtain still hung at my study window; I took it down and returned it, with the cheerful cushions, to his room. Cutting breakfast, I left the Studies by the back door and made my way down the wild lawn, aiming a disconsolate kick at the gnarled old bench as I passed. The downpours had ceased some time ago, and the ground underfoot on the Lower Field was dry. The winds, too, had lulled, and the air was quiet as I skirted the field with a slow, ruminative tread. From the chestnut trees at the top of the Passchendaele Steps, the view of St Clement's across the Upper Field was that which, confronting the punishment runner, would dissuade him from questioning the justice of his punishment; an imposing view, subduing, it was on this morning a comfort. The grey, solid, buttressed battlements of the Main School, the proud, clean lines of the long, red-bricked chapel, even the blowsily constructed Beckett Wing – they had always been there and were there now, mercifully unchanging like a doctrine, and grand. I borrowed their grandeur.

Amanda was pregnant? Swept off her feet on her summer holidays? Poor Amanda, but how frail! This was not the sort of behaviour one had a right to expect. Good riddance! And thank goodness I had torn up the drink-inspired love-letter!

Passing the white picket fence at the front of the green-shuttered pavilion, I moved over dead leaves as quietly as possible, as though beneath its pretty thatch, someone I valued slept.

Amanda overwhelmed by an Italian? What sort of Italian? A coach-driver, swarthy, in tight black trousers and a white frilly shirt, offering guided tours in despicable English? A yellow pigment to his flesh, perhaps, the Dennis Penney of the Rialto? Or a hotel waiter who played volleyball on the beach all day in scant, precarious trunks? It was sure to be someone she had met on the beach. A frog, maybe; I pictured a voluptuous specimen, with a vast gulping bubble for a throat, its backside dipped in a briny puddle, clearing its eyes of grit and tics with an upward-blinking membrane.

I trailed my hand through the cold leaves of the evergreen hedge bounding Starvecrow Hall.

And had this lover, this frog, chosen for her that awful dress that had so embarrassed me at the Tennis Club dance? So what! I cared not. I decided to throw her letters in the river.

The proprietor of the school outfitter's shop, a notorious bungler, made his first mistake that day when he chose to open up at the very moment I passed his door. I marched in and demanded to know the whereabouts of my new coat, now long overdue. *En route* from Huddersfield, he assured me, it would be arriving any day, there had been a mix-up. This was not the sort of service one had the right to expect, I informed him, and marched out, closing his door with a bang.

'For what we are about to receive, may the Lord make us truly thankful,' said Garland. We sat down for lunch. It was toad-in-the-hole. Twenty minutes later when a junior came up to collect our plates, not a word had been spoken on the top table. This was due to a highly concentrated charge in the atmosphere local to Ambrose, brought on by the impossible intensity of his demeanour. His atrabilious visage seemed, more than ever, petrified, and his dark brown eyes stared straight ahead, as shiny as buttons, as though the frozen tears that held them open had tightened their grip to prevent his eyeballs rotating. No-one dared speak. Jonathan, maintaining the air of a man who has noticed nothing unusual, nonetheless restricted his imaginary activities to hoisting slow lobs with a ping-pong bat from below the level of the table on Ambrose's blind side. Bosco, at the end of the table, peeped over a stockade of American sauce bottles from time to time, to regard the tutor with looks of affectionate, almost soppy concern; he adored Ambrose in this mood. Mrs Binks, at the hot plate, nervously tasted the food.

Eventually the monumental head gave utterance, in a clipped, unprojected voice. 'If you lot could manage to pay attention for a few moments, I've got something to say that concerns you all.'

We paid conspicuous attention.

'During the winter holidays the school is hosting a conference – educational psychologists, or something. Some of the people attending this conference are coming from far afield, so they'll be resident for a few days. Now, the Headmaster's decided we've got to have them here, so we're going to be using the Senior Studies for their accommodation. During the course of the afternoon, therefore, probably while you're off doing Corps—'

There was a murmur from Bosco's end of the table.

'I'M SORRY?'

'Why, ah jest said ah don't do Corps, Perry.'

'So what?'

'Nothing. Excuse me, sir.'

'As I was saying, during the course of the afternoon the school carpenter will be here to fit locks on the study doors, so don't be surprised to find them when you get back. The reason we're doing this now and not at the end of term is because two or three of you have expressed a wish to have locks on your doors already.'

The others at table looked nonplussed.

'I think it's a perfectly ridiculous idea, myself. I will of course have duplicates of all the keys, so don't go away with the idea that just because your door's locked you can hide things from me. It's bad luck on you two who are staying on, Garland and Palfreyman. I'm afraid at Christmas you'll have to clear your studies completely, and refurnish them again at the beginning of next term.'

I waved my head to indicate that this would be no inconvenience at all.

'But sir . . .' began Garland.

'Would you please have the courtesy to let me finish! And by the way, Andrew,' he turned to focus dangerously on the porky cadet, 'what was that I saw you bringing into the House yesterday evening?'

'Yesterday?'

'Yes, you know what I'm talking about. After prep. I had my hands full wih the juniors at the time.'

178

'It belongs to the Alpine Club, Perry, we had a meeting . . .'

'I SAID, WHAT WAS IT?'

'It was an ice-axe, Perry.'

'Yes, bring it to me after lunch, will you? I'll look after that from now on. In fact I think we'll have – what d'you call it? – an amnesty, shall we? Anyone else got deadly weapons in their rooms – knives, guns, hatchets and so on? Bring them up to me after lunch, would you? The school rules on this, I believe, are fairly clear.'

Garland, in a pink rage, puffed out his cheeks and seemed to hyperventilate.

'Now, I'm only going to say this once,' continued Ambrose. 'This is not a hotel, and I am not the porter. If you lose your key, that's it, you will not be getting another one. And if – no, *when* you lock yourselves out, I will let you in again when it suits *me*, not when it suits you. Is that understood?'

We nodded, we understood.

'Good. Does anyone have any sensible questions?'

There were no questions.

By the time I returned to my study after Corps, a Yale lock had been fitted. I let myself in with a key which had been left in it. When I closed the door behind me, the lock made an extra, decisive click; as I put the key on my keyring, I felt that it betokened a giant step towards adulthood. A place of my own, at last.

After tea, I re-read Amanda's letters. My lack of sympathy melted at her cussed good humour, which had never flagged, and her girlish enthusiasms. Her news had all been of school outings and hockey matches, the saga of the anonymous letters – Cheryl's work, I was sure – her pony, my trip to Brighton as I had falsely reported it; everything, in fact, except the

179

one thing that must have been always on her mind. It occurred to me that my letters had failed her in just the same way. I had not reported the real events of the term, the goings-on upstairs, the adventure of my relationship with Gaby, my emancipation; all of which, I felt certain, had contributed to a new maturity in my outlook. Our correspondence, this term, had been entirely bogus, an exchange between children who had been too polite to tell each other that they had moved on and were no longer children. The letters took on fresh significance: they would be the last things of my childhood. Throwing them in the river would be a profound gesture, a statement of my manhood. Later, I had an even better idea.

In the Studies cubbyhole down at the Main School, I had found a note at lunchtime, requiring me to attend a prefects' meeting at Collingwood that evening after roll-call. I cycled down to the House at about half-past eight. Digby Letts and Le Fleming were playing darts in the prefects' room, and arguing incessantly about the score. To keep the peace, I offered to be their scorer. In search of a piece of chalk, I opened a drawer in the large table at the centre of the room, and spotted, among other confiscations, a cigarette lighter. When the bell rang for assembly, I returned the chalk to the drawer and slipped the lighter into my pocket. Amanda's letters were in my saddlebag; I would make a fire of them and scatter the ashes to the river, it would be splendidly significant, a ritual!

When the roll had been called and the assembly broke up, Summers approached and handed me his imposition, the fair copies of the first psalm, which I had forgotten to ask for.

The prefects' meeting turned out to be a disciplinary affair. The boy to be disciplined was Peter Reed, whose move from the Studies had not been a success. It had taken him less than two weeks to collect enough black marks to warrant a boot-room beating.

'I'm not going to beat him, though,' said Digby. 'Marjorie won't hear of it. She only moved him over here because his parents have just split up.'

'Yawn, yawn.'

'What was he like at the Studies, Mark?'

'From what I could see he was settling in all right. The seniors and juniors don't mix, of course.'

The derision died down quite soon. Reed was summoned. He was a small, dark, attractively featured boy with fast eyes which foretold a capacity for mischief and which soon took in the riding-crop, laid out as an exhibit on the table. As Digby lectured him darkly, he looked quite suitably contrite. When the lecture took a lenient turn, however, and it became clear to him that this was only a warning, his attention immediately began to wander.

'Thank you,' he said, when Digby dismissed him; then he turned to the rest of us and fired off a wildly inappropriate, but winning, grin that felt compromising merely to receive. 'Thanks,' he said again, as though we had all pleaded for mercy on his behalf. It did not endear him to the company.

'Bloody tart!' said one. I worried for him; he had been no trouble at all at the Studies.

I cycled out of the Collingwood yard and down to the London Road, where instead of turning right and following the road round to the Studies, I turned left. Below the Headmaster's house, I took a side street which led to the edge of the hopfield. Dismounting, I followed a mud-path which, half a mile on, would lead down to the river flats and the towpath, where I planned to perform my ritual. It was a still night, clear and very cold. Ahead of me, low in the violet sky, hung a sombre moon. The hop-poles looked stark, like a plantation of trees neatly beheaded by a single mow from a cruel, celestial scythe. In the dead light of the moon, some of the hop-poles and their shadows on the naked earth formed perfectly straight lines and it was impossible to know where substance became shadow. This gave me the illusion that I was walking slightly above the earth through a black and white network, like a spider's web. Wearing no coat, I was soon tensed against the cold, a sharp, dry, penetrating cold that felt like a property of the moonlight. As I wheeled my bicycle along the rutted track, the saddlebag joggled and made a clumping sound, which seemed to carry. Where the path curved out to the edge of the field, I thought I heard other sounds, and stopped. There was silence. A few paces on, I thought I heard sounds again, and spun round to see if I was followed. There was no-one else in the web; it must have been the echo of my footsteps, walking my shadow along the hedge. I looked up at the moon. It stared down, a large, blind, yellowish eye channelled with faint pink veins, hopeless and dispirited; unfriendly, too, as though I trespassed.

Why was I taking the long way home on this forsaken night? It was to burn Amanda's letters, childish things which were to be the last of my childish things; it was to be a profound gesture, an initiation which I must not fail. Initiations were not meant to be easy. I pushed on. There was still far to go to the river.

But progress was slow. I shivered with the cold. The profound gesture began to seem futile. Midway across the field, I decided to have my small fire there, on the mud-path, and be done with it. I laid down the bicycle and its rear wheel continued to spin; as it lost momentum and clicked round ever more slowly, it seemed as though time itself was clicking to a halt. With the last click came a silence that was absolute and shocking. The stillness was unnatural, and seeing that the rigescent furrows in the mud resembled frozen waves, I imagined that it was really so: that time had stopped, and the sea and the tides and the waves had stopped with it, and the winds and the turn of the earth. The night seemed not to breathe. Setting to work, the spell was broken by the lighter, a petrol lighter, which roared at Amanda's letters; but they refused to conflagrate, and so, crouching on the path, I lit them singly. As a flapping, colourless flame consumed the last of them, the absolute silence returned.

Then, from nowhere, a voice descended: 'Not playing with fire, I hope, Mark?'

I jumped to my feet. There he was, a distinct silhouette, leaning against a hop-pole in front of the moon, his arms crossed, his well-made head cocked at an enquiring angle, crowned by a pool of silver light. I knew his invisible features would be forming a superior grin.

'I didn't startle you, did I?' He chuckled and came down the path at me. Although moving, for some reason, with a pronounced limp, his mood and manner were jaunty.

'Nice lighter. Is that one of those petrol things?'

'Mm.'

The extreme cold seemed not to affect him. He had an air of casual command, as though this ill-favoured night was familiar territory.

'Don't you ever feel like burning it down?' he said, nodding to the side of the field. I turned; through the bare bones of the high hedge, St Clement's was clearly visible. 'I do,' he sighed.

The Passchendaele Steps, in the pallid moonlight, shone with an eerie, spectral grace; beyond, the principal buildings loomed, sinister and gaunt. The Beckett Library was a huge, winged beetle, feeding on the Main School, which it obscured – all but the far tower, in outline a ghostly fist. From the dark mass of the chapel, the cloister extended like a black, rootling snout.

'I was going to burn it down on the day I left, but we can do it now, if you're in the mood, it's a nice, dry night for it,' said Gaby.

'Oh, I don't think so,' I said. 'There's the chaps in College House to consider, it wouldn't be quite fair on them, would it?'

'Yes, that's a drawback, I suppose,' he said. He turned towards the Studies; all that could be seen of them was the smoke-like canopy of the pine trees. 'What about setting light to your place, then? There's a perfectly good fire-escape for the residents, I know it well.'

'La Péri wouldn't like it.'

'Oh, he wouldn't mind.'

He lit a cigarette. 'I know, let's burn down the pavilion. Think of the thatch, it'll go up in no time!'

'That's very true,' I said, 'but a pity. I rather like the pavilion.'

'So do I,' he said, 'forget I mentioned it. Your turn.'

'My turn for what?'

'Which of our glorious school buildings would you most like to see in flames? The Beckett Wing, the Art School, the chapel?'

'This requires more planning, doesn't it?'

'Nonsense! Listen, you won't actually have to put a match to anything. I can make things catch fire just by staring at them very hard and concentrating, didn't you know?'

'What an extraordinary talent.'

'It's a great responsibility.'

'Of course it is. How long does it take?'

'You mean you want a demonstration?'

'I'd love one, but things like that don't really happen, do they? Not in real life?'

There was an odd pause, before he replied in a voice for which our conversation had not prepared me; a small voice without emotional charge that I had never heard from him before: 'But I don't like real life.'

The words seemed to hang on the air, and to gain weight in the silence. It was as though this unfamiliar voice had obediently recited the inalienable governing truth of his existence, and knowing how well this truth accorded with the perceptions of my second sight, and knowing, too, that I had nothing to offer but condolence, I felt stripped of insulation and longed to throw my arms around him, to warm and console this strange boy, with his far-fetched innocence, sometimes dazzling, always solitary, who chose for his territory the comfortless night and for company the disenchanted moon. I would have set light to the pavilion for him at that moment.

'I know you don't, Gaby,' was all I could say.

'You think so?' he said. Then, he turned towards me, and it was frightening, for the light of the moon made of his face a flat, featureless, ashen mask, with two black cavities for his eyes and a dark mobile gash for his mouth.

'You don't know the half of it,' said the ashen mask in the voice without emotional charge. My pity became terror. It's a trick of the light, just a trick of the light, I told myself, but then he sucked on his cigarette and in each of the blind cavities, a red, reflecting glow flickered briefly at an infinite depth, like distant intimations of satanic fire. Who was this, whom I had so nearly embraced?

'If you knew what I was really like . . .' he went on, but now I felt like screaming, because the ashen mask had begun to warp and buckle, the mask was taking on a new shape, the mask was trying to smile!

'What?' I gasped.

'Well, being the Undertaker,' he said, 'you'd probably have me buried, dead or alive!'

His head jerked back as though yanked from behind, the mask flew off and he laughed, a long, hard-hatted cackle. He was still cackling as he moved off down the path, seeming, on account of his limp, to be dancing to a macabre rhythm deeper into the network of shadows, deeper into the web.

'Good night, Mark,' he called back, and laughed again.

It was the first time we had ever been alone together. I felt utterly drained.

Ambrose was still in a grim mood.

'Oh, hallo, reporting back?'

'Yes.'

'You haven't locked yourself out of your study, then?'

'No.'

'Pity. He's not here, by the way. Where've you been tonight, in the pub?'

I told him about the prefects' meeting, and Peter Reed's troubles.

'He never wanted to go, you know,' said Ambrose. 'He was perfectly all right over here. He's a very nice boy, as it happens, I expect this'll ruin him. Pity, but no-one listens to me. Good night.'

At least we were speaking again.

I had started down the stairs before I noticed Jonathan, ascending. He had a small case in his hand.

'What ho, Mark,' he said, grinning genially. The reason for his good humour was below him on the stairs. Judy had arrived for the weekend. Cradling a

186

large bunch of blue and yellow flowers, she looked up at me and smiled; her blue-green eyes, steadfast and serene, smiled too.

'Hallo, Mark.'

Her wonderful voice cut into me, and resonated in that region still raw from my encounter in the hopfield.

'Hallo,' I said. 'How nice to see you.'

'It's nice to see you, too.'

As she climbed the stairs and that part of her which I most wanted to touch, the top of her head, came tantalizingly nearer, I clutched on to the banister to occupy my hands. This gave her an unnecessary amount of clearway, and, as though to match my extreme politeness, she edged by close to the wall, so that we passed each other at quite a distance, as if we were leaving space for someone else, unseen.

'What lovely flowers,' I said.

'Yes, aren't they. Here.'

She inclined them towards me. Their fragrance, mingled with her perfume, was as the essence of the feelings, powerful and fresh, that rushed like intoxicants to my head.

'Lovely,' I gasped.

We said good night. Wrenching my hands from the banister, I hurried along to my room. When I closed the door behind me, and the new lock made its extra, decisive click, in a place of my own at last, magically I was not alone, for Judy's essential presence, the scent of the flowers and her perfume, swirled in the air about me.

'Hallo, Mark,' said the wonderful voice.

'Hallo. How nice to see you.'

'It's nice to see you, too.'

'What lovely flowers.'

'Yes, aren't they. Here.'

'Lovely. And you're lovely too, you're beautiful.'

I told her that there had been no-one else, unseen, on the stairs; it was a vision we had made room for, a vision that we shared, of the two of us as one; a vision of our embrace. Now that we were alone, it was time to realize that vision. I put on a record, a Bach violin concerto, wrapped my arms around Judy, and rocked her to its heartfelt opening theme. The dark-timbred voice of the solo violin disclosed, like the voice of Miss English's violin, intimate longings for which I had no words.

One of my neighbours, Redley, knocked on the door; the music was distracting him from his work. I turned it down a fraction.

'Don't worry about him,' I murmured, taking her in my arms again. 'He's a dull fellow, no imagination.'

Judy's wonderful voice spoke in my ear very quietly. 'Is this the day of judgement, then?'

Her meaning eluded me; but she could be droll, could Judy. I just grinned. Then Garland knocked, to complain that the noise would be waking up the juniors.

'Typical,' I muttered. 'He never thinks of anything but the juniors, that one – it's a wonder that he doesn't get on better with Ambrose.'

I turned to the gramophone and pressed 'reject'. Over my shoulder, Judy spoke again, but this time, impossibly, the wonderful voice had a hard, un-adoring edge.

'This is the day of judgement, in your world is it, then?' I caught my breath. 'Good thing, for a change, you've not been drinking.'

A prickly heat crept up my spine.

'I don't know what you mean.'

'What's happened to you, recently, Mark? You never used to be like this.'

'But I haven't done anything wrong.'

'Would you really have burned down the pavilion?'

I hung my head. How could I have looked her in the face – her beautiful just face, where I knew I would find an expression of disappointment and regret?

'You know better than this, Mark, you've always known better than this.'

'Don't go, please don't go.'

But her essential presence had begun to shrink away.

'I've missed you since half-term,' I said.

'Oh no you haven't, Mark. And I'm not the one who's been away, I'm not the one who's been lost.'

I sat down on the bed, abject and ashamed, and plunged my hands in my pockets. There, I found a piece of folded foolscap; Summers's imposition. I opened it – ungrateful brat, he had written out the psalm twice, as required, but in a manner calculated to annoy:

Psalm I   Psalm I
Blessed is the man
Blessed is the man
Who walks not in the counsel of the wicked
Who walks not in the counsel of the wicked

Wicked? I remembered the red, flickering glows in the blind eye sockets.

'If you knew what I was really like . . .' said the voice without emotional charge. But I did know what he was really like. He was wicked.

'It's Gaby who's come between us, isn't it?' I said. But Judy had gone and my heart ached. I read again: 'Blessed is the man . . .'

The 'man', was that me? Yes; I had burned Amanda's letters as the last things of my childhood – that, at least, had been the purpose of the ritual. And 'blessed'? No, absolutely miserable. Why not 'blessed'? Who had been there to witness the ritual? Who but 'the shadow over the blessed' – they were his words, it was his judgement, not mine. How I hated him, and how abhorrent, now, the relationship I had thought would cost me nothing. The bargain!

For hours I lay awake, acknowledging my iniquities by the light of that code that Gaby had so totally eclipsed, and from which – fool that I was! – I had considered myself emancipated. I made resolutions and promises to the image now in the forefront of my mind, Judy's image, which was clouded by disappointment and regret. Then, I recalled a conclusion I had once formed, that where I was in discord with Judy, there, also, would be madness and lies, and this was my plea – that I had come through a period of madness. Her countenance softened.

'Oh, Mark, I'm so pleased you've seen reason.'

I knew she was giving me another chance. She said nothing about the wicked boy who had led me so far astray, but where Judy could make no favourable remark, she would make no remark at all, and I understood from her silence, therefore, that all she had for Gaby was animadversion.

15

A Golden Hour

After lunch the next day, Elwyn-Jones came round to
my study – he of the broken thumb and the chronic
giggle. His thumb was out of plaster by now, and protected by a sticky bandage. We had a match to play in
the chess knockout tournament, and we were hoping
to get it finished before two-thirty, when the 'fifteen'
was playing 'The Town' on the Lower Field, a fixture
that all were required to watch. As it turned out, we
never got started. We were sitting opposite each other,
crosslegged, on the bed, setting up the board, when
along the corridor outside came a familiar heavy tread.
There was a single rap at the door, which at once
almost caved in under tremendous impact. 'Oof!'

The heavy footsteps recoiled. Ambrose had forgotten about the lock. Elwyn-Jones looked startled. I
opened the door, and beheld the tutor rubbing his
shoulder resentfully; a long strand of his smarmed hair
had come adrift and dangled over his ear.

'Do you have to lock yourself in?'

'Sorry.'

He peered behind the door to see if anyone was
hiding, and found Elwyn-Jones beginning to succumb
to the giggles.

'What are you two up to?'

Elwyn-Jones let out an involuntary snort.

'We're playing chess,' I said, pointing closely at the
chess set so that it should not escape his attention for
another instant.

'Something amusing you, Elwyn-Jones?'

But the boy was crimson, and silently racked, and could only shake his head. Ambrose tutted.

'Does your father own a racehorse, Mark?'

'Yes. Half of one, anyway. Mister Moonshine.'

'That's right. I thought when the name Palfreyman was mentioned it must have something to do with you. It's about to run in a race on the telly.'

'I didn't know you were interested in the gee-gees, Perry,' I said, which kept Elwyn-Jones going.

'I'm not in the least interested, it just happened to come on. You can come up and watch, if you like, it should be over before the match starts. I suppose you two were planning to cut the rugger. Well, it's too bad, I've seen you now, so you can't.'

'Can I come?' piped Elwyn-Jones.

'Yes, anyone can come, I don't care,' said Ambrose.

Bosco tagged along as we passed, so did Hammond. On filing into Ambrose's flat we found Jonathan and Judy, dressed for the rugby match, watching the television. Judy wore leather boots, jeans, a sloppy blue jumper and a dark green beret. She looked fun, and formidably lovely. She smiled when she saw us. I wondered if it had been her idea that Ambrose should come and fetch me.

Mister Moonshine won his race quite easily, to cheers all round and a whoop from Bosco. Soon after, we left the Studies, the seven of us, and trooped out into the cold sunshine, a high-spirited group, susceptible to its own jokes, most of which concerned a black cossack hat sported by Ambrose, which, topping his hurry-footed gait, like an appalling wig, gave him the look of a truculent hooligan eager for an affray. The game had already kicked off. Most of the spectators, four hundred or more, were situated on the other side of the pitch, on the steep grassy bank which made a natural grandstand. Jonathan soon detached himself from the group, and with a colleague, shuttled up and down the field in line with the play. He left Judy sitting on his shooting stick, next to me. Nervous, I kept my eyes fixed on the game until she spoke.

'Goodness!' she said, as heaving players in front of us contested a speechless maul. 'Do you do this sort of thing, Mark?'

'Some of it, but by no means all,' I replied. 'I don't do much of the catching and kicking, but I do a fair amount of the grovelling in the mud. I'm a bit short-sighted, you see.'

Encouraged by her look of amusement, I recounted a few incidents in my sporting career, embarrassing blemishes all, at which she laughed. Cheers floated over from the natural grandstand, which I felt like acknowledging.

'Where's your coat, you must be cold?' she said.

I reported the problems I was having with the school outfitter's shop, and said that the only coat I possessed was the one she had seen me in on my return from Brighton, which she must have noticed was far too small.

'I didn't notice, actually. Did you ever find out what happened to your aunt?'

I told her about Aunt Lucy, that she was an artist (not that the family had her down for a lunatic) and about the picture she had sent to compensate for missing me that day.

'That was nice of her.'

'Yes, it's a picture of Brighton by moonlight.'

'I'd like to see it sometime.'

'I'll bring it up one day.'

'Do.'

Everyone took an interest in Judy. A couple of young

masters from Starvecrow Hall came by, friends of Jonathan, and took her to one side, almost out of ear-shot. From their exchanges, I learned that she was planning to stay on the following week. They produced their diaries and pencilled in an evening. I supposed that they would now monopolize her, that I had had my moment, but quite soon she was at my side again.

'Anyone winning this match, Mark?'

The young masters were on their way, and, incredibly, she had come back to me!

'Yes,' I said. 'The school's winning at the moment.'

'Judy, darling!'

She turned and fell into the widespread arms of Gorgeous Geoff.

'Hallo, Geoffrey,' she replied from the depths of his vast, calf-length fur coat. I caught the shooting-stick as it fell to earth.

'Oh, it's lovely to see you!' said the giant, wetly. 'When did you arrive?'

'Only last night.'

'You must get your man to bring you round to see me this time.'

'I will.'

'And here we are watching rugger, darling, when was it we joined the philistines?' He chuckled, clasped his hands together, regarded her fondly and trundled on – only as far as the black-hatted Ambrose, who tried to trip him up. The giant squealed. They were a famously disrespectful pair. Judy returned to the shooting-stick, which I had re-planted firmly beside me, and put her hand to the top of her head to check that her beret was still in place. I dearly wished that I could follow suit. I wished, too, that someone would fly-hack the rugby ball directly at her, so that I could dive on it and save her. There was nothing I would not protect her from. The chaplain sailed by on a puff of earthly splendour, his lower jaw retracted in a lupine grin.

'Hallo, my dear,' he sang.

'Hallo.'

She passed no remark on him. On the field, our strapping wing three-quarter, Forest-Nicholls, craving her attention, thrust out his chest and tore at the earth with his studs; Dennis Penney, another three-quarter, posed for her with one hand on his hip and the other priming his hair. Burnett and the Wizard passed behind us, eyeing me with envy. I breathed in the crisp, salubrious air and felt that with this, the most beautiful woman in the world at my side for all to see, I was uniquely gifted.

The boys from the junior studies obviously adored her, and came forward sheepishly in groups.

'Hallo, Peter,' she said at one point, with more than the usual allotment in her voice. I turned round to see, standing off a bit further than most, and not in a group but on his own, Peter Reed.

'Hallo,' he said, with a sweet smile that bore no relation to the flashy effort he had fired off at the Collingwood prefects.

'He's such a dear little boy,' she said when he had moved on. 'I shouldn't have favourites, really.'

Others came and went, but from every hail-and-farewell she would return and pick up the conversation again. What was I going to study at university? Law. What sort of lawyer did I plan to be? A barrister.

'I'm sure you'll make a very convincing one.'

'Thank you.'

Applause ran round the ground, we had scored again. The late November sun, sinking behind us, set light to the tracery of the chestnut trees, and burnished the red-bricked chapel like a precious copper casket.

Beneath the deepening purple sky, fire raged on the Beckett roof, a crest of yellow flame danced along the battlements, the central tower wore a sparkling coronet, and the Main School façade, molten and unstable, trembled like a sheer volcanic flow. The school was brilliantly, gloriously on fire. I thought about the boy who claimed to set light to things simply by staring at them – was he standing, wide-eyed, behind me? But we were casting long shadows in front of us by now and, reading the shadows, there was none for which I could not account. Where was he on this golden afternoon? I shivered.

'You are cold,' said Judy, promptly. 'Why don't you wear a waistcoat like Bosco?'

Bosco was fixing a camera to a tripod nearby.

'Ma'am?' he said.

'Did you get your waistcoat at the school shop?' she enquired.

'Oh sure.' His head wobbled with pride and he opened his jacket: 'D'ya like it?'

I promised her I would go and buy one straight after the match.

When the final whistle blew, she went off with Jonathan, Ambrose and Gorgeous Geoff to the staff room for tea. The crowd soon vanished through the chestnut trees. Alone, I strolled across the field and sat on the Passchendaele Steps. The sun set quickly, painting a flock of distant clouds scarlet, amber and purple, like the fallen petals of an exhausted flower. I was not sad at the sun's going down, but inspired and elevated, for I knew that I had been granted something that would not die with the light. I felt that, for an hour, the path of reality had merged with my dreams; that, for an hour, reality's sole purpose had been to animate my dreams, and that this hour could never die, nor fade, nor lose its joy, because the world of dreams in which it was enshrined was deathless and eternal. That the undying glow of this golden hour would be a positive inner resource seemed axiomatic.

One of my resolutions the previous night, when all had seemed lost, had been to make amends, where possible, to Ambrose. On leaving his flat that afternoon, I had noticed, on a salver in his hallway, the spare keys to the studies, scattered and untagged.

After tea, I reported to his flat with a gift, a square of hardboard I had found in the woodwork school, to which I had screwed eight hooks – one for each of the study keys, plus a spare, which I thought might be handy for the key to the fire-escape. Above the hooks I had printed: 'Bosco', 'Garland', 'Pal'man', etc. Ambrose agreed that it might be fairly useful, and sent me away with the salver of keys, to sort them out. On the senior corridor, I quickly found the right key for each hook. In the end, there were two keys left. I quickly deduced that one must be the spare key for the absent Ostler's study. I put this on the hook marked 'Pal'man', and transferred my own spare key to 'Ostler' – anyone could make a mistake. It was petty, of course, and not in the spirit of my resolution, but my privacy had been hard-won, and it pained me that Ambrose should have a key at all. The remaining key had a leather tag, and was not a doorkey; Bosco identified it as the key to his car, which, since the beginning of term, had been parked next door, outside the Binkses' cottage. I hung the car key on the spare hook, and above it printed, boldly, 'Bosco's Car'.

On the landing outside Ambrose's door, I somehow knew that, in the short time I had been away, Gaby had arrived. I paused. How could I possibly know? What sense informed me that I was about to enter the presence of Wickedness Incarnate, for so I thought of him now? I traced the sensation: there was a sort of heat in the air on the landing through which he had lately passed, not a bodily heat, but elemental, of the sort created by energy. In view of his other, known characteristics, I reckoned that this must be the energy of elemental particles, struggling for stability after the passage of chaos. It was impressive, and I doubted I should enter his presence at all, but I had the keys to deliver and an orchestra rehearsal to get to, as a valid reason for keeping my visit short.

I knocked. Ambrose was passing through his hall with a whisky in hand.

'Come in,' he said. 'Gaby's here now.'

He went straight into the sitting-room, paying no attention at all to the key-frame. I stood it up on a table near the door.

'Undertaker!' I was hailed from the settee.

'God, I do wish you'd stop calling him that,' said Ambrose.

'Nonsense, Mark doesn't mind,' said Gaby, aiming a blazing smile in my direction. 'We get on like a house on fire, don't we, Mark?'

'Of course,' I replied, averting my eyes and counting myself fortunate not to burst into flames.

'There you are, Perry. Mind your own business.'

Suddenly he produced a squash ball and slung it at the opposite wall, catching its rebound.

'Oh, thanks a lot!' yelled Ambrose. 'Look! It's left a filthy mark!'

'Never mind,' said Gaby, 'I'll do a few more – people'll think it's the pattern.'

He slung the ball again, but this time it struck the edge of the coffee-table and fell at Ambrose's feet. Gaby grabbed for it, but the tutor pushed him in the chest and he fell back heavily on the settee, clutching his knee.

'Aaaagh! You bastard! You know I've hurt my leg.'

'Diddums.'

'Give me back my ball.'

'Come and get it,' said Ambrose, presenting his fists and jigging, none too nimbly.

'Hit him, Mark!'

I was not to be drawn into horseplay, I was wearing a brand-new waistcoat.

Ambrose, however, had his back to me, and, still jigging, stuck out his bottom in case I was about to scrag him. Gaby, who had been reaching for his sheath-knife, instead said scornfully: 'Honestly, Perry, you look like a big fat dancing bear.'

Ambrose, hurt, stooped to pick up the ball.

'You can have this back when you leave,' he said. 'You can leave now if you like, I don't care. And don't bother to draw your silly little knife on me, or I'll knock your block off with that.' He indicated the Alpine Club's presentation ice-axe, now adorning his mantelpiece.

'No, that's for blocks of ice, Perry. I'm a hothead, remember?' replied Gaby immediately. He made himself comfortable on the settee and rubbed at his knee.

'Is there something actually wrong with your leg, now?' I said, confused, 'or is it just the – um – old trouble?'

His eyes gleamed.

'Of course,' he said, 'we haven't really spoken since the dance, have we? You haven't heard what happened to me then? Oh, I must tell you – you'll never believe it.'

His story was that a girl had come up to him at the dance, and introduced herself; seeing his condition, she had suggested that he might benefit from a breath of fresh air, and had taken him by the arm and led him outside; there, he had come to his senses, an experience which always put him in need of a cigarette; the girl had also wanted a smoke, so he had led her off to the cemetery; on the way, he had put a question to her, 'What do you do for casual sex?'; he recommended this question to us as a masterpiece, whose response was invariably silence – while it dawned on the recipient that casual sex was the one thing she had always denied herself – followed by intense, compensating activity; on this occasion, the compensating activity, on a gravestone, had been astonishingly intense; unfortunately, when it was over, he had rolled off the gravestone heavily, and dislocated his knee; with a sharp rabbit-punch he had snapped the kneecap back into place, whereupon the girl had helped him limp back to Clancarty; there, Pamela had taken over, and ministered to his almost unbearable agony with a compress and a bottle of brandy; since then he had been in constant pain.

Ambrose, sponging the black marks from the wall, had heard all this before and seemed actually to believe it. 'Doesn't sound much fun to me – making love in a cemetery.'

'I don't make love, Perry.' Gaby screwed up his face in his look of foolish lust. 'I commit it!'

'Oh, Christ!'

'The trouble was, of course, there was no time to take precautions, so Mark, if you find any girls hanging around the front gate asking for me, deny all knowledge, right? It could be her.'

'All right,' I said, playing along politely. 'What did she look like?'

'Who, this one? Oh, quite pretty, not tall, very long hair, name of Cheryl.' Gaby smiled happily, 'Absolute slut.'

It took a moment to sink in. Cheryl? There could

have only been one Cheryl of that description. The last I had seen of her, she had been dancing with Riley; so she had tangled with both Head Boys — what a complicated girl! And since I had decided that this was the girl who had sent herself the anonymous letters addressed to a 'slut', how strange that Gaby, even though his story must surely be lies, should use exactly the same word. What a satanic characteristic, to know the worst in everyone! It seemed he could hit on the truth even when he was lying, so Forked was his Tongue. He lounged back in the cushions, languid and conceited, engrossed by a gloating self-regard I instinctively wanted to crush.

Then he gulped at his drink, and to all appearances, exploded. I had seen this reaction before: the instant the first mouthful hit the back of his throat, he would splutter as though rejecting a deadly poison. The seizure was more dramatic on this occasion because it racked his knee, which caused him to gasp, and choke again.

'Ah,' he sighed when it was over, whisky dripping from his nose, 'nectar!'

He swallowed the last of the drink without gagging and held out his glass.

'Perry, I don't think I've heard you offer Mark a drink?'

'No, no,' I said, retreating, 'I've got an orchestra rehearsal now.'

From the position to which the earlier events of the day had exalted me, this downward view into his abysmal world had been vertiginous, and I was not sorry to note in the hall that the words 'Bosco's Car' stood out, on the upright key-board, as a flagrant enticement.

'See you later, Undertaker,' he called after me. I made sure that he did not. After roll-call I went straight to my study. Footfalls on the fire-escape paused outside my window at about eleven o'clock, but by then I was in bed, my light was off, and I was living again my golden hour with Judy.

16

A Return To Earth

It was a shock to learn, at Sunday lunch, of the disruptions caused to Collingwood House by the theft of a lighter from the prefects' room. Dormitories had been searched, cubicles raided; Jacobsen, the boy from whom it had been confiscated, had been questioned, as had other suspects; resentment and mistrust were rife. I had brought the lighter with me. It felt heavy; and fearing that its outline was visible, I covered my pocket with my hand. After the meal, Bill Rivers issued an ultimatum: if the culprit had not owned up by nine o'clock that evening, he would impose on the whole House a week-long gating.

'That means no activities outside the House for anyone, except classes and compulsory games. It's a rainy day,' he gestured outdoors, 'so I'll be in my study all afternoon. I *do* hope someone comes to see me.'

It all seemed so unfair. I had always intended to return the lighter, it had been no theft, and, in any case, this was something I had done in my time of madness, before redemption, before Judy. I had changed – was it too much to ask for a clean sheet? There was normally a prefects' meeting after lunch but it was put back until after the evening roll-call, the deadline, and so hard was it to focus on my responsibility, I hoped vaguely that, by then, somehow the matter would have sorted itself out.

That afternoon there was a meeting in the Music School of the Green Room, the theatrical society to which I had been elected an honorary member on account of my services behind the scenes. Since *Trial By Jury*, stage-lighting had become an interest, and at every school production I had been either backstage, assisting Mr Edie, or, more often, in the gods, directing spotlights. The purpose of the meeting was to read *The Merchant of Venice*, which would be the school play in the spring term. Naturally the parts were to be read by the boys who would actually be playing them, so having no part to read myself, I was under no obligation to attend. When Gorgeous Geoff swept in, late and perspiring in his fur coat, I earnestly regretted that I had come, for with him was his assistant producer, Jonathan – and Judy. It was nice to see her, of course, but I felt that there was no need, really, for her to have turned up. She was with me already, in unassailable spirit, and it was too much to expect another golden hour – more, even, than I wanted. I had a strange, ominous feeling, a presentiment that some-how I was vulnerable. When extra chairs were drawn into the circle diametrically opposite me, I made no attempt to catch her eye, and was glad she was no closer.

Gorgeous Geoff kicked off with an attention-winning gambit.

'Appleby's balls have dropped, boys. It's lovely for him of course, but it does mean I've got to re-cast Portia. However, the good news for this afternoon is, we're very very lucky because we've got a real lady with us – Judy – and she's going to read Portia for us.'

A polite cheer.

'Now, is everyone here?'

Someone informed him of an absentee, whose small part was allocated to me: Balthazar, A Servant to Portia. Judy smiled approvingly; I felt that I blushed.

'Don't get too excited,' said my neighbour, seeing me

flapping through the text. 'He's only got one line.'

'Where is it, then?'

'Dunno.'

When the playreading commenced, it was soon apparent to the company that there was, in the wonderful voice that spoke out Portia's lines so clearly and well, a spirit most aptly endowed for the role: good, witty, just, conductive of mercy. Suddenly she was addressing her lines to me.

> 'Now, Balthazar,
> As I have ever found thee honest – true,
> So let me find thee still . . .'

I ran my eye quickly down the page, and found my line. It was an unsayable line. I opted to deliver it heavy with sincerity: 'Madam, I go with all convenient speed.'

Everyone laughed, and Portia looked delighted with her amusing and popular servant.

She read the trial scene beautifully, and at the end, the Green Room's applause for her was warm. As Gorgeous Geoff and Jonathan conferred, I caught her on her own. 'You're the one who makes a convincing barrister.'

'Thank you.' She curtsied modestly. 'Oh, look, you've bought a waistcoat.'

I stepped back and opened my jacket, à la Bosco: 'D'ya like it?'

'Yes, it's very becoming. I think you should leave the top button undone, though. There, that's better.'

Our eyes met; was exchanged, a fateful look. Fleetingly, I had the impression that she saw all that I wanted her to see – the sincerity of my love, the power of my feelings – and that of these, she was not afraid, neither was she indifferent. My impression, in fact, was that she returned my feelings with her blue-green gaze, in a hundredth, perhaps only a thousandth part. It was enough. I felt sick with anxiety and remorse. Anxiety for all that she did not see, because of course I was unworthy; in an instant, the heights at which I placed her and to which I aspired became the measure by which I fell short, the measure of my baseness. And remorse, because it seemed that this baseness had escaped her eye; how could this be, except that I had duped her? Should I now point out to her my shortcomings? I felt that I had traded gifts with a goddess; hers to me, unique – a tiny, but priceless measure of love; mine, shoddy and impaired. Soon, she would discover this, and then, to her face – her beautiful, just face – would come the look I could not bear, the look of disappointment and regret. Not regret, distaste; that was how people looked on those who had cheated them. She might even fall from those heights at which I placed her, because if she depended on my being as I had presented myself, as I had wanted her to see me, it was a dependence I knew I could not sustain. But I would have to sustain it, at all costs. No effort, no sacrifice, would be too great to ensure that Judy did not fall, did not regard me with disappointment and distaste. I saw that I would have to dissemble. But if I dissembled too well, what then? Would there be more love, putting her in even greater jeopardy? The kindest thing would be to withdraw and never speak to her again, but here was one of the very things that she must never know: I could no longer do the kindest thing, and withdraw, because I loved her, and had, therefore, a dependence of my own. When Jonathan came and took her away, it was a great relief.

Later, as nine o'clock pressed, I realized that there was no question of owning up to the theft of Jacobsen's lighter. News travelled at St Clement's, and it would make a rum tale indeed that I, a non-smoker, had removed the lighter – for what possible reason? – and retained it while the House suffered upset and upheaval. The story would be sure to reach Judy, she was staying on the following week. It would hurt her, it was unthinkable. Only one person knew that I possessed the lighter: Gaby. He had remarked on it in the hopfield. Typical! He hit on the worst in everyone. I wondered where he was. Ambrose had announced at tea that he was going to London for the evening and would not be back until late, so Gaby was not upstairs. He was in The Blue Posts, or the winter fields, or the cemetery, I supposed, and cursed him. I reckoned it was at least half his fault I had taken the wretched lighter in the first place, I had been under his dark aegis at the time. I hid the lighter in my tuckbox.

At nine o'clock, I cycled down to the House. The roll-call was in progress. I went upstairs to the prefects' room. There was a deep hush below, and I assumed the collective punishment was being confirmed and dumbly received. When the assembly was dismissed, for a long time none of the prefects came to the room. Then, Digby entered, looking grim.

'Hallo, Mark. The others are down in the boot-room.'

'Why?'

He picked up the riding-crop.

'A beating, I'm afraid.'

'Oh no, you don't want me to come, do you?'

'Well, of course, you're a prefect, aren't you?'

'Who is it?'

'Peter Reed, he's owned up.'

'Owned up to what?'

'Pinching the lighter. Come on.'

I rushed down the stairs after him.

'Has he given it back, then?'

'No. He says he threw it away in case it was found. Then he owned up anyway.'

'But you can't beat him, he's only been over here a fortnight.'

'Bill's authorized it. Let's face it, he has rather asked for it, hasn't he? I suspected him anyway, he was on the cleaning duty, he had every opportunity.'

Peter Reed was very brave. When, in accordance with tradition, he shook hands with each of us after the beating, there was a tear on his cheek, but no sobbing.

I pedalled home furiously through drizzling rain. At the Studies, I ran up to my room and retrieved the lighter. If it ever got out that I had allowed this to happen – and to Judy's favourite, too! It was too much, it would destroy her. I raced back out of the yard, I would throw the lighter deep into the apple orchard. Looking over the Binkses' garden fence as I passed, I saw Bosco's car in the shadows. I wished that it was mine. I wished that I could simply jump into it and drive away.

At once, the car moved. Slowly, it emerged from the shadows into a pool of light cast by a streetlamp, moving as though by magic, for there was no-one at the wheel. Then I glimpsed a movement at the back of the car. A white garment. Gaby's anorak! He was pushing the car down the drive so as not to disturb the occupants of the cottage, from which no light shone.

'Gaby!' I hissed. He vanished out of sight behind the car. A few seconds later his head popped up. 'Gaby!'

'Who's that? Mark?'

I tiptoed up the drive.

'What are you doing?'

'Fancy a spin?'

He dangled the car keys in front of me.

'No.'

'Give me a hand, will you? Just to the gate.'

The little sports car was very light. At the gate, Gaby jumped in. The engine started at once. I glanced nervously back at the cottage; no light came on. Gaby patted the passenger seat.

'Hop in.'

As we roared off down the London Road, away from the school and the town, he yelled: 'Don't worry, I've done this before.'

'What? Taken Bosco's car?'

'No,' he replied, 'driven.'

I leaned across and switched on the headlights. Noting that he smelled strongly of drink, I urged him to turn off the main road as soon as possible. Crashing the gears, he swerved into a narrow country lane, down which we careered at a thrilling speed, weaving to avoid pot-holes.

'Goes like a dream, doesn't she?' he trilled.

Now, Father was a shocking driver, but at least he paid close attention to the road and had the good sense to look terrified. Not Gaby: with the cold night air and the rain dashing in our faces, blind bends, crossroads, narrowings of the way – all were negotiated with one hand idly spinning the wheel, while the other rested on the gear stick; or fidgeted with the rear-view mirror, in which I had a nasty suspicion he was admiring himself; or rummaged in a pocket for a cigarette. At one point he had no hands on the wheel, as he hunted for a match. I plucked the cigarette from his lips and lit it with Jacobsen's lighter. Gaby glanced at the lighter and, oblivious to the hazards of the winding way, gave me a half-faced grin. After a humpbacked bridge over the river, at which we were briefly airborne, a bend in the road led us sharply uphill into woodland. Gaby accelerated. The trees were white, in the headlights, like a tunnel of bones. We slithered to a halt, for a T-junction.

'Which way?' he cried. 'Left or right?'

'Where are we going?'

'A pub, I should think.'

I sniffed the air.

'Right,' I declared.

'Right it is!'

We were off again, at a velocity that made the back of my soft leather seat feel hard. Soon we came to an inn, The Hawthorn, and pulled in as though arriving at the scene of an emergency.

'Great, eh?' said Gaby. 'I'm a natural driver, you know.'

'Are you, Gaby?'

'Oh yes. Do you know, my reactions are too fast to be measured.'

'Really?'

We climbed out.

'Strictly speaking, they're impossible.'

'They need to be, Gaby.'

'Got any money?'

A quiet, rural establishment with no expectation of passing trade, The Hawthorn had a chaste, reclusive air. The public bar was empty. A grandfather clock presided, its ponderous tick-tock advising against the raising of voices and haste of any sort. The service was obediently slow. A low buzz could be heard from the saloon, but there was no sign of the landlord. In front of a log fire, a ginger kitten dozed. We cleared our throats deliberately. Eventually, a puffy-throated man with an aviator's moustache and grounded eyes came through, and took in the pair of us with a look of dull mistrust.

'Eighteen?' he said.

'I should hope so,' said Gaby brightly. 'We came in the car, what? Ha!'

He grinned at me. At ground level, he kicked me.

'Ha, ha!' I responded.

'What'll it be, then?' said the grounded aviator, persuaded of nothing.

This was left to me.

'A half of shandy and a large scotch, please.'

Gaby limped off to a table by the fireplace. When I joined him, he had put his feet up and extended his arms over two chairs in a masterful pose. An unlit cigarette hung from his mouth. I gave him a light.

'Thanks.'

'This isn't really mine,' I said, putting the lighter down on the table between us.

'No,' he replied, 'I didn't think it could be. Where did you pick it up?'

The kitten rose and stretched, and began to slink away. Gaby swooped and whisked it off its feet. He held it up in front of him, behind its front legs, so that its neck receded into its shoulders.

'Tell God, thanks for the car,' he instructed the startled animal. 'It's lovely!'

He put the kitten down on the chair beside him, where unaccountably it changed its mind about running for its life, and instead, jumped into his lap.

'Hmm?' he said, still waiting to hear more from me about the lighter.

Unnerved, I continued.

'Oh, it was in the prefects' room at Collingwood, someone had confiscated it. I only borrowed it, really, there was something I wanted to burn – personal things, you know.'

'Oh quite,' he said deferentially. 'In the hopfield?'

'Yes. The thing is, it's caused quite a rumpus. In fact, things have got rather out of hand.'

'Oh?'

I told him of Reed's bogus confession, and the dreadful event of the evening. Being Gaby, I expected he would have difficulty grasping the moral pain of my dilemma – his response amazed me.

'You bastard,' he said quietly.

The kitten rolled contemptuous eyes and fixed me with a stare.

'But what could I have done?'

'Almost anything! I'm astonished you let them go ahead with it.'

'Well, I was astonished he owned up, what did he do that for?'

'Who knows? It's got everyone else out of a punishment, though – that should make him popular. You say he's been in trouble already, perhaps he was put under pressure to own up.'

'Yes, but if they'd found out even his confession was a lie, they'd have beaten him anyway. He was on a last warning.'

'Perhaps, but that's not the point, is it? Then he'd have been beaten for being a constant pest, which he is, not a thief, which he may not be.'

'Oh, I'm sure he isn't.'

He drained his glass. The kitten dropped delicately to the floor and trotted away.

'Then don't you think you ought to clear his name?' he said, as though this was the easiest thing in the world.

'Another large scotch, please,' I said, putting his glass on the bar. He was gazing into the fire when I returned, his chin resting on his hand.

In the silence, the loud tick of the grandfather clock seemed tauntingly measured and slow. At length, he resumed the conversation, now in a maudlin mood.

'Do you know, when I first got to St Clement's, I was so scared of the place I used to go and hide in the changing-rooms, out of everybody's way. Hours I was in there, sometimes. It used to get lonely, so I'd start talking to the clothes – no, really, I did. I had to stop all that, though. People saw me hanging about the changing-room too often, a rumour went round that I was stealing. I was even accused of it.' He took a drink. 'The point is, after that, there was some truth in the rumour. Sometimes I did steal. Five bob here, half a crown there. I don't do it now, I gave it up soon enough. I found it didn't suit me.' He stared hard at his glass. 'There you are, I said you wouldn't like it if you knew what I was really like.'

'But you said it didn't suit you, so that's obviously not what you're really like,' I felt compelled to say. 'It was probably just a stage.'

'It's not necessarily good to go through a stage, you know – it depends which way you're travelling.'

'And which way were you travelling, Gaby?'

'Inwards,' he said softly, and drained his glass. 'So you see, it's not going to do this chap any good, owning up to stealing.'

The grandfather clock chimed and whirred; at the bar, a bell rang.

'One for the road?'

By now, I was resigned to going back to Collingwood and turning myself in. As I waited at the bar, however, I saw the matter in a different light. Here we were, drinking under age, a stolen car outside, breaking the laws of the land and the school, and now that I had admitted something, what was Gaby doing but claiming the high moral ground and trying to shame me into something that would undoubtedly ruin me? It would hurt Judy, too, terribly. Truly, this boy had many ways to destroy me! So here was another satanic characteristic: the apprehension of a moral code, to which he did not himself submit, sufficient to apply it critically to someone else's conduct. What a necessary skill for a Devil's Advocate! And talking to the clothes? He had not had much to say to the clothes on the night of *Trial By Jury*; a pretty excuse!

'Another double whisky, please.'

By the time I got back, he had quite cheered up; the kitten was rolling luxuriously at his feet, having its tummy rubbed.

'This is a good wheeze, isn't it?' he said. 'It came to me in The Blue Posts. I was playing darts in the public bar there, when who should I see walk in to the saloon but Mr Punch and his very fuckable Judy.'

'Did they see you?'

'No. I waved, but they sat down before I caught their eye. I didn't like to go through, I thought it might embarrass them. Anyway, "Ho ho," I thought, "no-one's on the top floor at the Studies right now, what say I go and pick up the car key on Mark's very helpful little board."'

'Ah. And how are you going to get the key back, you can hardly breeze in at this time of night?'

'I've thought of that,' he said, producing a door key from his pocket. 'Fire-escape!'

'What time does Perry get back?'

'Don't worry, we've got ages. I tell you what, I wouldn't mind taking that Judy for a ride some time.'

'Yes, awfully attractive, isn't she?'

'She fancies me, you know.'

'No?'

'She does.'

'How do you know?'

He winked. 'I always know.'

This was familiar territory, the usual bilge, and yet, too close to my heart to be lightly dismissed. Judy with Gaby? The Most Beautiful Woman In The World, The Animation Of My Ideals, in the arms of Wickedness Incarnate? Portia with the Devil's Advocate? It was nothing less than a taboo.

The second bell rang. The kitten rolled to its feet, arched its back in a hoop and bounded away without a backward glance.

'Bye bye, pussy, you're a whore,' called Gaby, amiably. He was beginning to show signs of inebriation. At the door, he handed me the lighter.

'Don't forget this, will you? Try and sort it out if you can. Just say something to the prefects, anything would help.'

'You mean, if we get back safely in the stolen car?'

He grinned. 'It's not easy, is it?'

Outside, the full effect of the whiskies hit him. He supported himself against the wall for a few moments. In the light from the inn, I noticed the purple flames emblazoned on the side of Bosco's car, and approached it with considerable foreboding.

'D'you want to drive?' he said. 'It's your turn.'

'I can't, I haven't got a licence.'

'Nor me,' he laughed, and climbed in. 'Do they take that seriously, then, having a licence? It's not that important, surely?'

'Oh, I believe it is.'

'Huh!'

On the drive back, it was soon apparent that those reactions which were too fast to be measured and strictly speaking impossible had atrophied somewhat under the effect of alcohol and were no longer keeping quite abreast of our career. The sports car having no memory of its own, we shot past the junction where we had earlier joined the road and bolted to the top of Paddock Hill.

'We can't go this way, Gaby, it'll lead us right through the town!'

We started downhill. The rain was heavier now, and the road beneath us hissed.

'Gaby!'

'Wha'?'

'We can't go through the town!'

I waited for a reply.

'Gaby!'

'Wha'?'

'Why don't you let me drive, now?'

'S'all right, I'm a natural driver.'

The hedges at the sides of the road unwound chaotically, like rolls of wire wool.

'Gaby!'

'Isn't this fun!'

But we were closing on a bend in the road too fast. Gaby braked. Suddenly the headlights were illuminating a field towards which we were not travelling; we were sliding away from the illuminated field, slipping, floating sideways as though caught up in the powerful tow above a waterfall. Aghast, I closed my eyes and drew up my knees. An age seemed to pass before the rear of the car, on my side, smacked into something solid with a bang so loud it might have signalled a puncture in the planet. At once, I was flying through the air, still in the sitting position. When I returned to earth, I landed on my elbows and knees, which promptly splayed outwards, depositing me face down in mud. Seconds later, a hollow implosive crunch and a shatter of breaking glass announced a calamitous journey's end for Gaby and the car.

Shocked and battered, I made the frightening discovery that I was in no pain, which I assumed meant total paralysis. Reluctant to confirm this, I made no attempt to move. Then, a sensation of moist chillness seeping through to my knees encouraged me to try waggling my extremities. They responded, so I sat up. My glasses were gone, but I hardly cared.

I was sitting in a field. Through the pitch dark, I could make out a gate, not far away; we must have hit the gatepost. I got to my feet and staggered to the road. Down the hill, the car had come to a halt against a telegraph pole. One of its headlights was still shining, into a hedge not a foot away, as though to display the hedge's nocturnal life for a nature study.

Approaching the car, I called out: 'Gaby?' It came as a croak, so I tried again, 'Gaby?'

There was no reply. I could see him in the driver's seat. Done for, I supposed, the fool. Then, a clicking sound from the car; the engine gave half a gasp; another click, and the engine gasped again. He was trying to get it started!

'Gaby?'

'What?' He sounded cross.

'We've had an accident.'

He made a choking noise. I thought he had burst into tears, until he spoke: 'Look, please don't make me laugh, I've hurt my shoulder.' He tried the ignition again. 'Now the fucking car won't start. Do you think it's worth trying to give it a push?'

From my standpoint, I could see that Bosco's car was good for nothing, a heap of twisted scrap. Another turn of the ignition, another gasp; at the front of the car, a tinny bit fell off.

'It's a write-off, I'm afraid, Gaby.' I saw blood glistening on his forehead and trickling down his face. 'You're bleeding, you must have a cut somewhere.'

'Yes, but it's all right, it's not deep. You OK?'

'Just about.'

'It's my shoulder I'm worried about — yow! It seems to be out of place somehow.'

It was his right shoulder, it did appear to be at an odd angle.

'It looks as though it may be dislocated,' I said, and remembering the story of his kneecap, added: 'Do you want me to try and push it back?'

'No!' He recoiled, which jarred the injury. 'Ow! Fuck it! It's really very painful.'

'What do we do now?'

'You'd better get out of here.'

'I can't do that.'

'Course you can, don't be daft. Tell Perry what's happened.'

'I can't leave you here on your own.'

'Don't be silly, there'll be someone along in a minute. Look!'

Lights in the distance approached the foot of the hill. Gaby seemed quite sober now: 'Tell Perry I'm going to say that the keys were in the ignition, that that's where I found them, OK? There'll only be more trouble if they find out where I got them. Now get out of here, go on. Oh, and Mark, here, take this.' He handed me the fire-escape key. 'Don't let anyone see you arrive, you look a mess.'

'All right.'

'Oh, and Mark.'

'What?'

He looked up at me, a wistful expression on his bloodied face, and with his hand compulsively trying the ignition to the mangled wreckage around him; and with trouble, really serious trouble, unstoppably on its way, I allowed myself one last time – since this, surely, was our goodbye – to recognize the attribute common to both his dazzling and abysmal aspects: he was the picture of innocence.

'I'm sorry about this,' he said.

With the headlights getting steadily nearer, I wanted to say something, without knowing quite what; suddenly mad, I blurted: 'I go with all convenient speed.'

He laughed and then, clutching his shoulder, howled: 'Fuck off!'

I had not got far into the field before the oncoming

car reached the scene and stopped. He would be all right. No longer in his presence, my madness had soon passed. The police would take a very different view of his innocence. It was no thanks to Gaby that I was still alive! At a corner of the field I crossed a stile into a lane. Half-running, staying close to a ditch into which I would throw myself if a motorist came by, I followed the lane down to the river. On the towpath I looked back and saw a flashing blue light rise quickly up the black hill. The rain was pelting down, I lifted my face for its cleansing. On an iron bridge which led over to the St Clement's secondary playing-fields, I took Jacobsen's lighter from my pocket and dropped it into the river. I grinned. Things had worked out rather well for me. And did I have a surprise for Mr Ambrose! Only one of us was coming back from this caper, and, against all the odds, it was me!

From the bicycle shed at the end of the garden, I stared up at the Studies top floor. A light shone from Ambrose's sitting-room. Raindrops drumming on the dustbin lids covered the sounds of my advance down the path to the front of the house. The front door was locked. I went back to the fire-escape. It must have been assumed that I was in my study, from the light I had left on – I had thought I was going out only for a moment. I ascended the humming metal flight as stealthily as a killer. On the top platform, sopping wet, I hesitated. Should I knock? That would be the normal courtesy – but no, it would wake the house. My watch said twenty past eleven; more than half an hour had passed since I left Gaby. I wondered if Ambrose had heard the news already. Turning the key in the lock silently, I pushed open the door. Down the corridor, the sitting-room door was shut. I could hear music playing, Greek music – 'Dances From The Aegean' – which the tutor had brought back from a holiday visiting archaeological sites; Gaby only let him play it if he poured us all an ouzo. Before knocking on the door, I hesitated again. I could hear sounds that were not part of the music, hiccupping sounds. I realized that Ambrose was sobbing. I had never heard a man sob before, it was a dreadful, emptying noise. I fled with all speed.

On the top platform again, shivering, this was a circumstance I could have done without. Steeling myself, I did the only thing possible: to give him notice of my arrival, a little time in which to compose himself, I kicked at the door, rattled the handle and fumbled at the lock, until a light came on, within. Once again I pushed open the door.

Ambrose was in the hall, wearing pyjamas and a woollen dressing-gown, knotted at the waist. His hair, lank and surprisingly long, dangled over his ears. He looked disturbingly like a very ugly woman.

'You?'

The look of dark wonder on his face gave way to the blackest scowl.

'Don't tell me you were with him! I thought you were downstairs.'

'Yes.'

'You're a cretin!' he thundered. He squared up with the corridor, I thought he was going to charge. 'I suppose you just ran away and left him there, did you?'

'No. Look, he gave me the fire-escape key. He wanted me to give you a message.'

'Well?'

'He's going to tell the police he found the key in the ignition.'

'So what? I don't need his bloody lies! And he didn't, did he? He found it on this!' He stabbed a finger at the key-frame. 'Who asked you to do this? No-one!'

'I was only trying to be helpful.'

'Has anyone seen you?'

'No.'

'If they have, I'm not protecting you.' His eyes narrowed. 'Did you plan this?'

'Plan what, a car accident? Of course not, I didn't plan anything, I just happened to see him going next door. I went with him, that's all there was to it.'

'Then why? Why did you go with him?' He curled his lip and sneered horribly: 'You're not exactly noted for this sort of thing.'

'Because they beat Peter Reed,' I said instantly.

'What?'

'The Collingwood prefects, they beat Peter Reed.'

'Oh, no. Why?'

'I told you he was getting into trouble. And I had to watch it. I'm afraid I find that sort of thing rather upsetting.'

He fell silent. A black grin disfigured him. Then he sighed. I sensed the heat was off.

'Has someone telephoned, then?' I asked.

'Mm? Oh yes, Pamela's rung, hysterical, of course. She'd heard from the cottage hospital, they've got him there.'

'How is he?'

'Nothing serious. Multiple minor injuries. He's broken his collar bone, needed a few stitches.' He shrugged. 'The police are bringing charges, he'll be expelled, of course. You've been very lucky, haven't you?'

'Yes.'

'Are you hurt at all?'

'No, I was thrown out into a field.'

'Christ? Where are your glasses?'

'In the field.'

'I hope you've got some others.'

'Only National Health ones.'

'Well, you'd better get off to bed.'

He checked that the landing was clear, and whispered: 'For God's sake don't let anyone see you like this. I'll have to speak to Bosco in the morning.'

In my study, I put on my reserve spectacles to see myself in the mirror. With dried mud on my cheeks and chin, and unruly hair, and the goggling expression the unflattering glasses always gave me, I looked a fright. My Sunday suit was filthy and dripping wet; it would take a hard brush before I could even present it for cleaning, though I was relieved to find that my brand new waistcoat was unharmed.

I washed and went to bed before trying to get in touch with Judy. There was a lot of explaining to do, but the evening had wearied me, and all I really wanted from her was a sign, some token to indicate that I was not beyond the pale. At first, she would not be summoned; then I found her, sitting diametrically opposite me in the Music School.

'Gaby said you fancied him,' I said. 'He won't be coming back, I've seen to it.'

She smiled across approvingly; I felt that I blushed.

'I'm sorry about Peter Reed.'

She was clear now, as clear as the day.

'Can you forgive me? Please, please forgive me.'

Our eyes met and, as she spoke, there was still that precious measure of love in her steadfast, blue-green gaze:

'The quality of mercy is not strained,
It droppeth as the gentle rain from heaven
Upon the place beneath: it is twice blessed.'

17

A Collective Demon

As the school herded in through the Lady Chapel for the morning service, and Dr Rabbitt, on the organ, dawdled through an air of little moment, the assistant chaplain, the Reverend Mr Adams, appeared at the top of the loft's spiralling staircase. He beckoned.

'Would you ask the doctor not to play us out with anything too joyous today?' he murmured. 'The chaplain has unhappy news for the school.'

'Oh?'

'One of our boys has been involved in a road accident, I'm afraid.'

'Oh dear. I'll tell him.'

'Thank you so much.'

I passed the message on to Dr Rabbitt, whose hands at once abandoned the keyboard.

'Oh?'

He dipped his fingers into his billowing white curls and seemed to be tickling his brains.

'A road accident, eh? Dead or injured?'

He reached for a pile of sheet music.

'Hang on, I'll ask.'

At the top of the staircase, I called after the descending curate: 'Excuse me, Mr Adams. Dr Rabbitt says "dead or injured?"'

'Oh!' He smacked a hand to his mouth. 'Only injured, thanks be!'

'Only injured, sir,' I reported back.

Dr Rabbitt tossed most of the sheet music aside, impatiently.

'Who is it? Did you ask?'

'No, I'm afraid I didn't.'

'Oh well,' he squinted at a manuscript, 'why should you care?'

I smiled on him indulgently. I was in a splendid mood, quite confident I would get away with the night's adventure. When the chaplain asked that we remember in our prayers 'our young friend Martin Gabriel', who had been injured in a car crash, I marvelled that, at the very last, Gaby had managed to bring the whole school to its knees. And since, absurdly, I had begun to worry that Gaby was my very own corrupting demon, it was a comfort to lean over the parapet and witness the rows of bowed heads praying for this demon's welfare, for it allowed me to diagnose a collective visitation, and to reassure myself with the thought that, far from being my very own, the demon had everyone for a potential host and victim. He would have corrupted the behaviour of anyone so closely acquainted as I; not all would have finally suppressed him. I felt like an anonymous social benefactor.

All the classroom talk was, of course, speculation about the accident. Rumour inflated Gaby's injuries, so that at break, he had lost the use of his limbs and by lunch, fallen into a coma. David Burnett gave me a scare at one stage during the morning.

'Why have you got your silly specs on today, Mark? What's happened to the others?'

'A lens fell out, that's all.'

'You're sure they didn't get smashed up when you were out joy-riding with Gaby last night?'

The Upper Sixth laughed.

'No, of course they didn't.'

'I didn't think so really. Sorry, Mark, just my little joke.'

The little joke concentrated my mind. I decided that in a free period after break I must go in search of the glasses. They would be lying around somewhere near the scene of the accident, they might still incriminate me; and anyway, the wire-rimmed reserves were already starting to pinch.

When the bell went, I fetched my bicycle and rode off down the High Street. There, a strange encounter detained me. I was waiting at traffic lights above the redstone bridge, when I heard someone calling my name and glimpsed an arm raised on the crowded pavement, waving for my attention. It was Miss English – not usually the buttonholing sort. She was evidently returning to her houseboat from her allotment, which she tilled with great pride, for she was carrying a wicker-basket loaded with roots – potatoes, carrots, turnips and so on, enough for the most gargantuan stew.

'Mark, are you all right?' she asked urgently.

'Fine, thanks.'

'Have you broken your glasses?'

'No. A lens fell out, that's all.'

'Oh, I've been so worried about you.' Her hand covered her heart and she gave a short, not frivolous laugh. 'I almost came to find you at the weekend.'

'But I only saw you on Friday, what's the matter?'

'No, dear, nothing's the matter, nothing at all.' She touched my sleeve and lowered her voice: 'But it's nice to see you still in one piece.'

'Why? I mean, thank you, but why shouldn't I be?'

She tightened her grip on my sleeve.

'You can tell your chums I'm an old fool, I won't mind a bit, but I had a real frightener of a dream about you, Mark, d'you know, like a warning.'

'Gosh! What about?'

'Don't ask me what it was about, dear, because I don't really know myself, but I'd say it's time for you to go steady. Will you do that now?'

'Yes, of course.'

'Do go easy on your bicycle, won't you?'

'Yes, I always do. Look, I've passed my cycling proficiency, there's a badge on my saddlebag.'

'That's all very well, dear, but just don't take anything for granted.'

'Righto. But don't worry, I'll see you on Wednesday as usual. I'll be there as right as rain, you'll see.'

I pushed off from the kerb. Her dream was impressive and I would not have shrugged it off – any more than I would have described the independent, well-founded Miss English as an old fool – except that I took it for a prophecy of the car crash – a prophecy that had already been fulfilled.

On Paddock Hill, a strong wind gusted, plucking dead leaves from the sodden hedgerows and flicking them across the fields from one snag to the next. Small dark clouds hurried across a stone-grey background. To my surprise, the car had not yet been removed, and lay at the roadside, a poor piece of work. It had always been a small car, and it was even smaller now, being chronically compacted at the front. With its ripped bonnet clamping the telegraph pole in a mean bite between its wide-eyed headlamps, the car wore an expression of impotent fury; the emblematic flames down its side suggested it had escaped from a fairground. On the windscreen, where Gaby had cracked his head, was a stale, rust-coloured smear. One look at the passenger seat, which was overwhelmed by a jumble of metal, reminded me how miraculous had been my escape, and how deadly the demon at the wheel. I would have liked Judy to have seen it.

I moved on up to the gate on the other side of the road, where paint-flecked scars on the gatepost confirmed that here had been our initial point of impact. I wheeled my bicycle out of sight from the road, into the ploughed field where the accident had thrown me. My glasses were easily found, only a few feet from the gate, still open and, though crumby with mud, unbroken, which exceeded my hopes. Turning back, I saw with alarm that a black car had drawn up by the telegraph pole, nose to battered nose with Bosco's. Fearing it was the police, I kept my head down and crept along the hedge to a tree at a corner of the field, opposite the two cars. No challenge came from the road, I had not been sighted. After a few slow minutes I peered round the treetrunk. It was not the police, it was Pamela Watts. For a long time, she sat at the wheel of her car, smoking a cigarette. I picked impatiently at the bark of the tree; time was getting on and I had to be back for the last lesson of the morning. At last, she got out. With her hands plunged in her overcoat pockets she moved, with the grace of a woman twenty years younger, to the front of her car, leaned back until almost reclining on the bonnet, and, ignoring the wreck, lifted her face to the top of the hill. There, a copse of leafless sycamores waved in the wind like a black-boned, skeletal hand. It struck me that Pamela Watts must have been lovely once, but she was sallow now, drawn and drying. She tossed her head, as though to shake birds from her long hair which, russet-brown and silver, streamed behind her on the breeze. Her face wore an expression of exalted communion, as though all the voices in the free wind sang of Passion and Courage and Beauty, and none of Prudence or Duty or Thrift. Lighting another cigarette, from a red Embassy packet, she turned her attention to Bosco's car, tipping her head towards it slightly with a wry smile, as though it were muttering some endearingly improbable excuse. Suddenly, she flinched and stiffened. She took a white tissue from her pocket, moistened it with her lips, and rubbed Gaby's dried blood from the windscreen. Then she cast the tissue up into the wind, leaving her hand frozen in mid-air in a gesture of farewell, and watched as it flapped briefly before dropping – as theatrical props will – ingloriously into a roadside ditch. I was getting jolly cold behind the tree. Finally she got back into her car, drove up as far as the gate, executed a many-pointed turn in the road as ham-fistedly as could be imagined, and headed back very slowly towards the town.

Ambrose came to my study after lunch. He knocked softly on the door, waited for a response, and asked if he might come in. This unusual civility was the prelude to a lecture. In the past week, since the Sixth-Form dance, I had got away with a hell of a lot, he said. Drinking, car-theft, joy-riding, absence without leave – he was unsure how much more of this he could take. Where was it all going to end? I promised he would have no more trouble. He told me that Gaby had rung from the hospital to say that he was being held against his will and had run out of cigarettes.

'I'm going to visit him this afternoon, any message?'

'You can tell him from me he's a maniac.'

'I see you've got your glasses back.'

'Yes. I went to pick them up this morning.'

'Huh! You're a cool one, aren't you? By the way, have you got anything he can read? He's going to be down there a couple of days, apparently.'

The first thing that came to hand was a science fiction I had recently finished. Ambrose looked at it doubtfully.

'I don't know that he likes this sort of thing. You haven't got any *Mad* magazines, I suppose?'

''Fraid not. Try Bosco.'

'No, I think Bosco's been tried enough for one day.'

That evening during prep, mysteriously, Judy's image seemed to have moved into a new, almost physical dimension. It was as though she was sitting with me as I worked. If there was harmony between us, it was fragile and imperfect. When I went to bed, I felt that she was pleased I had stayed in my study all evening, where she could keep an eye on me.

By the following day, word had got around that Gaby's injuries were not serious, and the accident had already become a stale topic. His name might not have cropped up at all, had it not been for the careers officer, who posted in the great arch a list of Lower Sixth boys who had yet to see him for counselling. Carelessly, he had included the name 'M. Gabriel' on the list, which brought a short outbreak of mirth. 'Gaby goes to the careers officer' — it was the stuff of comic strips. When we tried to think of a career for him, nothing suitable could be found, and we wondered if this meant he was not going to have one: we decided that it did.

'I asked him once what he wanted to be, should he ever grow up,' said Burnett, 'but he just said "free". He was brilliant at closing conversations.'

'Well, can we now close this one?' said the Wizard crossly. 'There must be something more edifying to talk about.'

But from my life he could not be so peremptorily dismissed. More than a week earlier, I had plagiarized, from an optional text, a history essay for Jonathan, which, as was his dilatory way, the tutor had not yet returned. By now, two days had passed since the play-reading, two days in which I had neither seen nor spoken to Judy. I had fallen into lassitude and lethargy. My need for her was gnawing at me, loosening my judgement, so when Jonathan, at lunch, promised that he would be marking the work that afternoon, I gambled that he would not detect the plagiarism and angled for an invitation by remarking how interesting I would find a tutorial with him on the essay's subject.

'Come up and see us this evening, then,' he said, as good as gold.

He came to my study after tea, though, to cancel the invitation; Judy had already committed them to an evening at Starvecrow Hall. He went on to say that, anyway, he gathered from my essay that I had already benefited from the views of his favourite historian on the subject. Lurching towards me with a straight bat, he cited the optional text. I coloured, he grinned.

'Don't worry. So long as you can trot it out in the exams like that, you won't go far wrong. I do prefer it, though, when you find time to form ideas of your own.'

He could scarcely have treated the matter more lightly, but when he left, closing the door behind him with that final, still-novel click, I blinked moistly at Aunt Lucy's picture, which I had planned to take up to show Judy, and only with rubbery contortions of my face did I manage to restrain myself from bursting into tears. It was not just the disappointment of not seeing her; I was also worried that Jonathan might have told her about the plagiarism. And even if this worry could be assuaged – for why should Judy take the matter any more seriously than Jonathan? – and if the disappointment at not seeing her could be borne, still there were feelings from which there was no escape; the feelings of shame and inadequacy that beset me when I sensed that Judy's presence in my room – that strong, mysteriously physical presence – shrank from me, recoiled as though from an outrage, an enormity. Nowhere in my study could I hide from her, neither was I equipped to appease her, for all I could do was plead for forgiveness in that same voice which had failed her before, the voice of one not yet sufficiently endowed with those qualities of honesty and integrity that so distinguished her. So I went out. I wandered down to the school feeling unaccustomedly isolated. I had better acquire these qualities pretty fast, I thought, or life in the one place I had thought of as my own would be intolerable. Then where would I be? There would be nowhere for me, nowhere on earth. And pity Judy; in that new, mysterious dimension she too must be lonely.

Help was at hand in the form of a brilliant idea. Finding the Music School open, I went in and practised a piece to which Miss English had recently introduced me, a nocturne by Hummel. The nocturne opens with a theme that is neither dramatic nor ingratiating, but subtle, reticent; hinting, but demurely, at a passionate disquiet. My playing had greatly improved this term, since the loan of the Eileen Logan violin, and it occurred to me, as I tackled this opening theme with tolerable success, that I was listening to a voice with which I could address Judy adequately and without shame. The violin's intimate voice was the perfect medium; it could never contradict itself, it could never choose its words, it could never lie. Its only language was that of my dearest, innermost feelings, and I had no qualms about communicating them, for they were genuine, tender and true; they were passionate and disquieted, too, but there was no harm in Judy knowing that! My brilliant idea was that at the first opportunity, which would come in the morning after break when I had consecutive study periods, I would take the violin back to my room, and play so that she could hear. Then she would learn that, for all the temporal frailties for which she was so quick to condemn me, at least my feelings were worthy of respect!

Walking back, having practised unstintingly for almost two hours, I noticed that the wind had got up, and smelled so strongly of the sea, it seemed that an unprecedented tide must have risen and flooded the county, and that foaming waves must be near at hand, perhaps seething over the bridge at the foot of the High Street. Much later, I was in bed when an express train passed through the valley, hurtling along as though racing over a collapsing bridge, and the bluff winds blew its urgent rhythm up to the house, where it sounded like the beating wings of a colossal bird at my window.

18

On The Third Day

In the morning I sat restively through the lessons before break, thinking only of Judy, visualizing her alone in Jonathan's flat, cleaning, perhaps, or cooking, or doing a spot of housework. What if she went out? But the air was still powerfully redolent of the sea, strong winds stiffened the flag on the Founder's Hall, gulls flocked on the grand lawns at the front – surely she would stay indoors, with the elements so flagrantly portending a storm! The bell for break, by my watch, was ninety seconds late.

I collected the violin from the Music School. Someone had left the tuck-shop door open, and a gust of wind shut it with a crash. On the London Road, cars travelling towards me had headlights and windscreen wipers on. Rising behind them in the sky, a bank of massed black clouds dragged rainfall beneath it like a woolly grey beard. By the time I reached the front yard, the first fine flurries were whipping down diagonally on the wind. It was fresh, lusty weather. A light shone from Jonathan's flat: she was in. I hurried into the hall, hugging the violin-case to protect it from the wet; it was a presumption to have taken it from the Music School, I would take special care of it.

On the senior corridor, Bosco's door was open, but he was not at home; he never bothered to use his lock. The corridor was not deserted, though. A light showed through the glass above Garland's door. I cursed. This would confound my plan, he would be sure to have something to say about a violin recital. The idea was to charm and appease the Goddess, not treat her to a shrill altercation. Fortunately, just as the bell for the end of break would be ringing down at the school, he left. Since the advent of the study locks, Garland had taken to attaching all the keys in his possession to a clip on his belt, so he clinked like a jailer as he passed my door, and then jangled down the stairs. Apart from Mrs Binks down in the kitchen making a start on the lunch, I assumed that there was now no-one in the building but Judy and me. I opened the case and unwrapped the violin from the midnight-blue scarf. I knew the nocturne by heart, after the evening's long practice, but I had brought the music along anyway. Placing it open on the desktop, I removed my jacket, fitted the chin-rest, tightened the bow and set myself to play.

A wind-tossed volley of rain spattered against the window. It had grown very dark, the storm clouds were lowering. I put down the violin and turned on the light, and gave some thought to what I was doing. What was I hoping to achieve? The perfect outcome would be a visit from Judy, enticed from her room, curious to know who played. Was I prepared for this? No. How foolish to be unready for the perfect outcome. I retrieved Aunt Lucy's picture from the drawer to which I had sadly consigned it the night before. A quick glance in the mirror reminded me to undo the top button on my waistcoat, as Judy preferred. On the turntable of my gramophone, I placed the Bach violin concerto – Our Tune – in case she had time to come in and listen to some real music – a wonderful, frightening thought. Now everything was ready. I raised the violin.

A growl of thunder sent a sound-wave through the house at a frequency that made everything tremble in its fundament. But what was I thinking of, the door was shut! She would never hear me with the door shut, and even if she did, might she not be too modest to knock? I opened it; the old house was draughty at the best of times, and now streams of air whispered and sighed in the corridor like echoes of the turbulence outside. Once again I took hold of the violin.

But was there resin on my bow? It did no harm to apply some more. I had not expected to feel so nervous. I had another look down the corridor, just in case anyone had arrived, in which case I would have to try again some other day. There was no-one, only the whispering draughts. Then I spotted the name-plate in the case, 'Eileen Logan', and took heart; mine was a romantic enterprise of which she and the instrument's other ghosts would surely approve. First Love – it was said to be a trial. I began to play. Short, declamatory phrases announce the nocturne with a flourish; I attacked them boldly, as I had practised, and hearing that they were satisfactory, my nervousness fell away. Soon, the warm, dark-grained voice was singing out the nocturne's subtle theme, tremulous with vibrato. The piece is written for piano accompaniment and there are occasional pauses in the violin part. As I tapped out the rhythm in the first of these pauses, I thought of Judy, laying aside her book, or her duster, and smiling; surely she would have guessed whose voice was calling. Did her heart beat a little faster, like my own?

'One-two-three, one-two-three . . .'

How long before she came to find me?

'One-two-three-and-back-to-the-subtle-theme . . .'

At the second pause, disaster: a pounding drumbeat started up, threatening to swamp my serenade.

It came from above, from Ambrose's flat. The ceiling throbbed. I sat down on the bed, thoroughly outgunned, and glared up angrily. Gaby. He was back! How could he be? I had not heard him arrive. Had he been up there all along? Above the pounding drumbeat, I could make out other, thinner sounds – electric guitars, amplified wailing. He was using the harsh voice of cheap, popular music to shout down, to belittle, the voice of my innermost feelings. How dare he! I refused to be shouted down, refused to be belittled. But the racket made my study intolerable and sordid, so I snatched up the violin and strode along the corridor to the reading-room, which was underneath Jonathan's flat. Judy would hear me there. Once again, I announced the nocturne boldly. It seemed to exacerbate the storm. Rain sheeted against the windows, lightning flashed, and, one-two-three, the heavens unleashed an almighty thunderclap. Winds boomed around the house, trees and bushes seethed. I continued, bowing resolutely, hoping that Judy would hear this still, small voice beneath the fury. Perhaps it would draw her down to sit with me until the storm abated. A dustbin lid blew off and shrieked along the path at the side of the house. I played on. Nothing would stop this recital.

Nothing, that is, except the sound which now came from the corridor; the decisive click of a door, shutting. I froze. Had someone returned from school? I ran out to investigate. No light had come on. Bosco's door was still open. Mine was shut. The whispering draughts, the giggling draughts, had closed it. I pushed at the door, but of course it was locked; the key was inside, in my jacket.

I had either to go up and ask Gaby for the spare key, or to wait. I looked at my watch. It was midday, I would have to wait a whole hour before Ambrose came back. But standing, helpless in the corridor, I heard that the pounding music upstairs had stopped, and I sensed that this was Gaby's work, somehow, that he was waiting for me, summoning me. I would not be summoned. I returned to the reading-room and slumped in an armchair. The storm raged on. An empty fireplace sucked and gasped. And more persecution was on its way; 'Bolero', the war-machine, arrived upstairs, quietly, at first, and insidiously, as though it were the essential pattern to the storm, its secret, mechanical heart. I reached for the violin – but no; outgunned, belittled, excluded, I despaired.

Why me? I thought I had fought off this demon, and that anyway he was not my demon but Ambrose's, Pamela's, everyone's. So why had he come back for me? My mind went back to the Monday morning chapel service, when I had been the only boy he had failed to bring to his knees, the only one positively to rejoice at his suppression. Was it because of that ? Very well then, let him have his day. His parents, presumably, would be along some time to take him away, he was certainly not coming back to the school. Let him have his trashy revenge. Was 'Bolero' nearing its offensive conclusion? No, he had turned up the volume, its merciless crescendo was swelling still.

Then I thought of Judy. What must she be thinking? She must have heard the violin, she must know that I was in the house. Why did I not complain about this hellish row? Would she suppose that I condoned it? If not, why did I not rush upstairs and demand that peace be restored? She would be disgusted that I allowed it to continue. I got to my feet, I would go up at once. It was my duty.

In a bookcase by the door, a set of encyclopedias had been shelved in the wrong alphabetical order. The sight of them arrested me. I got the entire set of books out on to the floor, and then replaced them in the correct order. I knew that I was procastinating, but it made not a scrap of difference. It required nerve — nerve that took a bit of finding – to climb the stairs and lay down the law, it seemed hardly my place to do so. How fitting, that I must go up to the two of them! Not down, or along, but up. They were Higher Powers, they belonged in Upper Chambers. And more, even, than this, there was an ambiguity in the atmosphere, something I was loth to acknowledge. The raging winds uttered fervent pleas, the house was a labyrinth of sighs and moans, the sucking, gasping fireplace sounded almost human, and all these disturbances were as minor accompaniments to the fulminations upstairs. What was going on? What on earth was going on between these Higher Powers? I remembered Gaby saying: 'That Judy, she fancies me.'

'How do you know?'

He winked: 'I always know.'

Sacrilegious thought! I tried to banish it. But what of his 'masterpiece'? – 'What do you do for casual sex?'

How would Judy answer that? Surely she would just pat him on the head and laugh? Well, of course she would!

'Bolero' crashed to a halt. Now was the moment to act. I grabbed the violin and hurried along the corridor. At the foot of the stairs, the music started up again. He had turned the record over. More Ravel: an ecstatic female choir announced 'Daphnis and Chloë'. I ran up the stairs. The two doors were shut. Over the blare of the imploring sopranos behind Ambrose's door, the storm could still be heard, like an auxiliary, dissonant choir. From Jonathan's flat, silence. She must be feeling intimidated too. I rapped on the riotous door.

'Gaby!'

No reply. I tried again.

'GABY!'

Nothing. In the air on the landing, I could feel his elemental heat. It prickled on my skin. I knocked on Jonathan's door; it opened a few inches and then closed. It had been left on the latch. No-one came. I knocked again, and went in.

'Judy?' I said softly.

It was a very small flat.

'Judy?' I said again. She was not there. I stepped back out on to the landing. With my ear to Ambrose's door, I heard a long, high-pitched screech – but that was connected to the music; howls and moans – but they were the wind's; a scream – but that came from far away, probably the corrugated roof on the bicycle shed. I pressed closer to the door.

'Gaby!'

Pictures began to come into my mind: first, the ashen mask in the hopfield, and the red flickering glows deep in the eyeless sockets. It spoke: 'I can set fire to anything . . .'

Who could resist Gaby? Not Pamela – I saw her again, lovingly cleaning his blood from the wrecked car. Not Ambrose – I saw his picture in the framed mirror, on his knees in homage. Not I – 'Hop in'. He patted the passenger seat, tempting me with madness.

Who could resist Gaby?

Then, a cry. Just one, but female and urgent and quite distinct over the music, which had quietened. Still with my ear to the door, now the pictures came, thick and fast, from a prying, prurient lens. Powerful pictures, rich, lewd, lubricious pictures, licensed by the howls and groans and sighs – such deep-felt sighs! Stimulating pictures, pictures of the taboo: Judy with Gaby, the Animation of My Ideals locked in the arms of Wickedness Incarnate, the Most Beautiful Woman in The World thrilling to the Forked Tongue, Portia eagerly receiving the Devil's Advocate. Seeing it all, hearing their frenzied excitement, I was vilely, irrepressibly aroused. Fevered by a sort of negative rapture, bereft of all dignity, I banged repeatedly on the door.

'JUDY! GABY! STOP IT! STOP IT!'

I raised the violin and attacked the introductory phrases of the nocturne. As though in reply, the female choir returned stammered, repetitious, orgiastic gaspings. Crazed beyond all thought of consequence, I clutched the instrument that could never lie, the instrument of my most intimate feelings, and bashed it without restraint against the door, again and again and again, until it hung limp in my hands. When I stopped, I heard that the music had also stopped. Apart from the dying lamentations of the storm, there was silence.

'You slut!' I was sobbing, 'you fucking slut!'

I kicked on the door. From inside came a terse response: 'Who's that?'

It was Gaby's voice.

'Mark.'

He half-opened the door. There was a wild, wild look in his eyes, his face was desolate and grey. A half-faced smile lurched into place as though cranked by a weary mechanism. He wore a white bandage about his head, a sling for his arm, and Ambrose's cricket sweater. All were blotched scarlet with blood.

'Hallo, Undertaker,' he said, in the voice without emotional charge. 'She's ready for you now.'

He swung open the door.

She was on the floor in the hall, propped up against the wall. Her hands lay at her sides, upturned like a pavement beggar's. On the wall above her, in the shape of an aureole, was a red spray, like tiny flowers, some with dark, still-trickling stems. In that most hallowed region at the top of her head was embedded the Alpine Club's presentation ice-axe.

A scream exploded around me.

'NO!'

A sour stew of bile vaulted into my mouth. I choked it out and stumbled down the stairs.

'Mark! Wait!'

My legs buckled. I slumped to my knees. I could hear whimpering, my own. I trembled and shuddered convulsively, as though a nerve-louse worked a tooth into my neural core.

'I'm going to call the police,' said Gaby. 'Please wait there, don't let anyone else come up.'

I nodded and sucked at the air.

A minute or so later he came out on to the landing again, carrying a whisky bottle by the neck. He sat down on the top stair, swigged at the bottle and choked violently; so he was not already drunk. He swigged again and offered the bottle down to me. I shook my head and edged further away.

'They're coming,' he said. 'I'm sorry I showed you, I couldn't resist it.'

I struggled to get up.

'No, don't go, please, they'll be here in a minute.'

I slumped back. There was a very long silence. At last he spoke again, as though to himself: 'I've always been afraid of doing something like this.'

I said nothing.

'Always.'

He took another swig. Another long silence. Incredibly, he tried a joke: 'Bit like the car, eh Mark?'

'What?'

'Not much point in giving her a push?'

'Oh, shut up.' I pleaded.

Quite soon he spoke again.

'Aren't you going to ask me why I did it?'

'I know why you did it.'

'Oh yeah?' His face tightened. 'Go on then, genius.'

With all the cold hatred and loathing in my heart, I said: 'Because she wouldn't let you in.'

A ghostly shade washed over his face. He stood up. His eyes fell. He muttered something inaudible, twisting his lips in a scowl. Finding the battered violin at his feet, he kicked it down the stairs at me. He turned to go back into the flat, but this time recoiled from the abomination in the hallway, as though he had walked into plate-glass. He hesitated, and then, having nowhere else to turn, huddled in a corner of the small landing with his back to me. The whisky bottle fell with a thud. He dashed his hand to his mouth, sank his teeth into the back of it and started to weep.

I picked up the violin – and suddenly a rough-tongued sweat licked at my flesh. What exactly were the stirrings that had taken place in me; the innermost feelings to which the violin had been giving voice all term? Surely the violence with which I had destroyed it had also been an expression of those feelings. In my hands the violin now felt not only broken and useless but incriminating, too, like a played-out motive. I looked up at Gaby but now, when I needed most to see an outright Devil, worthy of all the blame, he let me down. Racking, almost silently, in his blood-splashed apparel, he made a tragic sight, more like a victim than a killer. He was not a picture of innocence, not now, but neither was he Wickedness Incarnate. He was scarlet and white. Scarlet and white, a picture of innocence defiled. And who had defiled him? There were no other suspects, only me. Hot tears came to my eyes, but I felt I had no right to them, and wiped them away with shame. I thought how wilful was my guilty heart to pound so strongly beneath my damp shirt when I so much yearned for it to stop.

'Oh Gaby, I'm sorry . . .' I began, but just then,

242

downstairs, the front door bell rang and he fled into the flat.

Mrs Binks, utterly bewildered, came up to the first landing with two uniformed policemen who thought they were answering a hoax.

There was no fuss when they entered the flat. One of them, a bearded sergeant, came back down the stairs, tightlipped, and suggested to the housekeeper, who had started to gargle, that she go down and make us all some tea. He radioed for assistance. More police, and ambulancemen, were quickly on the scene. Eventually, a short, bat-eared detective arrived and took charge. Having interviewed me briefly, he went up and fetched my door key.

'Here you are, Mark. Go and sit in your study, there's a good lad. We'll come and get you when we need you. I've got a man on the front door now, so no-one else'll be coming in for a while. All right? Good boy.'

Alone, I approached my door with dread. Judy's had been such a physical presence in my study, how would she be represented now? I put the key to the lock. It was the wrong key. I remembered the switch I had done with Ostler's. A lucky chance. I would be much more comfortable in his study.

No-one had told me that at the weekend – while I was at the play-reading, it transpired – his belongings had at last been collected. The plush curtain, the cheerful cushions, the warm furnishings – all had gone. The room was bare, save for a wooden chair, and a mattress, on which I laid the remains of the violin. By the time the bearded sergeant found me, I was stone cold, and ready with my confession.

19

Reincarnation

South Point,
St Osyth,
March 1989

The builders have gone. The last of them, the painters and decorators, left yesterday. The cottage's interior has been stripped, so I am sitting, once more, in a bare, unfurnished room. No-one heard my confession twenty years ago.

'It's partly my fault,' I told the bat-eared detective, at the police station. 'I was right outside the door. I was playing . . .'

'Now wait a minute, son.' He raised a palm. 'Hold hard. Let me just ask you this – were you in the flat at the time of the, er, incident?'

'Well, no.'

'No. Right.' He laid the palm on the table, and spoke as though giving dictation. 'I can tell you that that corroborates what Mr Gabriel – Martin – has told us himself. As a matter of fact, we don't see any mysteries here, except, of course, why he did what he did, and that's something he doesn't know himself. In his own words, he doesn't know what possessed him . . .'

'I possessed him!' I wanted to scream, but all that came out was a hopeless sob, and then tears, profuse and humiliating. Father collected me later and took me home, where I stayed for the rest of term. I was treated as merely a witness, unlucky but uninvolved. It afforded me grim satisfaction four months later, when a court ruled that, for his dreadful deed, Gaby had only a diminished responsibility. The judgement confirmed what I knew all along, that part of the responsibility – the part by which his was diminished – lay with me. I have found guilt to be like an instinct, subdued by no rational means. But work on the property is complete, now, the cottage is spick and span, and up for sale; and my task is finished, too. The events of the last twenty years may be briefly told.

The photograph of the St Clement's cricket eleven, 1969, testifies that I saw out my time at the school; since leaving, I have never been back. At the end of that summer I went to university, but my health failed, before the year was out, and I was obliged to abandon my course. A friend of my father's, a solicitor in the City of London, took me on as an articled clerk; eventually I qualified. I was still living with my parents when my father died suddenly of leukaemia. That left me with Mother to look after. Six years ago she suffered a stroke. A full-time nurse was required. An agency sent us Monica. As Mother's condition deteriorated, we grew close. We discovered a mutual interest in music. She is a churchgoer, like myself. When Mother died, we married. We think of our union as founded primarily on the third reason given for matrimony in the Book of Common Prayer: for the mutual society, help and comfort that one ought to have for the other, both in prosperity and adversity. There are no children.

Soon after Mother's death, I went into partnership with a colleague, Alan Dean. Our departure from the company at which we had both been apprenticed was amicable; the only client we took with us was my brother, Miles. Miles runs a computer company and lives in Reading with his third wife, Dee, an American. His business career has been rather like his golf: he has gone a long way, but not straight, and has therefore often had need of my professional services. I see little of him socially.

'Palfreyman, Dean' is flourishing. Monica and I live comfortably in a pleasant area on the outskirts of Colchester, twenty miles from here. Monica still takes on occasional work as a private nurse, but for the worthwhile occupation, rather than the money, and only when my health is good. Illness has dogged me through the years, nervous complaints that it would be unseemly to parade here. At the start of this record I had the idea that all my afflictions might spring from but a single source, a secret that was poisonous to hold, an allergy. It is too soon to know if disclosing this secret has drawn the poison. My life is not yet over. And Gaby?

One day, my parents and I set off to visit Aunt Lucy, who was dying of cancer. Soon we ran into heavy traffic. As Father drummed impatiently on the wheel, Mother turned to him: 'Are you sure you want to go through with this?'

'How do you mean?' said Father.

'You know how it upset you when we saw her last month. She's going to look even worse now, and, anyway, the poor thing's not conscious, she probably won't even know we're there. Wouldn't you prefer to remember Lucy as she was?'

A few minutes later, Father turned the car round. He would much rather remember Lucy as she was, what a humane idea. I was going to go down the next day but it was too late, Aunt Lucy died that night. Whether my parents were quite in touch with their true motive for turning back that day is open to question, but let it not for a moment be doubted that where Gaby is concerned, I much prefer to remember him as a schoolboy, than to think of him in the condition in which I last saw him, when 'real life' and dissipation, and years and years in institutions, had ruined him. It is only in the interests of completing this report that I bring myself to record his sad, seedy, mercifully brief reincarnation.

When he rang me in January, he was drunk. I got him off the phone as soon as possible, by making an appointment with him for the following day, at eleven-thirty. As the hour approached, I wished I had simply told him to go away, and hung up. The last time I had set eyes on him had been at the trial, but my attention there had been taken more by Jonathan, who, since the day of Judy's death, had never been seen at St Clement's. While I gave evidence, he was sitting in the crowded gallery, but he seemed alone, set apart by bereavement. When he noticed I was looking at him, he gave me a brief nod and a smile, as though mindful of his manners. I felt dizzy with shame, when he did that, and a strange terror seized me, that I was becoming transparent, and my dark secret, visible. The hearing gave Jonathan no satisfactory explanation for his loss. The story was that Judy had investigated noises in Ambrose's flat at about ten o'clock, and found Gaby. He was upset at having heard, from a telephone call to his parents, that they had been asked to take him away from St Clement's and that a place had already been found for him at another boarding school, further afield. Judy had stayed with him to give comfort, no doubt. No reason was given for the savage assault. Medical opinion guided the court to its judgement. Gaby's poem, 'The Wilderness Song', was read out; his father cried, his poor mother looked hunted.

Eleven-thirty came and went, with no sign of Gaby. Twelve o'clock. Twelve-fifteen. At twelve-thirty I left the office and crossed the road to The Crown, for my usual sandwich and lemonade. There is a games room at The Crown. Usually it is empty at lunchtime, but on this occasion, someone had found the juke-box: Andy Williams was singing 'Solitaire'. Twenty minutes later, when I was ready to leave, Andy Williams was still singing 'Solitaire', for the fifth or sixth time.

At the last moment, I remembered that my secretary had handed me some coins and asked me to buy her a packet of cigarettes from the vending machine, which is located in the games room. I went through. There was Gaby. He was shabbily dressed. His colour was high, with an artificial bloom, like make-up, which made him look feminine; so did his hair, which was thin and yellowish-grey, and wavy on account of being too long. Feminine, but not pretty; his good looks had gone weasel. From the tonic-water bottles that crowded his table and the slice of lemon in his empty glass, I guessed he had been on gin. He was fast asleep. *While life goes on around me everywhere, I'm playing solitaire . . .*

I backed out of the games room, fast.

He rang the office the next day. I pretended to be out. He asked my secretary for another appointment. I told her to make it later in the week, at ten o'clock or thereabouts, before opening time. This time, he turned up. He seemed to have shrunk. Shaking and clammy, he brought a sour sickly smell into the room; I thought he was probably dying. The half-faced grin was a permanent fixture, now, and the laughter had gone, leaving behind its hard hat – a mirthless 'heh-heh-heh'. And the oddest thing: as we spoke, I noticed that his voice became lower in tone, and quieter, and slightly ponderous, like mine. Automatically, he was imitating me, borrowing my voice as though he had none of his own. It was like talking to no-one at all, to an echo. And yet, to this impression that Gaby was really no-one at all, his eyes gave the lie. Perhaps they always had; perhaps it was only now, when, weasel-like, alcoholically rouged, his façade no longer dazzled, that Gaby could be clearly seen to possess the despairing eyes of a prisoner. I knew that I was not meeting this prisoner, that I never had and I never would. This feeling that the real Gaby, the true spirit, was a prisoner inside himself, made it once again impossible to say a prayer for him, for had I done so, I would have prayed for the release of this prisoner, I would have prayed for him to die. He is dead now, anyway, and my faith holds that his spirit is free.

He told me that he had been discharged six years ago, and that, with the advantage of a large inheritance, had made a living buying and selling property, mostly in the West Country. Now he had bought a holiday home somewhere near Clacton-on-Sea, and was going to spend the winter renovating it. But the week before, calamity. After a minor road-accident he had been charged with driving while drunk. At an initial hearing he had pleaded not guilty, in order to hang on to his driving licence for a few more weeks, until the case was brought. He was certain to be found guilty, and the consequences were likely to be severe. His liberty was only conditional, he was on lifelong parole, and any breach of his parole could lead to further, indefinite confinement. He would kill himself sooner than suffer that, he confided, in my very own, borrowed voice, but before doing so, had thought it might be worth consulting someone, in case there was an alternative. Being new to the area, he had stumbled on 'Palfreyman, Dean' in the commercial directory.

It happened that I did have an idea for Gaby, although, having no experience of the Parole Board, I was unable to guarantee him a good result. I asked him, as tactfully as one may, if it was possible that he was suffering in some degree from a problem with alcohol. He readily agreed. Why then, I suggested, did he not submit himself to an alcoholic rehabilitation programme? It would be viewed in his favour, not only by the parole officers but also by the magistrates' court, and who was to say it might not make him feel better? I told him about The Lodge, an establishment where Monica has done some private nursing, and gave him the address. I warned him that it was expensive, but this, he assured me, was no problem. He was pathetically grateful. Would I handle the court case for him? I could hardly say no. Meanwhile, he was going, straight away, to check in at The Lodge. A clammy handshake, another whiff of his sour smell, and he was gone. My secretary pulled a face.

A week later, the administrator of The Lodge, a Miss Fraser, telephoned my office. A Mr Gabriel had that day been admitted, in a dreadful state. He claimed to have no family, and had given my name as his closest friend. Did I know him? Yes. Would I be visiting him? No. Could I confirm that Mr Gabriel had the means to pay for his treatment, the cost was £480 per week? I confirmed it. Did I think Mr Gabriel sincerely wanted to give up drinking? I said that £480 per week sounded sincere enough to me. Was Mr Gabriel telling the truth about his family? I knew not. Could she have my home telephone number, in case of an emergency? I reluctantly agreed.

She said it would take a few days to detoxify Mr Gabriel, after which he would be joining in the recovery programme: group therapy, life stories, case histories and so on.

'Well, I shouldn't think any of that'll help,' I said, 'but look after the old soak if he starts drinking again, won't you? I think it's killing him.'

'Oh, no,' she said, 'if he starts drinking again, he'll

have thirty minutes to get off the premises – that's the rule. That's why I asked if he was sincere.'

He lasted less than a week.

I came home late from a day in court to be told by Monica that The Lodge had called, urgently, hours ago. When I rang, Miss Fraser said that she had telephoned to ask if I would come and collect Gaby, but it was too late now. He had been seen earlier that evening in a nearby public house, and on his return to The Lodge, smelling of drink, the duty nurse had refused to let him in. He had been handed his packed bag on the doorstep. This had not gone down well. The story had a familiar ring. For a full hour he had banged on the door, at the front, then the back, then the front again. At last the fearful assault had ceased, and the terrorized community thought he had gone away; then he was heard clambering about on the roof. Later, he had reappeared in the garden, shouting abuse and hurling gravel at the windows. In the end, she had called the police. When they arrived, Gaby had made a run for it through the grounds, and got away.

The following day, the Clacton police telephoned. They had been given my name by Miss Fraser. A body had been recovered from the sea at St Osyth. From documents on the corpse, the deceased was assumed to be a Martin Gabriel, for whom they had been watching out since a complaint the previous night. It was thought that while staggering home, drunk, across a causeway, he had fallen and knocked himself out, and slipped into the sea. Would I identify him?

As I drove to the hospital, I felt peaceful; at last, I thought, the spirit is free, the prisoner is released. It was only when I saw him that I realized I had work to do, work which I am here completing; for I have not rested easy, since the events of 1968, and I was therefore moved to envy when the orderly pulled back

251

the mortuary sheet, for it seemed, from the expression on Gaby's face, that after so long a nightmare, so much 'real life', so long in the Wilderness, at last there was occurring in his well-made head a sweet, peaceful dream.

THE END

The Death of David Debrizzi
by Paul Micou

'Marvellously stylish . . . an immense pleasure to read'
SUNDAY TIMES

Pierre Marie La Valoise is incensed. He has just read with disbelief what he considers to be a criminally unfair biography of David Debrizzi, the renowned French concert pianist.

Resting comfortably on the terrace of a Swiss sanatorium, La Valoise takes pen in hand to rebut Sir Geoffrey's *Life*. He weeds through its distortions and omissions, its exaggerations and personal attacks, and supplies the version of the truth that he intended to incorporate into his own biography, *The Death of David Debrizzi*. 'Never have I begrudged you your *Life*,' writes La Valoise, 'any more than you would deny me my *Death* . . . Given the state of my health, and the treachery of my *bastard* of a British publisher – who loathes me merely because I am French – I feel it is safe to say that your *Life* will stand alone on the shelves for posterity, while my *Death* will remain untold.'

Paul Micou's third novel at last gives La Valoise his say.

'It is so full of musical feeling that even the tone-deaf will feel thrilled . . . Above all, it is a good story . . . I have not enjoyed a book so much for a long time'
OXFORD TIMES

'His observation is as sharp as ever . . . telling a good story with considerable expertise'
NICHOLAS BEST, FINANCIAL TIMES

'Hugely entertaining. An odd, compelling book with a superb twist, and one which should clinch Micou's reputation as a writer to be reckoned with'
CARLA McKAY, DAILY MAIL

0 552 99461 8

BLACK SWAN

The Little Brothers Of
St Mortimer
by John Fergus Ryan

'A novel about likeable rogues, morally devastating, extremely
funny, with only one fault: it ought to be three times longer'
ANTHONY BURGESS

Belonging to a religious order can work wonders for business.
Especially in the Deep South where folks still respect a preacher. So
it doesn't matter that Brother Edgar is the only member of the Little
Brothers of St Mortimer. He makes a good living, in the small
towns on the Texas-Arkansas border, selling men's socks, trading
'antiques' and even running 'poetry contests'.

So all's fine and well, until the day Brother Edgar and his Mexican
ex-convict assistant stop for a plate lunch in Slovis Plumrod's Cafe.
That's when they run into the White River Kid (on the run from the
law); that's when they meet sex-crazed waitress Apple Lisa Weed;
and that's when all the trouble begins . . .

Brother Edgar is one of the truly great comic creations –
outrageous, cynical, well-meaning and wise. And the rude,
rumbustious and often sad tale he spins makes probably the
funniest and most original chase novel ever written.

'Wholly original . . . Ryan radiates his gnarled knowledge of the
human zoo via a truly wicked sense of humour'
ANTHONY HOLDEN

'Funny, tough, sentimental and subversive'
AL ALVAREZ

0 552 99425 0

BLACK SWAN

Max Lakeman And The Beautiful Stranger
by Jon Cohen

'A haunting, gentle book, with its feet firmly on the lawn and its head in the air . . . strange and lovely'
TERRY PRATCHETT

Max Lakeman is an utterly happy man. He is not merely content with his job caring for lawns, but crazy about it; not merely comfortable with his marriage, but madly in love with his wife; not merely satisfied with his two children, but thrilled by them. Can such a happy man be seduced?

Sitting alone in his back yard one evening, he is transfixed by the sight of a beautiful woman materializing out of his rhododendron bush. She blows him a kiss and vanishes. Fantasy and reality become dangerously intertwined when this visitation moves out of Max's dreams and into his neighbourhood – and he is drawn into a passionate affair which threatens to take him away from everything he knows and loves, for ever. In a novel that introduces one of the most original voices in recent fiction, Jon Cohen creates a funny, wondrous, and thoroughly captivating story – a modern tale of marriage, mystery, and temptation.

'Hilarious . . . an auspicious debut indeed'
NEW YORK TIMES BOOK REVIEW

0 552 99441 3

BLACK SWAN

A SELECTION OF NOVELS
PUBLISHED BY BLACK SWAN

THE PRICES SHOWN BELOW WERE CORRECT AT THE TIME OF GOING TO PRESS. HOWEVER TRANSWORLD PUBLISHERS RESERVE THE RIGHT TO SHOW NEW RETAIL PRICES ON COVERS WHICH MAY DIFFER FROM THOSE PREVIOUSLY ADVERTISED IN THE TEXT OR ELSEWHERE.

☐	99198 8	The House of the Spirit	*Isabel Allende* £5.99
☐	99313 1	Of Love and Shadows	*Isabel Allende* £5.99
☐	99474 X	The Best There Ever Was	*John Ed Bradley* £6.99
☐	99356 5	Tupelo Nights	*John Ed Bradley* £3.99
☐	99421 9	Coming Up Roses	*Michael Carson* £4.99
☐	99380 8	Friends and Infidels	*Michael Carson* £3.99
☐	99348 4	Sucking Sherbet Lemons	*Michael Carson* £4.99
☐	99465 0	Stripping Penguins Bare	*Michael Carson* £4.99
☐	99441 3	Max Lakeman and the Beautiful Stranger	*Jon Cohen* £4.99
☐	99141 4	Peeping Tom	*Howard Jacobson* £4.99
☐	99063 9	Coming From Behind	*Howard Jacobson* £5.99
☐	99408 1	The Cover Artist	*Paul Micou* £4.99
☐	99381 6	The Music Programme	*Paul Micou* £4.99
☐	99461 8	The Death of David Debrizzi	*Paul Micou* £4.99
☐	99419 7	The Redneck Bride	*John Fergus Ryan* £4.99
☐	99425 0	The Little Brothers of St. Mortimer	*John Fergus Ryan* £4.99
☐	99360 3	Unnatural Selection	*Daniel Evan Weiss* £4.99
☐	99437 5	Hell On Wheels	*Daniel Evan Weiss* £4.99

All Black Swan Books are available at your bookshop or newsagent, or can be ordered from the following address:
Corgi / Bantam Books,
Cash Sales Department,
P.O. Box 11, Falmouth, Cornwall TR10 9EN

UK and B.F.P.O. customers please send a cheque or postal order (no currency) and allow £1.00 for postage and packing for the first book plus 50p for the second book and 30p for each additional book to a maximum charge of £3.00 (7 books plus).

Overseas customers, including Eire, please allow £2.00 for postage and packing for the first book plus £1.00 for the second book and 50p for each subsequent title ordered.

NAME (Block Letters) ....

ADDRESS ....

....